Praise for Rosanne Bittner

MYSTIC DREAMERS

"Sure to please Bittner's fans and to win over new converts, especially as sequels are planned."

—*Booklist*

SONG OF THE WOLF

"Powerful, mystical, and eloquent . . . Historical fiction at its very, very best. A stunning achievement."

—*Romantic Times*

"Despite the violent events that punctuate this tale, Bittner's historical romance is, ultimately, a gentle work, thoughtful and sympathetic."

—*Publishers Weekly*

THUNDER ON THE PLAINS

"So full—with likeable characters, realistic dialogue, and details about frontier life—that she balances the predictable love-conquers-all plot."

—*Publishers Weekly*

WILDEST DREAMS

"Bittner is one of those writers whose talents have grown over the years; that talent truly blossoms. . . . [The characters] are extraordinary for the depth of emotion with which they are portrayed."

—*Publishers Weekly*

OUTLAW HEARTS

"Filled with vivid description of the raw, unsettled land from Kansas to California in the 1800s that evoke images of a wilderness too quickly tamed by civilization."

—*Publishers Weekly*

"Rosanne Bittner has been around for a good many years, concentrating most of her efforts on Indian novels that became known for their impeccable research and true-to-life characters. . . . With *Outlaw Hearts,* she has definitely entered a new and exciting phase."

—*Los Angeles Daily News* (four-star review)

"It is a masterpiece of fiction that cannot be forgotten when you turn the last page. . . . Put your life on hold. . . . It is marvelous!"

—*Affaire de Coeur*

TAME THE WILD WIND

"Bittner may have written the Western romance of the year with this incredible character study. The story line is exciting and fast-paced. . . . A Western romance reading phenomenon."

—*Affaire de Coeur*

MYSTIC DREAMERS

ROSANNE BITTNER

FORGE®

A TOM DOHERTY ASSOCIATES BOOK
NEW YORK

This is a work of fiction. All the characters and events portrayed in this book are either products of the author's imagination or are used fictitiously.

MYSTIC DREAMERS

Copyright © 1999 by Rosanne Bittner

A Forge Book
Published by Tom Doherty Associates, LLC
175 Fifth Avenue
New York, NY 10010

www.tor-forge.com

Forge® is a registered trademark of Tom Doherty Associates, LLC.

ISBN-13: 978-0-7653-5939-1
ISBN-10: 0-7653-5939-1

First Edition: April 1999
First Mass Market Edition: February 2000
Second Mass Market Edition: September 2007

Printed in the United States of America

0 9 8 7 6 5 4 3 2 1

This book is dedicated to the Lakota Nation and to all Native Americans. I have done my best with what I know, always aware that it is nearly impossible for a modern-day *wasicu* to properly portray Native American people in full depth of understanding. However, I hope these stories will help bring respect, wonder, and attention to their spirituality, and to their beautiful outlook on the circle of life, death, and the hereafter.

AUTHOR'S NOTE

Dreams and visions remain significant to Native Americans as part of the mystic circle of birth, life, death, and rebirth. Such visions, usually experienced after willing physical torture, often dictated every decision made. Today many Native Americans still turn to important prayer rituals, including physical sacrifices such as the sweat lodge, to find guidance in their lives. Deep spirituality is vital to their religion. Native Americans cannot be understood without respecting their belief that all life exists for a purpose and that human beings are no more important than the bear or the wolf or the tree. These beliefs and practices literally ruled their lives during the time period in which this story is set, the early 1800s, shortly before the white man's invasion of the West.

In this book, certain Native American tribes are referred to as the enemy, and sometimes spoken of in a disparaging manner. This is only because those tribes were the natural enemies of the tribe about whom I have chosen to write. I mean no disrespect for any particular tribe; I am only following the course of history as it reveals relationships among the tribes in the times of which I write.

Finally, although in this book I show my characters' dialogue in English, they would, of course, have used their own Siouan tongue in conversation.

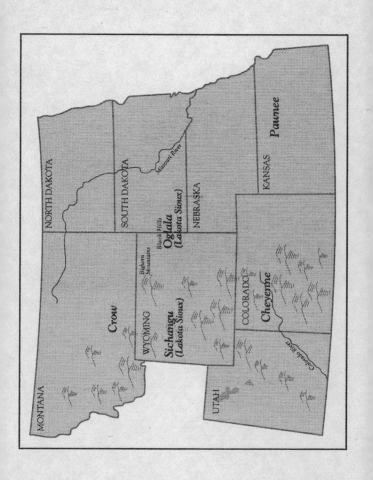

CHAPTER ONE

BY WHITE MAN'S terms, the year this story begins is 1832, during the Moon When The Ponies Shed . . . in May.

"Take pity on me. Show me the way, and protect my people."

A naked Night Hunter trembled from four days of hunger and thirst. The red heat of the afternoon sun penetrated his skin, but he ignored the pain, celebrating his suffering. Four days ago, his uncle, Runs With The Deer, had warned that he must come to the Big Waters of the sacred Black Hills to seek a vision.

"A wolf spoke to me about you in a dream, my nephew. It told me you must go to the Big Waters. There the wolf will come to you and tell you of a woman you must seek, for without her, you cannot become a true leader of the People. This woman has power, and she will help you become a leader of the Oglala."

As a member of *Naca Ominicia,* men who represented the entire Lakota Nation, Runs With The Deer held a position of great importance and his dreams held great significance. Thus Night Hunter now sat alone on a high ledge that overlooked the Big Waters, waiting faithfully for the wolf to come to him.

As he listened to the gentle flow of the river at the bottom of the canyon, he breathed deeply of the sweet, cool air that hung rich with the scent of wet pine needles. These sacred hills, nearly black with thick groves of deep green pine trees, harbored powerful spirits. Other Oglala men, and sometimes women, came to this hallowed place to seek visions.

Again, Night Hunter drew on his sacred pipe, letting the sweet smoke fill his lungs. He held the pipe aloft and sang to the God of the Sky.

"Take pity on me," he repeated. "Show me the way, and protect my people."

Despite his powerful build, weakness consumed him, and raising his prayer pipe took great effort. With shaking hands and arms, he offered the sacred pipe to the four corners of the earth. At each point, east, west, north, south, he again sang his prayer, his voice husky from a dry throat. He lowered the pipe toward the ground, praying to sacred Mother Earth. Here he had experienced his first vision at fourteen summers of age. In that vision, the moon and the sun moved side by side, and then the moon passed over the sun, blocking its light. After that, Moon Painter, the Oglala priest, told him that he should be called Night Hunter.

He had lived up to his name, hunting at night, his vision sharper in the night's darkness than others of his clan. Unafraid of the spirits of the darkness, he once killed a buffalo after dark, an accomplishment that brought him great praise and adoration from his fellow warriors, even from the wise old men of the Big Belly Society. For the next ten summers he pursued his quest to be a leader among the Oglala, a *Wicasa*, Shirt Wearer. From there he hoped to become *Wicasa Itacan*, one who ruled the Shirt Wearers.

Night Hunter swayed, then fell. The gravelly earth cut into his elbow and forearm, and he grimaced as he managed to ease himself back up. He crossed his legs and laid his pipe across his knees. Taking a deep breath for courage, he slid his hunting knife from its sheath and deftly sliced into his left arm, then stretched it out so that the blood from the wound dripped onto Mother Earth. He must show the Great Spirit his willingness to sacrifice even his own blood for the gift of a vision.

Could the woman of whom the wolf spoke be Fall Leaf Woman? He had enjoyed her slippery depths many times since the day two summers past when she caught him alone and boldly offered herself to him. She had dropped her tunic, exposing her womanly mysteries, enticing him with licks and caresses that caused him to fall under her power. Since then, she had continued to brazenly offer herself to him without reservation.

Fall Leaf Woman truly seemed to care for him, but he did not feel deeply for her. Lately she annoyed him with her constant pestering, and it seemed that wherever he turned, she hovered nearby. Surely such a woman could not be his intended. She held no special powers. Whomever he chose to call first wife must be a woman of great honor, one who would cost many horses, and who would not offer herself physically without a great price. Fall Leaf Woman did not hold such honor; he could have her for no price at all.

As the sun lowered, the western trees and hills cast a shadow over Night Hunter. His body shook with a chill, and he nearly passed out again. Thunder boomed overhead, rousing him from his stupor. The earth began to shake, and a powerful dizziness overcame him as the thundering noise grew so loud it hurt his ears. Then he saw it, a herd of buffalo stampeding toward him. Their pounding hooves shook the ground, yet they did not touch the ground at all. They charged out of the sky, so many and so fast that he could never run fast enough to avoid being trampled.

He sucked in his breath and waited for whatever must come, and just before reaching him, the herd suddenly parted and thundered around him on either side. Wild, black eyes glared at him as shaggy heads darted past. He heard their snorting, felt the hot breath from their nostrils, yet their feet stirred no dust once they touched the canyon ledge where he sat.

The herd suddenly vanished, and silence reigned once again. Then, from where the great beasts had charged out of the sky, a bright white cloud approached, swirling and eddying as it floated closer. Finally it came to rest on a nearby outcropping of rocks at the edge of the great chasm before him. Gradually the cloud changed shape, forming a white buffalo.

Then a black cloud, outlined in yellow, swirled and tumbled toward the white buffalo, settling beside it. The black cloud slowly took the shape of a wolf with yellow eyes. The menacing beast began to prowl around the white buffalo as though stalking it. When the wolf seemed ready to pounce, the head of the buffalo quickly transformed into a woman's face, her long hair white and shaggy like the buffalo's mane. She looked down at the wolf, and the animal backed away. Then one leg of the white buffalo turned into a slender arm that reached out and touched the wolf's head.

"One day you, Night Hunter, will be my husband," she told the wolf. "But then your name will be Stalking Wolf."

She withdrew her hand and became a buffalo again. She ambled away, and the wolf turned to Night Hunter, its yellow eyes filled with wisdom. "She is the woman you must marry," the beast told Night Hunter. "She is blessed by the white buffalo. When you find her, do not let her go."

The wolf turned and chased after the white buffalo. Night Hunter watched until both figures again became only clouds, which soon disappeared into the red sunset. Then a blinding flash of light exploded across the sky, causing Night Hunter to cup his hands over his eyes. A great warmth enveloped him, and when he dared look again, he saw a man standing before him with outstretched arms and a hairy face. He wore a simple robe, his long hair and the hair on his face lighter in color than Night Hunter's hair.

The man's gentle, comforting gaze held Night Hunter in rapture for several minutes, but the vision did not speak. As Night Hunter watched, the man spun around and his robes fell away, until he wore only an apron about his loins. His hair and skin turned darker and his outstretched arms bulged with more muscles, until he grew into a powerful giant of a man with feathers sprouting from his arms and back. Finally, the feathers covered his entire body, and his head transformed into the head of an eagle. He opened his beak and spoke.

"The man who appeared first represents peace, as will the woman you take as a wife. I am the Feathered One, and I represent the power of the Oglala, as do you, Stalking Wolf. Go and seek the woman of peace among the people of the Burnt Thighs. Some call her the White Buffalo Woman."

The Being soared away, disappearing into the clouds. Night Hunter stared after it in awe and confusion. A terrible dizziness washed over him then and he fell, hitting his head on a rock. He breathed deeply of the sweet smell of pine before lapsing into unconsciousness.

The next morning, Runs With The Deer and other Big Bellies came to check on Night Hunter. They found him lying near death, his head and left arm encrusted by dried blood.

"Take him, quickly," Runs With The Deer ordered. "Moon Painter must pray over him, and his mother and sister can tend to him."

The others managed to maneuver Night Hunter onto a travois tied to a horse. They hauled his limp body back to camp, but Runs With The Deer remained behind, staring out over the valley below.

"What have you seen?" he muttered, wishing his nephew could speak. He noticed a feather on the ground, and he stooped to pick it up, but a sudden wind whisked it away. It floated out over the valley below and disappeared.

JUNE 1832

Rutting Time of the
Buffalo Moon

CHAPTER TWO

STAR DANCER LISTENED attentively to the Oglala messenger called Runs With The Deer. Like her father, the visitor belonged to the Lakota Big Belly Society. More important, he belonged to *Naca Ominicia,* which represented the entire Oglala tribe before the *Wicasa Yatapickas,* the four great leaders of the Lakota Nation.

A mixture of burning curiosity and undeniable fear coursed through Star Dancer, for upon arrival, Runs With The Deer had specifically asked to speak with her father, Looking Horse. For a *Naca* to come so far, the reason must be of utmost importance; and Runs With The Deer had looked at her strangely when he first entered her mother's tepee.

Star Dancer sat unmoving in the shadows with her grandmother, Walks Slowly, keeping quiet while Looking Horse entertained his important guest. She noticed her mother, Tall Woman, seemed nervous as she served the men a meal of venison and wild onions; but she saw excitement and pride in her father's dark eyes. He obviously enjoyed playing host to such an esteemed visitor from the Oglala tribe.

"He must be here to talk about you," old Grandmother whispered.

Star Dancer hoped her *Uncheedah* was only teasing, as the old woman often did, but somewhere deep inside, she knew Walks Slowly might be right. Runs With The Deer continued to glance at her repeatedly.

His dark eyes showed deep wisdom and awareness. His mostly white hair hung in long braids over his bare chest, and sweat glistened on his dark skin. Star Dancer thought it fitting that he belonged to the Big Bellies, for his belly did indeed hang over his lap. Her father, however, retained a fine build in spite of his advanced years, and Tall Woman often bragged about her husband's still-handsome appearance.

Following their meal, Looking Horse offered Runs With The Deer a pair of beautifully quilled moccasins, for custom required a host to present his honored visitor with a gift. Runs With The Deer graciously accepted the moccasins, and he in turn offered Looking Horse a brightly quilled, wide, leather banner, as a sign of friendship and good will.

"This is a fine gift," Looking Horse told his guest. "I will drape it over the neck of my finest war pony when I ride to the next Lakota Council gathering on Medicine Mountain." He carefully laid the banner across his lap and shared a pipe with Runs With The Deer. Star Dancer waited impatiently to discover the reason for Runs With The Deer's visit, and finally her father asked the burning question.

"And why does a great Oglala leader such as yourself honor the Sichangu and my own dwelling with his presence?" Looking Horse asked cautiously. Star Dancer knew that even though her father held a high position among his people, Runs With The Deer enjoyed much greater importance among the entire Lakota Nation. Thus Looking Horse chose his words carefully, in order not to offend the Oglala man.

Runs With The Deer thought for a moment, obviously weighing his words before he spoke. Then he leaned forward, resting his elbows on his knees.

"I come to the village of the Burnt Thighs to speak about my nephew," he answered, using the Siouan dialect that most tribes understood. "He is called Stalking Wolf, because of a vision that came to him one moon past at the Big Waters of *Paha-Sapa.* He suffered many days with no food or water, and he cut his arm in an offering of blood to *Wakan-Tanka.*"

Runs With The Deer stopped and frowned, thinking for a moment before continuing. "My nephew has suffered two vision quests, and has also twice sacrificed his blood in the Sun Dance, once at seventeen summers, and again at twenty summers. Both times, he braved the pain of the skewers piercing his breasts and the calves of his legs. He did not cry out, and he danced longer than the others, dragging the leg weights and straining against the skewers at his breasts until they tore away. Even then, he made no sound, for he takes honor in suffering for the prosperity of the Lakota Nation."

Looking Horse frowned with intense interest. "Your nephew must be a very brave and honored man."

"*Ayee!* At twenty-four summers, he is already a Shirt Wearer. Crow and Pawnee scalps decorate his lance, and many of their horses are now in his possession. He cleanses himself in the sweat lodge often, and he prays constantly to be blessed with the powers of the sky spirits and the animal spirits. He rides against the enemy with no fear, and he has killed many buffalo with arrow and lance. I come here on his behalf."

Star Dancer glanced at her grandmother, thinking what great wisdom the hundreds of wrinkles around her eyes represented. Still sharp-minded, her mother's mother listened closely to the visitor's words, her dark eyes sparkling with curiosity. Walks Slowly loved to gossip, and a visit from a mysterious warrior of another tribe promised to provide much for her to chatter about.

"And what is it your nephew would ask of me?" Looking Horse inquired. "Why did he not come to me himself?"

"He chose not to come because he believes that here

among your people there is someone so special that he must not look upon her face until he has your permission. He has gone to hunt buffalo. His father was killed many seasons past by the humpbacked bear and Stalking Wolf must provide for his mother and sister. When we all meet for the annual Council on Medicine Mountain, he will then present his petition before you."

A refreshing rush of air swept through the dwelling, and Star Dancer could smell Runs With The Deer's perspiration. She longed to go out and wade into a nearby stream to cool herself, but she dared not leave.

"And what is Stalking Wolf's petition?" Looking Horse asked.

Runs With The Deer sat a little straighter. "It is said among the Oglala that a young Sichangu girl has seen the white buffalo, and that she carries the hairs of the buffalo in her medicine bag. Because of this, she is considered holy. It is said that this girl is your own daughter."

"It is true that at ten summers my daughter saw and touched the white buffalo," Looking Horse answered.

Star Dancer's throat constricted with a sudden rush of dread when the stranger nodded. Runs With The Deer again turned to her with a critical gaze, and she looked down, feeling embarrassed and afraid. She took pride in the fact that she'd seen and touched the sacred white buffalo, an experience that brought honor and attention to her father. Even as a young girl, she had held little doubt that Looking Horse had always wished for a son. Tall Woman had never conceived again after giving birth to her, and that had brought much grief to her mother's heart. When Star Dancer had told her parents about seeing the sacred white buffalo, presenting to them a fistful of hairs she'd pulled from its mane, Looking Horse had shown a new pride in his daughter, and that had helped soothe Tall Woman's disappointment at not being able to give him a son. Star Dancer's value as a holy woman had made her just as important as a son to him.

After her experience with the white buffalo, the tribal priest had declared Star Dancer destined for great things and high responsibilities. Until now, that destiny had always seemed far away, part of a remote future that would never come to be; but suddenly it had come upon her, in the form of old Runs With The Deer.

"Stalking Wolf believes that a vision he experienced one moon past has meaning that involves your daughter," Runs With The Deer continued. "So says our holy priest, Moon Painter."

As he explained the vision, Star Dancer knew it indeed held great meaning, for no warrior shared such a personal event with utter strangers unless it was vital to the future of the Lakota Nation.

"The black wolf then spoke," Runs With The Deer finished, "telling Stalking Wolf, 'She is the woman you must marry. She is blessed by the white buffalo.' " Again, Runs With The Deer paused and looked at Star Dancer. "The vision is a sign that Stalking Wolf can marry only a woman who shares the spirit of the white buffalo."

Star Dancer's cheeks began to burn, and she fought an urge to cry. Had Runs With The Deer come to take her away?

"Among the Lakota Nation," he continued, addressing Looking Horse again, "only your daughter has seen and touched the white buffalo. Stalking Wolf wishes to meet Star Dancer and ask for her hand in marriage."

Star Dancer glanced at her grandmother again, and the old woman grinned with excited delight. Her *Uncheedah* surely considered this announcement a wonderful event, and the thought of making her grandmother happy helped Star Dancer swallow her dread. Tall Woman's face showed no emotion. She would not embarass her husband.

"And would Stalking Wolf take my daughter away from us?" Looking Horse asked.

Runs With The Deer nodded. "His sister is not yet married, and his mother never took another husband. He will not take his mother away from her people. It is easier for the young ones to learn to live with a new people than for the old."

Looking Horse frowned and nodded, then turned to look at Star Dancer, who waited with pounding heart, trying to tell her father with her eyes that she did not want this union, did not want to leave her family.

"I must give this much thought and prayer," Looking Horse informed Runs With The Deer, his eyes still on his daughter. "As yet, I have not approved of any of the young men who have come to me asking for my daughter's hand." He turned his gaze back to his guest. "Just as this man called Stalking Wolf feels he must marry someone very special, so do I believe my daughter must do the same. The one called Stalking Wolf seems worthy, and his vision has much importance."

"More than you know." Runs With The Deer drew a deep breath, and Star Dancer could see he was trying to pull in his belly. "Listen well, my friend, for I have not told you all of my nephew's vision."

The man's words were spoken with great reverence, a portent of yet another revelation about the warrior Stalking Wolf. Star Dancer momentarily forgot her own concerns, and *Uncheedah* leaned forward, cupping a bony hand behind her ear to be sure she heard well.

"Stalking Wolf had yet another vision," Runs With The Deer said, lowering his voice. He looked around at all of them, then back to Looking Horse. "He has seen the Feathered One."

Looking Horse straightened in shock, and Tall Woman gasped.

"My, my, my," *Uncheedah* murmured quietly, putting her hand to her mouth. The announcement even piqued Star Dancer's interest. She had been taught since her first moment of understanding that a vision of the Feathered One constituted the most sacred vision any Lakota man or woman could experience.

"The Feathered One!" Looking Horse spoke the words reverently.

Runs With The Deer held his chin proudly. "At first, he appeared as a man wearing robes. Then he became naked and grew feathers. His head became that of an eagle's. He told Stalking Wolf that he would find the White Buffalo Woman here, among the Burnt Thighs."

Looking Horse sighed deeply and studied the banner still draped across his knees. "In one moon, I will bring my daughter to the annual Council at the great circle of stones on Medicine Mountain. Until then, I will think about all you have told me. Tell Stalking Wolf he may speak with me about this at the Council."

Star Dancer felt dizzy from this sudden decision that could change her life forever. Her father knew little about Stalking Wolf. Was he handsome? Ugly? Kind? Cruel? How could her father so easily agree to consider giving her over to a complete stranger? And at Medicine Mountain! She'd gone there only once, when her father took her to a special Sichangu Council meeting to talk about her experience with the white buffalo. The place seemed to hold magical powers.

"My daughter is only fifteen summers," Looking Horse continued. "From what you have told me, this man seems worthy of her hand, but Star Dancer must first meet him and approve of him. She will come to the Night Dance. She will throw her blanket over Stalking Wolf, and they will talk."

Throw her blanket over a stranger? Such an act indicated a young maiden's preference, and in her heart, Star Dancer loved and wanted only Kicking Bear, the brother of her good friend, Little Fox. Since playful childhood, an unspoken bond had existed between herself and Kicking Bear, each secretly sure they would one day wed. Looking Horse, however, did not consider Kicking Bear worthy of her hand.

"Stand up, Star Dancer, and let this man look at you," Looking Horse commanded, "so that he can tell Stalking Wolf how beautiful you are."

Star Dancer breathed deeply and forced her legs to move. Her father expected her to be brave about this, to show pride and honor. She held her chin high, fighting tears as she rose and faced Runs With The Deer. He scrutinized her intensely, so that she felt self-conscious of every part of her body.

"She is indeed pleasing to the eye," Runs With The Deer said, finally turning his gaze back to Looking Horse with a grin of satisfaction. "I thank you for your hospitality," he added, rising. "Stalking Wolf also thanks you. I will tell him he is free to speak with you about Star Dancer when we meet in the mountains of many sheep with horns." He paused a moment, then said, with arrogance and pride, "The Crow dogs try to keep us out, but always they fail."

Looking Horse also rose, folding his arms in front of him. "We, too, have many Crow scalps," he said with a slow grin.

Runs With The Deer picked up his gift. "I have a ride of many days to return to the sacred Black Hills. There is still daylight left, so I will leave now." He looked at Star Dancer once more. "You will be pleased with my nephew. Stalking Wolf is a handsome man, one any Lakota woman would be proud to call husband."

But I do not know him, Star Dancer wanted to answer. *It matters not to me how he looks or how honorable he is.* But she said nothing aloud. She wrapped her fingers around the medicine bag worn at her waist. Because of the white buffalo hairs it held, she apparently must wed a fierce Oglala warrior. She could not change what the Wolf Spirit and the Feathered One himself proclaimed must be.

LATE JULY 1832

The Heat Moon

CHAPTER THREE

FLICKERING FIRELIGHT CAST an eerie glow on the Night Dancers. Star Dancer's heart pounded in time with the rhythmic beat of the drummers, who sang songs of love, using teasing words of flirtation for the women who danced around the stone Medicine Wheel atop Medicine Mountain, some of the women stopping to sway seductively in front of their husbands or chosen favorites.

> *Do you see me?*
> *I dance for you.*
> *I am your special one.*
> *Do you see me?*
> *I will throw my blanket,*
> *And we shall be together forever.*

Just yesterday, the mysterious Stalking Wolf had arrived at this place of power and mysticism called Medicine Mountain. His presence generated excitement and gossip. He had brought eight horses with him, surely a gift for Looking Horse in offering for his daughter's hand.

Until the Night Dance, Star Dancer had remained out of sight. Young virgins were required to avoid prospective suitors, for sometimes a young man tried to run off with his intended, or to tempt her into sexual intimacies.

This one could never tempt me into such a thing!

Star Dancer thought. *I will take him to my bed only when I am ready.*

She leaned back and watched the great expanse of heavenly stars, wishing she could join them. High on this mountaintop, she must surely be halfway to heaven already. Magic filled the air here at the sacred circle of stones around which she danced. Built by the Ancient Ones, at a time and for a reason unknown even to the Lakota, the stone pattern resembled the structure of a Sun Dance lodge. From a central cairn, stones expanded outward in twenty-eight rows, connecting the central cairn to a much larger outer circle of stones. Six smaller cairns outside the circle's rim burned with fires that helped guide the dancers and kept them from stepping within the larger circle, a sacred area entered only by men and women of special honor.

According to legend, when the Feathered One physically appeared to the Lakota Nation someday in the future, he would come here, bringing all of the Lakotas' ancestors with him. Forever after, there would be an abundance of grass and buffalo for the Lakota, and there would be no warring, no sickness or sorrow, and no death.

The narrow, flat top of Medicine Mountain did not allow enough room to accommodate the thousands of Lakota who came here for a Council meeting. And so only the most respected warriors and their wives attended, and those men with marriageable daughters showed them off to eligible young men. The rest of the Lakota Nation gathered at the foot of the mountain, preparing the Sun Dance lodge for the ritual of manhood that would take place in a few days.

Star Dancer watched how the more experienced dancers moved, and she tried to imitate their seductive sway. Kicking Bear had deliberately stayed away from the dance, and she ached to talk to him, but her father would not allow it. Her father sat with the other husbands and suitors in the circle around the dancers, his eyes filled with his love for Tall Woman, who danced only a few feet in front of Star Dancer.

Tonight Star Dancer wore a white tunic adorned with colorful quills, a gift from *Uncheedah*. Quills wrapped around each tiny fringe decorated the bottom hem and side seams of the dress, and the fringes swished enticingly with her body movements. Walks Slowly had braided quilled leather strips into her hair and painted flowers on her cheeks and arms. It irritated Star Dancer that she had to make herself as beautiful as possible for a man she did not even want.

Her stomach tightened when the married women began throwing blankets over their husbands, and some of the young maidens did the same with their heart's intended. Star Dancer continued dancing, bashful about approaching Stalking Wolf, and keenly aware of his penetrating gaze. White circles painted around his eyes made him appear more menacing than handsome. He showed no emotion when she twirled in front of him, and Star Dancer wondered if he felt disappointment with her. An air of mystery enshrouded him, and his all-knowing eyes held her gaze in much the same way a wolf or a hawk could sometimes glare right at a person . . . or its prey. Maybe the wolf actually lived in his soul.

Tall Woman threw her blanket over Looking Horse and sat down beside him, leaving Star Dancer the only remaining dancer. She had no choice now but to approach the stranger vowed to win her. She trembled at the power that radiated from Stalking Wolf's very presence, glad it was too dark for him to see how tightly she gripped her blanket.

Then, as though sensing her fear after all, Stalking Wolf reached up and grasped one of her hands firmly before she could throw her blanket over him. She jumped at his touch, for at the same moment, a bolt of lightning cracked through the black sky, accompanied by an instant explosion of thunder.

Women screamed and warriors gasped in surprise. Looking Horse and Tall Woman tossed aside their blanket and looked wide-eyed at the sky, and several warriors leaped to their feet. Startled, Star Dancer tried to pull away, but Stalking Wolf tightened his hold.

"Look up!" he commanded.

Star Dancer slowly followed his gaze, raising her eyes to see only a profusion of stars.

"It is a sign," Stalking Wolf told her. "There are no clouds, yet you heard thunder and saw lightning."

Others whispered among themselves over the surprising event.

"Indeed, it *is* a sign!" Looking Horse exclaimed.

The singing and drumming ceased, and Star Dancer's legs felt weak. Then Looking Horse asked the drummers to resume their love songs. He glanced at Stalking Wolf and nodded, then went off into the darkness with Tall Woman. Other husbands and wives followed suit. Feeling abandoned, Star Dancer threw her blanket over Stalking Wolf and grudgingly sat down beside him. Nearby she heard teasing laughter and suggestive comments, something all couples endured when they courted under the blanket.

Star Dancer waited nervously, still shaking from the ominous clap of thunder and the white lightning. Not sure of what to say, she felt a mixture of dread and curiosity at being so close to such a great warrior. How could she possibly please such a man? She didn't even *want* to worry about pleasing him.

"I am Star Dancer," she said quietly. She hunched her shoulders defensively, afraid to let her body touch his. "Say what you wish," she added, trying to pretend confidence. That confidence quickly dissipated when Stalking Wolf raised a hand and brushed her cheek, as though to warn her he could touch her any time he wished once she belonged to him.

"You are more beautiful than Runs With The Deer described."

Star Dancer's determination to hate the man wilted a little at the surprising and flattering comment. Stalking Wolf leaned closer, and she could smell him. He smelled clean, like he had bathed in cold water and rubbed cedar on his skin.

"You should know that I intend to marry another," she told him, refusing to acknowledge his compliment.

"And you should know it is written in the stars that you will marry me," he answered gently but with authority.

Star Dancer could not keep from shivering. "How can you be so sure of this?"

He took his hand away. "You saw the lightning. You heard the Thunder God. It frightened you and the others, but I was not afraid. I know it is a sign that you are the woman the Feathered One told me I should seek. You know we must follow where the Great Spirit leads."

Star Dancer made no reply, and they sat in silence for several seconds. Finally, Stalking Wolf sighed as though irritated. "I must know if it is true that you have seen the white buffalo," he said. "I must hear it from your own lips."

Reluctantly, Star Dancer answered. "I have seen it . . . five summers past. I carry some of the white buffalo hairs in my medicine bag."

He paused, and Star Dancer waited.

"And how do you come by your name?" he finally asked, touching her hair.

His touch disturbed her, and she wanted to run. "Two summers past, some of the leaders of our clan asked me to dance a war dance with them. They felt I would bring them good luck because of my having been blessed by the white buffalo. I was only thirteen summers, and so I took great honor in being allowed to dance with them. I danced until I could no longer stand. I prepared myself first by going many days without food. This was my sacrifice."

She wished he would not lean so close. She could not think with his shoulder touching hers. The commanding air about him not only made her feel compelled to answer his questions, but also made her worry over how forceful he might be with her if she belonged to him.

"I fell to the ground," she continued, "and when I looked up at the stars, they came closer, so close that I could climb onto one of them, and I danced among them. They were all around me, under my feet, falling like dust on my hair, and I heard the sound of light laughter. It was—" She hesitated. Did he believe her, or think her a foolish child? "—wonderful," she finished. "When I told the priest what happened, he gave me the name Star Dancer. I used to be called Little Buffalo Girl. I know when all this happened, because my father keeps a circle of pictures, showing the seasons since I was born and the important events in my life. In this way, I can count my age by counting the seasons in the circle."

Stalking Wolf leaned away from her. "The stars watch you now. They smile on us, and they will dance when you become my wife. Tommorow I will speak with your father." With that, he slid from under the blanket and left.

Star Dancer breathed a sigh of relief and pulled the blanket close around herself. Stalking Wolf disappeared into the darkness, and Star Dancer hurried back to her mother's tepee.

CHAPTER FOUR

WALKS SLOWLY SAT resting inside her daughter's tepee when a breathless Star Dancer arrived. Star Dancer sat down near a lingering central fire, bending her legs and wrapping her arms around her knees. She rocked as she fought what others would probably consider childish tears.

"You sat with him under the blanket?" Walks Slowly asked.

Star Dancer did not miss the sly teasing in her grandmother's voice. She closed her eyes, not wanting to talk right now, but also not wanting to offend her beloved *Uncheedah*. She remained turned away when she answered. "Yes."

Walks Slowly chuckled. "What was it like, Grand-daughter?"

Out of respect, Star Dancer had no choice but to turn and face the woman. Walks Slowly shifted her position against her backrest, and Star Dancer felt renewed worry over her grandmother. Lately, Walks Slowly seemed to have more trouble sitting and rising. She had also started coughing more the last few days.

In spite of that cough, the old woman put her favorite pipe to her lips. She had fashioned it herself from elk bone. Staring thoughtfully at the small tepee fire, she quietly drew the sweet-smelling smoke into her lungs, so that when next she spoke, smoke puffed from her mouth with each word. "I only saw him from a distance. Was he as fine-looking as I suspected?"

Star Dancer saw the curious twinkle in the woman's eyes. "I am not sure," she answered with a shrug. She hated to admit she thought Stalking Wolf might be handsome. "There was only the dim firelight, and under the blanket, I could not see him well. He appears to be very strong. His voice is deep, but he did not speak harshly. White circles were painted around his eyes, and he . . . smelled good. He asked about my dream of the stars, and about seeing the white buffalo."

"Hmmmm." Grandmother rubbed at her lips. "I hope you know that you are greatly honored. I have heard he is very fine-looking, too, from those who have seen him closely. It is easier to take a man when he is fine-looking."

"It does no good for a man to be fine-looking if he is a stranger, and if he is cruel," Star Dancer pouted.

"He would not be cruel to someone so special as you. It would only anger the gods and bring him bad luck."

Star Dancer felt more tears sting her eyes. "I am afraid. I only want to be with Kicking Bear. I know him. He cares for me. We are good friends."

Walks Slowly picked up a stick and poked the fire. Star Dancer noticed the skin on her hand was so thin that the blue veins underneath stood out prominently, as though nothing covered them at all.

"Kicking Bear is a good man," Walks Slowly told her, "but he cannot match the one called Stalking Wolf, from what I am told. The women here all envy you." The old woman coughed again before continuing in her cracked voice. "Many of them would enjoy sharing their bed with a Shirt Wearer, one who will one day surely join the *Wicasa Itacans,* perhaps one day the *Naca Ominicia.* I assure you, Granddaughter, that a woman learns to love the man who plants his life in her. It is the way."

Star Dancer clenched her jaw tightly to keep her

lips from quivering, and silent tears spilled down her cheeks.

"Do not judge him so quickly, Granddaughter. Perhaps it is also difficult for him. You share the same problem, don't you see? He, too, cannot marry just anyone of his choosing. The People come first, what is best for them. He is very respected, a member of the Brave Heart Society. His father belonged to the Big Bellies, as does his uncle, who is also a *Wicasa*. It is from the old men of that society that all leadership comes. All of them are wise men. You can be sure that Stalking Wolf has been taught well. He will know his place inside the tepee."

"But I don't *want* to share a tepee with him!" Star Dancer told her in a quivering voice.

Grandmother chuckled again, and much as Star Dancer loved her, Walks Slowly's sense of humor irritated her now.

"You will not always feel this way," Grandmother assured her before drawing on the pipe again. "The men of the Brave Heart Society are only the bravest warriors. They are taught strength and patience. They will fight to the death to protect family and friends, and they have vowed to take care of the needy, to provide for widows and children when necessary. They must be of high moral character. This is not a man who would abuse you."

Star Dancer angrily wiped at her tears. "I could refuse him. It is my right. Maybe he *wants* me to refuse. Then he would be free to pick someone else."

"Yes, you could refuse. But you have been taught that if there is anything we can do to bring prosperity to the People and to bear children of the finest blood, we must do it. The People always come first. The Feathered One chose this man to be your husband. It is your destiny, my child, something that cannot be changed."

Star Dancer felt sick. "I know this better than anyone."

"And you will make your father proud. Together, you and Stalking Wolf will make the whole Lakota Nation proud. Tomorrow he will speak for you. It will be a grand day for both of you."

"Perhaps," Star Dancer answered. "I think it will be a grander day for my father, who will receive many gifts."

Uncheedah nodded. "Your father loves you. Do not ever forget or doubt that, Granddaughter."

Star Dancer stared at the fire. "He gives me away to a stranger."

"No, Star Dancer. Only you can do that. Even if you agree to this, you can set the rules inside the tepee. This man cannot touch you until you say it is right. Do not be afraid. I think he will not want to offend you. Remember, he, too, is marrying a stranger."

Star Dancer felt no sympathy for Stalking Wolf. "I am tired, Grandmother." She removed her tunic and crawled into her bed, pulling a buffalo robe over herself. No matter how hot the season, nights were always cold high in the mountains . . . but tonight she shivered from more than the cool night air.

CHAPTER FIVE

WALKS SLOWLY SET aside the quill comb she had used on Star Dancer's lustrous black tresses, then tied the girl's hair to the side with a piece of beaded rawhide and fluffed her hair over one shoulder.

"You look beautiful, Granddaughter."

Star Dancer read the pride in her grandmother's misty eyes. "Thank you, *Uncheedah*. And thank you for the dress." She looked down at the colorful quill design on the front of her soft deerskin dress. Walks Slowly had spent many hours making it for her, saving the dress for a very special occasion. She insisted that today was a suitable day to wear it for the first time.

"You will make a fine wife for a fine warrior," Walks Slowly told Star Dancer.

Before Star Dancer could reply, Tall Woman called from outside the tepee. "They are ready, Star Dancer."

Using a sturdy branch for a cane, Walks Slowly struggled to her feet. "Now I can see your lover for myself, Star Dancer."

"He is *not* my lover!" Star Dancer frowned at her as they walked outside to greet Tall Woman.

"Your father is so pleased," Tall Woman said excitedly. She grasped her daughter's arms and smiled with a mixture of joy and sadness. "You are my only living child. I would die before I would allow you to be unhappy, but I am telling you, Star Dancer, that this man *will* make you happy. Your father and I both believe this is the will of *Wakan-Tanka*. I know of your feelings for Kicking Bear, but those are the feelings of a child. This one will turn you into a woman, and you will not regret becoming his wife."

Star Dancer swallowed at the painful lump in her throat. "But I do not know him in the friendly way I know Kicking Bear."

"You will learn and grow together. Kicking Bear can never be more than a friend. Stalking Wolf will become much more to you." She pressed Star Dancer's arms supportively. "Come. Be a proud, strong woman for us today."

Walks Slowly shuffled closer and patted her back. "Let us hear what he has to say. And we will see for certain if he is fine-looking!"

Star Dancer rolled her eyes in exasperation. If not for the seriousness of her situation, she would laugh at the old woman's near-childish attitude. They walked with Tall Woman to the gathering, and some of the women watching whispered and giggled. Star Dancer wished she could enjoy the moment as much as the rest of them. In the distance, the wind groaned through the mountains, as though in empathy with her dread, as finally she faced her father . . . and the man who stood beside him.

Star Dancer's heart leaped unexpectedly. Stalking Wolf wore no paint on his face, and his soft, fringed, buckskin pants and shirt were beautifully quilled. His nearly waist-length black hair hung loose, a colorful hair ornament tied into one side of it. He held a staff decorated with red-dyed deerskin and eagle feathers, a symbol of the Oglala Brave Heart Society.

Stalking Wolf met her gaze, and Star Dancer found herself surprisingly attracted. Here in the light of day, without the painted face and the mystery of darkness and firelight, he did not seem quite so frightening to behold. Indeed, he stood as tall and strong as she surmised him to be when she sat with him in darkness the night before. One short scar marked his right cheek, and a longer one ran sideways across his left cheekbone and partway across his nose. Somehow they did not detract from his handsomeness, for they were only the marks of a man well experienced in battle.

"Stalking Wolf stands before you, Daughter," Looking Horse spoke up, "and before the Council, to ask that he be allowed to take you for a wife. He has brought eight horses, all sturdy, two of them good war ponies."

Stalking Wolf turned to Looking Horse. "I bring even more," he said. He left them and walked to a horse brought forward by a young boy. He untied several skins and a buffalo robe. "I also bring these." He walked over and handed the skins to Tall Woman, who took them gratefully. Stalking Wolf then laid the buffalo robe at Looking Horse's feet. He took a pipe from its casing tied to the horse, then turned and gave it, too, to Looking Horse.

"This is my sacred prayer pipe. The feathers that decorate it are eagle feathers. I took them from an eagle's nest myself. This is the pipe with which I prayed when I received the vision that your daughter should become my wife. These gifts I bring you, and I will bring more, if you will but tell me what you would require. I know it is a great loss to have your daughter taken from you, and it is my promise that she can come and visit you often. I tell you truly, my family will make Star Dancer welcome in our village. My mother will become her mother, my sister her sister."

Looking Horse fingered the pipe reverently, then handed it to the Sichangu priest, Beaver Singing, who stood beside him. The constant wind at the top of the mountain blew Stalking Wolf's hair to the side, and small pieces of tin tied into his hair ornament made little tinkling sounds. Star Dancer wondered if he had traded something to white men for the tin. She had yet to see one of the hairy-faces who lived in the land of the rising sun.

"Your gifts are generous," Looking Horse spoke up, "but my daughter is very valuable. You ask her to leave her family and go to a people she does not know. I will need more than this."

Star Dancer heard the women around her whispering, and she noticed several of them were literally gawking at Stalking Wolf.

"Wait!" Kicking Bear's shouted demand interrupted the mystique of the moment. He nudged his way through the crowd and came forward to face Looking Horse. "I, too, wish to have Star Dancer's hand in marriage. You know I have always planned to marry your daughter. At times, you were like a father to me, yet you would never let me court Star Dancer. Now I *demand* that you allow me the chance to win her! I am Sichangu! With me, she could remain close to her own people. Do not let her go to a stranger, to live away from her mother and grandmother. Tell me what you want of me and I will do it! Already I own nine horses. This you know. I will give *all* of them to you!"

The whispering stopped and all grew quiet as everyone waited for Looking Horse to reply. Star Dancer felt a rush of love for Kicking Bear, proud of the brave stance he took now. He stood nearly as tall as Stalking Wolf, but of a more slender build. Star Dancer thought him just as handsome, but he did not hold the same prestige as his opponent, and he bore no battle scars. Still, he cared enough about her to bravely offer any sacrifice for her hand.

Star Dancer could see that her father enjoyed the attention he gained from this sudden interest from two brave men for his daughter's hand. He rubbed his chin and paused before answering.

"You know that when Stalking Wolf touched my daughter's hand at the Night Dance, lightning flashed and the Thunder God spoke, even though there were no clouds. This is surely a sign that he should be her husband."

"Perhaps it is a sign that he should *not* be her husband," Kicking Bear suggested. "A sign that such a union is *wrong!*"

Now a quiet mumbling erupted among the others, and the men of the Council frowned.

"The Feathered One himself told me to come here for your daughter," Stalking Wolf reminded Looking Horse, speaking with a calm sureness. "If a man does not abide by his visions, he might as well not exist."

Several men of the Council nodded. "I agree," Looking Horse replied. "But my daughter will not go to *any* man for only a few horses." He looked at Stalking Wolf as he spoke, then turned his gaze to Kicking Bear. "And it is true that Kicking Bear has had feelings for Star Dancer for many years. Because he is Sichangu, he must be allowed a chance to prove he should wed my daughter."

Star Dancer felt a hint of relief, mixed with apprehension.

"What is it you ask of me?" Kicking Bear demanded.

"It is something I ask of *both* of you," Looking Horse answered. "There will be a contest for my daughter's hand."

Pleased excitement swept the faces of the men who sat in Council. The Big Bellies smiled, their wisdom wrinkles deepening.

"This is how it must be," Looking Horse continued sternly. "Stalking Wolf must bring me one more horse, to match the nine Kicking Bear gives me."

Kicking Bear grinned with satisfaction, and irritation showed in Stalking Wolf's eyes at Looking Horse's apparent greediness. "You know she must belong to me," he reminded Looking Horse. "My vision says it must be so!"

"I will share the horses with the rest of my Sichangu

brothers," Looking Horse added. Star Dancer suspected he made the remark so that he would not appear selfish.

"I will bring you *more* horses!" Kicking Bear declared.

Others mumbled among themselves. Capturing horses was dangerous, as the most common way to do so was to steal them from the Crow or Pawnee, which could cost a man his life.

"That is not necessary," Looking Horse told Kicking Bear. "Here is what else I require."

Kicking Bear stiffened, and Stalking Wolf folded his arms with an arrogant air and frowned.

"You must each bring me the fresh skin of the humpbacked bear. He who returns first with the bearskin will win my daughter's hand," Looking Horse finished.

Star Dancer heard the others gasp. This was an enormous price her father asked for her hand! Star Dancer felt embarrassed.

"It is too dangerous!" Kicking Bear's father, Whistler, shouted. "Do not ask such a thing of my son, Looking Horse!"

"I am not afraid!" Kicking Bear kept his eyes on Looking Horse as he spoke. "The bear is my Guiding Spirit. I *accept* your demand."

Stalking Wolf stepped closer, dropping his arms at his sides and looking down his nose at Kicking Bear. "Although my own father was killed by such a bear, I do not fear the humpbacked beast." He turned to Looking Horse. "I will bring you the fresh bearskin, *before* Kicking Bear can return with his. You will see that it will be so, because the Feathered One himself means for your daughter to belong to *me!*"

Looking Horse turned to Star Dancer. "You see that I give Kicking Bear equal chance to win your hand. Do you agree with what I have asked?"

To agree could mean a death sentence for one or

both of these men. Still, Star Dancer knew how she must answer. She could not ruin this great moment for her father. The air suddenly seemed to hang still and heavy, and a complete silence engulfed the moment. Even the wind stopped howling as all waited for Star Dancer's reply.

"I agree," she answered, thinking how small her voice sounded on the mountaintop. She breathed deeply for the courage to say what she must say. "He who returns first with the fresh bearskin will become my husband, but I will not be a wife to him in all ways until I am *willing*." She glared at Stalking Wolf on her last words, feeling a little silly saying it. He could break her in half if he chose.

"It is done then," Looking Horse told them. "My daughter has given her word, and I have told you what I require." He turned away, and the others began talking excitedly among themselves. She watched Stalking Wolf's eyes, and saw both challenge and victory in his gaze. She glared at him with defiance and authority, as though to dare him to win her, until finally he turned and left. She watched him go, stunned that the moment was so quickly over. The challenge had been made, and she must go to the best man.

She watched Stalking Wolf as he slid his staff into the leather shaft that held it secure on the side of his horse; then he leaped onto the animal's back in one easy motion. He slung a quiver of arrows and a bow over his back, and another Oglala man from the Council walked up to him. Star Dancer saw them grasp wrists in friendship.

"Watch over my mother and sister as they go home to *Paha-Sapa,*" Stalking Wolf said. "I will come when I have done what I must do."

Star Dancer noted the caring tone of his voice as he spoke of his family.

"We will hunt along the way and take our time," the young man answered. "We will leave signs so that you can find us in camp. I wish you well, my friend."

Stalking Wolf nodded, and without another word, he headed down the mountain. Star Dancer turned to see Kicking Bear standing near her, determination in his eyes.

"I will not let you go to him," he promised. "I will return first with the skin of the humpback."

She could tell he wanted to hold her, and she in turn wanted to be held. "I have missed talking with you, Kicking Bear."

He blinked, yearning in his dark eyes. "And I have missed being close to you."

"I will pray for you to be the first to return."

Star Dancer watched him leave, and she felt a last piece of her childhood leaving with him. She turned to help her grandmother walk back to the tepee.

"My, my, my," the old woman said, patting Star Dancer's arm. "The one called Stalking Wolf is the finest-looking man I have ever seen. He makes me wish that I was young and pretty again." She made a clucking sound. "You will not mind being alone with that one. I predict that Stalking Wolf will be first to return with the bearskin."

Star Dancer held her chin high. "We shall see, *Uncheedah*."

AUGUST 1832

Moon of Dry Dust Blowing

CHAPTER SIX

Bear Spirit, be with me.
You took my father's spirit into your heart.
Now, my father, come to me.
Offer yourself, for it is right.

STALKING WOLF CROUCHED in a thick grove of chokecherries. His diligent search for the humpback had covered three weeks so far, and anxiety wore at his patience. He yearned to be with the Oglala, hunting buffalo so the women could begin storing meat for the winter.

At last, only five days before, he had discovered bear tracks and followed them to the wide stream nearby. Colorful trout danced and jumped in the water, creating an ideal feeding place for bears. This was the time of year the beasts feasted intensely to store up fat for their long winter's sleep.

He yearned to finish this hunt. Since first catching a glimpse of Star Dancer, her long black hair fluttering in the gusty wind at the top of Medicine Mountain, he felt more determined than ever that she should belong to him. He had seen fire in her dark eyes, a challenge in her demeanor. A woman like Star Dancer could not go to just any man. She had seen the white buffalo, and she must go to a warrior worthy of her special status. An ache deep inside at the thought of making her his wife would not go away. He would never be satisfied until he claimed Star Dancer as his own.

He closed his eyes and forced away the distracting thought. His search had brought him to the mountains north of the place of the steaming waters, where Looking Horse told him the Sichangu would make camp after the Sun Dance. Nearby were slate-gray mountains rising to jagged points resembling a woman's breasts, snow decorating their peaks. This land of the Sichangu was beautiful. Still, he missed the pine-covered hills of home.

Again he sang his prayer in a soft whisper, waiting, listening, watching. Finally, the Great Spirit granted his wish. He heard a crashing sound in the underbrush and stopped singing, his heart hammering with anticipation. Whatever was moving closer was big. It could be a moose or an elk, but when it came even closer, he heard panting, with a deep grunt to each breath. A bear! There was no mistaking the sound. When the great beast finally came into view, he saw it was indeed a humpback, one of the biggest grizzlies he had ever seen.

Fear coursed through his veins, but quickly he drew on deep reserves of courage learned over years of physical and mental training for just such moments. The Bear Spirit had answered his prayers, but this bear might have come to take him to the place where his father waited with the Feathered One. Whatever the Great Spirit willed for him, he must accept. The memory of his father's mangled body when brought back to his village many years before remained vivid in Stalking Wolf's mind. He had barely recognized his father. To face the same kind of bear now presented a true test of courage. Looking Horse knew that. So did all the leaders of *Naca Ominicia*. This kill could be his greatest victory, or his most horrible defeat.

Carefully, he pulled an arrow from the quiver at his

shoulder, then positioned it against the bowstring. The grizzly sniffed, looked around, then ambled over to the stream. Except for the babbling water, no noise came from the eerily quiet forest. Even the birds had stopped singing.

Stalking Wolf's heart pounded in his ears. His first shot must be true. He could not hesitate, for the only thing more dangerous than a feeding humpback was an angry one! The bear slapped at the water and tossed a large trout onto the bank. The fish lay flopping while the bear made another grab in the water, tossing up a second trout. Before reaching into the stream again, the animal hesitated, sniffed the air and looked directly where Stalking Wolf hid.

Stalking Wolf quickly rose, bowstring drawn. The startled grizzly grunted and stood up on its hind legs, towering a good three feet taller than Stalking Wolf.

"Thank you, Bear Spirit," Stalking Wolf muttered. He released the arrow. It landed deep in the middle of the bear's chest, but the beast did not falter. Stalking Wolf felt a sudden chill. He snatched another arrow from his quiver and positioned it.

The bear let out a deep growl of fury that shook the trees, then stepped forward. Stalking Wolf again released the bowstring. This time the arrow landed in the bear's throat. Stalking Wolf expected the beast to fall, but it kept right on coming.

Stalking Wolf released a third arrow. This one also stuck in the animal's throat, and by then, the bear was too close for him to get another arrow into position. Stalking Wolf tossed the bow aside and ripped the quiver of arrows from his shoulder, then pulled his hunting knife from its sheath. He held out his arms as though to fight, growling and screaming at the bear, but his voice was lost in the grizzly's much louder roar. Still, the bear hesitated, apparently put off and momentarily confused by Stalking Wolf's shouting and waving. Then, enraged by the arrows embedded in its chest and throat, the bear suddenly regained its strength, and it thrashed closer.

Stalking Wolf felt the grizzly's huge claws dig into the flesh of his left shoulder as the beast whacked him with a swing that sent him sprawling to the ground. He hung on to his hunting knife and staggered to his feet, but the bear was quickly upon him again. Another blow followed as the bear batted at him as though he were a small toy. Stalking Wolf landed with a grunt against a tree trunk. Fighting dizziness, he turned to face the bear again. He did not have to look to know he was bleeding badly. He must not give the beast a chance to swing at him a third time.

Quickly and deliberately, Stalking Wolf dived at the bear, burying his hunting knife deep into the animal's chest several times. At the same time, the bear dug its claws into Stalking Wolf's back. Stalking Wolf's shrill screams matched the bear's growl. He could smell the animal's hot, rancid breath as the grizzly prepared to clamp its huge jaws around his head. Stalking Wolf found the inner strength a warrior possesses when his life seems doomed, and he quickly buried his blade again, this time into the bear's ear. The animal pulled back slightly, and Stalking Wolf stabbed again, ramming his blade into the bear's eye.

He jumped away then as the beast finally crashed to the ground, which shook from its weight. The bear landed in a great lump of fur and blood. Stalking Wolf stared at it, stunned and breathless. At first, he did not even feel the pain of his wounds. He waited to be sure the bear was dead, then dropped to his knees, looking at the bloody knife still in his hand. He bent close to the bear and saw it was a male. He reached out and touched its head, then closed its eyes.

"Bear Spirit, my father, I thank you for offering yourself to me." He wiped his knife on the bear's fur and returned it to its sheath. Then he reached to his wounds and smeared some of his blood onto his hand, wincing as the pain began to set in. He placed his bloody hand against the wound in the bear's throat. "Your claws have dug into my skin. Now our blood mixes together, and we are one in spirit. Bear animal, man animal. They are the same." He put his head back and stretched out his arms, then let out a long, loud cry of victory. He had earned what he needed that he might claim the Sichangu woman called Star Dancer.

CHAPTER SEVEN

"HE COMES, STAR Dancer!" Kicking Bear's sister, Little Fox, shouted as she ran toward Star Dancer. A hefty young girl, she panted from the exertion, and strands of her sweat-soaked hair stuck to the sides of her face. She pushed the hair behind her ears. "Scouts say my brother comes! He is back before Stalking Wolf!"

Star Dancer looked up from where she sat sewing porcupine quills onto tunics made from freshly tanned deerskins. A full month had passed since Kicking Bear left to hunt the grizzly, and Star Dancer worried that he would never return. "Does he bring the hide of a humpback?"

Little Fox's dark eyes widened with happiness. "I do not know! I did not even ask. I came right away for you."

Grandmother set her sewing aside. "Let us go and see," she told both the girls.

Star Dancer helped the old woman to her feet, but her blood ran cold when suddenly women began keening a death song. Little Fox's smile vanished, and she shared a look of horror with Star Dancer. "Kicking Bear!" She ran off, and Star Dancer saw several warriors and women begin gathering around an incoming rider. Even from a distance, Star Dancer could see that something was terribly wrong. Alarm filled her when Kicking Bear slumped from his horse, and his mother screamed.

"I have to run, Grandmother!" Star Dancer hurriedly left Walks Slowly and hastened to the scene. When she reached the commotion, her stomach lurched at what she saw. Kicking Bear's face was nearly ripped away, and his stomach had been torn open, exposing his insides. How he managed to get on his horse and return to camp, no one would ever know. His mother wept bitterly, falling to her knees beside him.

"The great humpback did this to him," Looking Horse said, shaking his head in remorse.

"*You* did this to him!" Kicking Bear's grief-stricken father, Whistler, retorted. "You asked too much for Star Dancer. Now my son is dead because of your demands!"

Looking Horse faced him squarely. "Kicking Bear is dead because he chose to challenge Stalking Wolf. I am sorry, Whistler, for what has happened to your son, but I did not do this. I only said what was required, and Kicking Bear chose to go after the great bear. Now he has died with honor. It is even possible that Stalking Wolf will be killed. If not, we will know it is the will of *Wakan-Tanka* that he wed my daughter. It is the way."

Star Dancer turned away, unable to look at Kicking Bear any longer. She felt sick inside. When she looked over at Little Fox, her childhood friend stared back at her accusingly, as though this was her fault. She left the crowd to go back to her grandmother, her grief over Kicking Bear enhanced by the fact that now, if Stalking Wolf returned with the required items, she would have to go away with him.

She met Walks Slowly as the old woman shuffled toward the sight. "You do not want to see, *Uncheedah*. He was mauled by the bear."

The old woman shook her head and reached out to Star Dancer. "I am sorry for you, child. I realize that you cared much for him. Now we know what your own choice must be."

"But what if Stalking Wolf is also killed?"

"He is a visionary, child, destined to be your husband. He will return with the skin of the humpback. Of this I am sure."

Star Dancer blinked from tears. "But if he had not come to us saying I must be his wife, Kicking Bear would still be alive! I *hate* him! I hate this man who is to be my husband!"

"What has happened is simply the will of powers we cannot control, child. Kicking Bear was not strong enough or clever enough to do what he had to do to prove his worthiness. This is not the fault of Stalking Wolf."

Star Dancer closed her eyes as the cries of keening women filled the air. Some of the men also began chanting the death song. Kicking Bear's body would be wrapped and taken to the summer burial ground, where it would be placed on a scaffold, his medicine bag and most important weapons placed around him to take with him to the place in the sky where he would join his ancestors. Star Dancer felt responsible for his horrible demise, and she wept at the thought of how he must have suffered . . . just to try to keep her from having to marry a stranger.

"I will never forget him," she sobbed to her grandmother.

The old woman put an arm around her. "Kicking Bear was happy to show his bravery to us, and today he is happy in death. Now we can only wait to see if Stalking Wolf survives. Think good thoughts for him, Granddaughter."

"I cannot," Star Dancer replied. "I will *never* think good of him!" She ran off to cry alone.

EARLY SEPTEMBER
1832

When the Leaves Become
Yellow Moon

CHAPTER EIGHT

AN UNUSUAL QUIET hung over the large Sichangu camp. Star Dancer carefully worked the sharp edge of her elkhorn scraper across a staked deerskin, peeling away the remaining membrane on the underside. The hard, busy work helped soothe her grieving heart. Indeed, a cloud of grief hung in the air, and Star Dancer felt drained from her own weeping over Kicking Bear's death.

Several of the younger men had left to hunt, and the women remained at camp to cure fresh meat and scrape and stretch hides. A contingent of older warriors stayed to guard them.

Walks Slowly sat near Star Dancer, sorting quills by their size. Later, the softened and dyed quills would decorate the new skins when they were fashioned into clothing and moccasins. Star Dancer marveled at how fast her grandmother could sort. Her gnarled fingers bore many old scars and calluses from working with quills for so many years.

Star Dancer wiped sweat from her brow. Even though late summer was upon them and the aspens showed a hint of yellow in their leaves, heat still visited this place of bubbling waters, and the surrounding mountaintops remained mostly bald, except for small patches of snow that never disappeared.

The tranquil camp came alive when scouts rode in, their horses' hooves pounding against the soft soil and spewing dirt as they passed. The riders dismounted in front of Tall Woman's tepee.

"Stalking Wolf comes!" one of them announced to Looking Horse. "He brings even more horses, and the hide of a humpback!"

Star Dancer's heart fell. After an absence of over six weeks, she thought Stalking Wolf might never return. She left her work and walked closer, meeting her mother's gaze as the woman hurried to meet her. "He has come for you. Go and wash yourself, and put on another tunic, Star Dancer. You are soiled from cleaning the skins."

Star Dancer obeyed, but with no joy in her heart. She ducked inside the tepee to get a clean tunic, wondering why it mattered how she might look to a man she did not even want to marry.

"He is wounded," she heard one of the scouts telling her father. "The bearskin he brings is the biggest I have ever seen! He also brings the fresh meat of an antelope."

"This is a great moment," Looking Horse answered.

Star Dancer went back outside. In the distance, she saw others gathering to watch Stalking Wolf ride in. She hurried away to wash. Angrily she tore off her tunic and walked into the creek, sinking back into its warm waters. She liked this place of magic, where in certain areas the ground bubbled, and sometimes water gushed from underneath in great spouts. Here they were closest to Mother Earth. Here the waters were always warm for bathing. She wanted to stay forever.

Reluctantly, she scrubbed her hands and body with sand, then rinsed and came out of the water to stand in the hot sun. She let its warmth dry her skin, and with her hair still damp, she pulled on her clean tunic. She decided not to brush her hair or to do anything else to make it appear as though she wanted to look pretty for her husband-to-be.

"Good enough for a stranger," she mumbled to herself.

She pulled on her moccasins and let her hair hang loose and tangled as she stomped away from the creek toward the gathering on the other side of the village. As she drew closer, she saw a truly magnificent bearskin spread out on the ground. Everyone there exclaimed among themselves as to its size and the thickness of the fur. Already, Looking Horse busily directed others to divide and smoke the meat of the antelope Stalking Wolf had presented him.

"Stalking Wolf left the bear meat for the wolves," Tall Woman told Star Dancer. "There was no time to divide and smoke it, since he had to hurry back with the skin. He killed the antelope only yesterday, wanting to bring us meat as an extra gift. He is a fine hunter, Star Dancer, and a great warrior! In spite of his wounds, he stole horses from a Crow camp before returning, just so he could present more to your father to show how much he values his new wife."

Star Dancer glanced at Stalking Wolf, who stood back watching, perspiration gleaming on his skin. Even from a distance, Star Dancer could see lingering, puffy scars on the man's left arm and shoulder, and she could not help feeling a hint of pity for what he had suffered to win her. She stiffened when Stalking Wolf's gaze then rested on her. He said nothing, but his hypnotic dark eyes drew her in, and she felt herself leaving her mother and walking closer to him, her emotions ranging from fear to curiosity, from hatred to an acceptance of her fate. When she came near, he nodded toward a black mare standing beside his own horse.

"I took this one from before the door of a Crow warrior's tepee," he told her.

Star Dancer knew that such a daring act could easily cost a man his life. Horses tethered in front of a man's tepee were kept there because they were the warrior's favorite ponies, tended by only the owner himself. It took great courage to sneak into an enemy camp and steal such a horse.

"She is strong, but gentle," Stalking Wolf added. "She is a gift for you. I call her *Sotaju.*"

Smoke. It was a fitting name. Star Dancer felt a little of her resentment leave her. Not all Sioux women owned horses. To own one such as this beautiful black mare would bring her even more prestige. She ran her hands along the sleek animal's neck and side, admiring its fine lines.

"I thank you for the gift," she told Stalking Wolf. "I am honored."

A hint of a smile crossed his face. "I am glad."

Their gazes held, and to realize she would eventually have to be intimate with this man made Star Dancer's cheeks burn. Here was the one who would be her husband . . . not Kicking Bear. She looked away to hide her tears. "Did they tell you about Kicking Bear?"

She started when he touched her shoulder. "I am sorry about your good friend. It was the will of *Wakan-Tanka.* Perhaps this same bear killed him. If so, then it, too, has given up its spirit. It is proper."

"Your gifts are even finer than I hoped for," Looking Horse spoke up, coming over to stand near them. "You have greatly honored my family and my daughter, Stalking Wolf."

Stalking Wolf proudly nodded. "I must ask if you have moss. Most of my wounds are healing, but I fear some of them are not. They are still painful, a deep pain that may make me sick."

Looking Horse walked around him, studying the great gashes from the bear's claws. Most were scabbed over, a few of the scars turning white now instead of pink. But two of the gashes festered in the way he had seen cause some men to die. "*Aye,* you must come into our dwelling and let Tall Woman and her mother treat the wounds. You will eat with us."

Stalking Wolf followed Looking Horse to Tall Woman's tepee, and Star Dancer gave *Sotaju* to a young boy to tend, then joined her family. Inside the tepee, Walks Slowly glanced at Stalking Wolf as he sat down with a grunt from pain and weariness. Her aged eyes became bright with eagerness. "What have we here?" she asked. "My granddaughter's new husband?"

Stalking Wolf managed a grin, but anyone could see that he was in pain. "Not until we have a ceremony," he reminded her.

Looking Horse directed the women to tend to Stalking Wolf's wounds. Walks Slowly set a stirring spoon aside as Tall Woman took from her supplies a leather pouch that held fresh moss. She began packing it against the still-raw claw marks.

Walks Slowly used her cane to support herself as she eased down in front of Stalking Wolf. She watched him silently, a sly, all-knowing look in her eyes.

"I am sorry to take your granddaughter away, but you know it must be so," Stalking Wolf told her.

Walks Slowly nodded. "You understand that most of our young girls are close to their grandmothers, but my Star Dancer is more special than most. She is a good girl, and she is afraid. You must be kind to her."

"You have my promise," Stalking Wolf answered.

Walks Slowly nodded, looking over at Star Dancer with a grin and a nod of approval. Star Dancer stayed out of the way, unable to bring herself to talk to, or even to look at, her future husband in such close quarters. She could not help admiring him for his courage and skill . . . yet part of her would not have minded if his wounds had been fatal.

It was done now. Stalking Wolf had returned with the required bounty. Her marriage to him would be *wiyan he cinacaqupi,* a marriage wherein a man simply stated he wanted a certain woman, and for the required gifts, her family gave her to him. She would enjoy no courting beyond that one brief conversation under the blanket.

CHAPTER NINE

SLEEP REFUSED TO visit Star Dancer. She listened to the occasional yip of coyotes and the howls of wolves far off in the foothills. Their wailing seemed to reflect the agony in her soul at knowing she must soon leave her family.

She slept next to her grandmother, wanting to remember everything about this most special woman—her wrinkled hands with their callused fingers, her scratchy breathing, her patience, her comforting arms, her familiar smell, and her words of wisdom that seemed to come in an almost constant chatter. She rubbed at one of the old wrinkled arms, and Walks Slowly stirred and opened her eyes. She smiled as she reached out and pulled Star Dancer closer and gently stroked her hair.

"I will miss you, Granddaughter," she whispered.

Star Dancer clung to the old woman, letting her tears come. "And I will miss my *Uncheedah*."

Walks Slowly patted her back. "One day you will be a true woman, and you will bear children for Stalking Wolf. Your children will warm your heart and make you happy. And I believe Stalking Wolf also will make you happy. Someday you will understand that this is a good thing, this leaving of your family. It is the way."

"I want to believe you, Grandmother, but it is hard to think I can ever be happy again."

"The white buffalo will not allow you to be so

unhappy for long. It represents only good things and will always protect you. Remember that, and remember that you are very special and must always be treated with respect. Hold your head high, Granddaughter, and make your father and mother proud. Most of all, you must make your husband proud. One day you will desire Stalking Wolf in every way, and he will be the one you never want to leave. You will ache for him, as I sometimes still ache for my own long-dead husband."

"Did you love him when you wed him?"

"No. He first wed my sister, but she died and left him with two small children. I was just then old enough to wed, and I loved and wanted to care for my sister's children, and to give her husband more offspring. And so I went to his tepee, and we made love. It was not long before I truly did love and desire him. It will be this way for you."

Star Dancer could not imagine allowing Stalking Wolf to come to her bed at any time soon. "At least you knew your husband. You did not marry a stranger."

"This is true, but you will get to know Stalking Wolf better as you travel together, and you will be as happy as I was. I promise you, Granddaughter, or I would fight to keep you here. So would your mother and father."

Star Dancer closed her eyes, weariness enveloping her. She could only trust that her parents and grandmother were right. After tomorrow, it would be too late to change any of it. "I just want to stay here with you, *Uncheedah.*"

Walks Slowly patted her back, smiling through her own tears. "Of course you do. I felt the same way once about my grandmother. To this day, I feel close to her."

Star Dancer tried to picture Walks Slowly as a young girl, but it was impossible. Grandmother had always just been Grandmother, and after tonight, it was very possible she would never see her again.

"I hope that someday I am as wise and brave and strong as you, *Uncheedah*."

The old woman chuckled, but when she breathed in, Star Dancer detected a quick little jerk and only then realized that the woman's light laughter was mixed with tears. She hugged the frail body gently.

"I will always love you, Grandmother."

"As I will always love you. Neither distance nor death can part us, Star Dancer."

"Will you dream about me sometimes?"

"Yes. And you will dream about me. In that way, we will always be together. Remember all the things I have taught you, and when you are an old woman yourself, you can teach your own granddaughters."

"That is a long time away."

Walks Slowly chuckled. "Not as long as you think. It goes quickly, Star Dancer, like the blink of an eye. And one day you will wonder why you were so afraid to leave your grandmother's arms. You will wrap your own arms around a granddaughter of your own, and you will give her the same advice. Love your husband well, and always be pure and honest. Most of all, have courage. You are a Sichangu holy woman. *Wakan-Tanka* and the White Buffalo Spirit will always protect you."

Star Dancer finally felt sleep beginning to overcome her. She snuggled closer to her grandmother. For this one last night, she just wanted to be a little girl and not think about being a married woman going off to a strange new land. Tonight was for *Uncheedah*.

CHAPTER TEN

MORNING CAME TOO quickly. Star Dancer reluctantly left the safety and protection of her grandmother's arms to rise and dress. She helped prepare something to eat, but she had no appetite herself. After filling his belly, her father left, and Walks Slowly and Tall Woman began the preparations for what should be a happy wedding day. Star Dancer felt no happiness. She sat still while Walks Slowly combed her hair, a task the old woman always loved doing. The realization that this was the last time she would enjoy Walks Slowly's attentions brought silent tears to Star Dancer's eyes.

"Remember that if Stalking Wolf should be cruel to you, you can throw him away and come back to us," the old woman told her. "You can declare you are no longer husband and wife. You have the right."

Star Dancer nodded and sniffled.

Walks Slowly ran her hand over the girl's thick, lustrous hair. "Now you must have a woman's heart, Star Dancer. Today my granddaughter will become an honored wife. I will paint flowers on your cheeks, and you will wear the special dress I made for you, the one with the quilled fringes that you wore for the Night Dance. Stalking Wolf has chosen the most beautiful and most special woman among all the Lakota. He knows this, and he will honor your wishes, as well he should."

Star Dancer waited patiently while Walks Slowly

finished combing her hair. Tall Woman joined them then, helping Walks Slowly prepare the paint for Star Dancer's cheeks, using ground roots, flower petals, and berries for colors.

"I am sure my mother already advised you well, my daughter," she told Star Dancer, "as she always has done. I can only say how proud I am, and how much my heart will miss you. I will live for the day when you can come back and see us." She sat down beside Star Dancer with a wooden bowl filled with red berry juice. "Stalking Wolf has promised to bring you next summer."

She kissed Star Dancer's cheek, then held her hand as Walks Slowly painted flowers on her daughter's cheeks and forearms. Star Dancer noticed how Walks Slowly's bony hands were amazingly steady for her age.

"If I were marrying Stalking Wolf, I would remove my chastity belt the first night," Walks Slowly teased, smiling slyly.

Tall Woman laughed, but Star Dancer did not appreciate their humor.

"I intend to wear my belt a very long time," she declared.

Walks Slowly only chuckled. She finished her painting, and Tall Woman braided Star Dancer's thick, dark tresses into one heavy braid at her back, weaving quilled rawhide strips into it for color and beauty. She then helped Star Dancer slip into her wedding tunic, after which Walks Slowly tied a colorfully quilled hairpiece into the side of her hair.

"There." The old woman leaned back. "Your intended will be pleased."

Star Dancer did not care much if she pleased the man or not. Outside the women already sang a wedding song, one that spoke of love and courtship, of a man and woman sharing a life together, of bearing children who would continue the life of the Lakota Nation.

Star Dancer faced her mother. "I am ready."

Tall Woman frowned. "Do not let others see that look on your face," she warned. "You look as though we are leading you to the torture pole." She smiled and shook her head, and the three of them left the tepee to join the singing well-wishers outside.

People smiled and followed along as Star Dancer walked toward Stalking Wolf, who stood with Beaver Singing and Looking Horse. He wore a bleached-white fringed shirt adorned with a colorful circle of quills in a sunburst design. A round hairpiece made of dyed quills decorated his shiny black hair, which hung clean and loose, and a bone hair-pipe necklace graced his throat.

Star Dancer supposed that his mother or sister had made the shirt and necklace for him. They represented hard work, which told her his family loved him. Looking Horse stepped forward and took her arm, then held her hand out ceremoniously to Stalking Wolf.

"This day I give to you my daughter as a wife. I trust you to treat her well, to honor her as one who has been blessed by the sacred white buffalo. I accept the gifts you brought as fitting payment for the honor of taking Star Dancer to your people and to your dwelling."

Stalking Wolf nodded and took Star Dancer's hand. She felt so numb that she hardly felt his clasp. She heard whispers of excitement and approval all around, and she recognized Little Fox's giggle. It reminded her to be grateful that her good friend did not blame her after all for Kicking Bear's death. How happy and proud she should be at this moment she shared with her family and friends, yet she wished someone else stood here beside her.

A gentle wind blew at strands of Stalking Wolf's

hair, and his dark eyes held her captive as he spoke in a deep, sure voice.

"As a member of the Brave Heart Society of the Oglala, and a Shirt Wearer for the Lakota, I pledge my honor. I will protect and provide for you all my days."

Star Dancer managed to find her voice. "As a daughter of the Sichangu . . . and . . . as one who walks with the sacred white buffalo, I—" she forced the words "—I pledge my honor. I will be your loyal and dutiful wife all my days." If only they could each also pledge their love.

Beaver Singing raised his arms and called a chant to the Great Spirit to bless this union, then took an already-lit prayer pipe from Looking Horse and drew on its sacred smoke, which he blew onto the couple to bless them. "I declare that you are husband and wife," he said, speaking so that all could hear.

That was it. Star Dancer now belonged to an Oglala warrior. Stalking Wolf bent close to touch her cheek with his own, and Star Dancer knew that if this were Kicking Bear, he would whisk her into his arms and carry her off now, and she would gladly go.

Drummers sounded their rhythmic recognition of the union, accompanying the trills and singing of the women. Star Dancer moved through the expected celebrations, the center of attention at the grand feast held by Tall Woman. Walks Slowly bristled with excitement, and by early evening, all were teasing the newlyweds with suggestive remarks, leading them to a tepee the women had collectively constructed for the young couple to use for the night. It sat well away from the main camp. Stalking Wolf stood aside and motioned Star Dancer inside, and among trills of encouragement from the other women, Star Dancer reluctantly entered. Once inside, she felt totally intimidated by Stalking Wolf's powerful presence, and she scurried to her own side of the tepee.

"The others will leave food at the entrance, so we need not rejoin them today," she told Stalking Wolf. "We will stay inside and let them think what they wish, but I will not be a wife to you tonight." She dearly wished she could read his dark eyes. Was he laughing at her? Angry? He gave a wry smile, looking her over in a way that reminded her of how helpless she would be if he chose not to honor her demand.

"I will not make you my wife until *I* feel you are ready. I still see some of the child in you, so go to sleep. You need not fear my advances."

He moved to his own side of the dwelling, removing his shirt and crossing his legs, taking up his pipe. He lit the pipe with a burning stick from a small central fire, then held it high. He closed his eyes, whispering something Star Dancer could not understand. He drew on the pipe, then raised it again, whispering another private prayer.

Star Dancer plopped onto the bed of robes made up for them to share. "Do not come near this bed," she warned, secretly angry that he had practically called her a child.

Stalking Wolf did not answer, and Star Dancer turned away, pouting. This certainly was not how she had imagined her wedding night if she could have married Kicking Bear. She felt a distinct urge to run back to her grandmother's arms, but that would humiliate everyone, including herself.

Tired from the strain of the day, she moved under a robe, deciding not to undress. Now she must trust this new husband of hers to keep his word.

CHAPTER ELEVEN

STAR DANCER AWOKE to daylight gleaming through the tepee smoke hole. She turned over to see Stalking Wolf gone. Quickly she rose and changed out of her wedding tunic so no one would know she had never removed it last night. She ducked outside, hurrying behind a bush to relieve herself. On her way back, she saw Stalking Wolf with a group of men and women walking toward the tepee, the women talking and laughing.

Pain gripped the pit of her stomach. How could she have slept so hard and for so long? She needed time to visit her mother and grandmother, but it looked like Stalking Wolf meant to leave right away. He led Sotaju and his own horse. Sotaju pulled a heavily packed travois.

Too soon the well-wishers reached her, many of the women teasing her about being "worn out" from her wedding night. Star Dancer blushed as she smiled and pretended they were right. She did not want to spoil the leave-taking for her mother by letting her know how terribly unhappy she really was; nor should she embarrass and shame her husband by admitting she had ordered him to stay out of her bed.

Her mother hurried ahead then to embrace her, followed by other friends and relatives. Her arms still around her mother, Star Dancer looked pleadingly at Stalking Wolf. His gaze remained hard and determined. She wondered if he rushed her along out of anger about last night.

"We must get an early start," he said firmly. "We have a long way to go."

Star Dancer fought hard not to break down and cry. She turned to hug Walks Slowly, and the old woman returned the embrace with surprising strength. She and Tall Woman, as well as several other women, wept amid smiles, laughter, and good wishes. Even Little Fox wept. Star Dancer turned to her father, who only smiled and nodded. His eyes betrayed his sadness, but Star Dancer knew he would not show emotion in front of the others. There would be no embrace from Looking Horse.

Women threw wildflowers on top of the newlyweds' supplies, gifts of deerskins, buffalo hides, moccasins, quills, tools, smoked meat, turnips, roots and berries, and more, all offered freely and joyfully by kind friends Star Dancer feared she might never see again.

Stalking Wolf finally grasped her and pulled her away from more hugs. He lifted her with ease onto Sotaju's back. "We must go." He mounted his own horse in one graceful leap. The eager gray-spotted gelding tossed its white mane and trotted around in a circle. Tall Woman reached up, as did old Grandmother, and Star Dancer touched their hands one last time.

"Remember what I told you, Granddaughter," Walks Slowly said. "We will always be together in spirit."

"I will remember, *Uncheedah*."

Stalking Wolf calmed his horse and grasped a lead rope tied to Sotaju. He rode away from camp, heading east. Near panic engulfed Star Dancer as she looked back, taking a last, long glance at her father and mother, her grandmother, her friends. She wanted to scream at Stalking Wolf to wait a while longer. She waved until her arm ached, and finally the camp faded into the western horizon.

"Your neck will be stiff," Stalking Wolf called to her.

Star Dancer turned to see him looking back at her with a scowl. She bowed her head, not knowing what to say.

"It is time to look ahead, my wife, not behind."

When I look ahead, I see only a stranger, Star Dancer thought, *taking me to a strange people in a strange land*. She refused to cry, but the effort made her head ache.

CHAPTER TWELVE

"YOU WILL LEARN to love *Paha-Sapa*," Stalking Wolf told Star Dancer. "My homeland is a beautiful place."

"And so is the land of the bubbling waters, the land of the Sichangu," Star Dancer replied.

Stalking Wolf continued riding in front of his wife, perfectly happy to avoid looking at her, for to watch her was to want her. For four days they had traveled almost in silence. Star Dancer spoke to him only when he spoke first. Her flippant arrogance annoyed him so much that he did not find it terribly difficult to stay out of her bed.

"I agree your homeland is beautiful," he told her. "But one day you will gladly call the Black Hills home."

"Perhaps."

Stalking Wolf frowned. Nothing he said or did impressed the woman. He had tried to reason the ways he might win her affection and desire. Any other Lakota woman would be proud that he had suffered through two Sun Dances and held the honor of Shirt Wearer. He had risked his life to win this woman, and during their trek to his homeland, he'd killed fresh game for her every day, demonstrating his skill with bow and arrow. Sometimes he almost wished they would be attacked by the Crow so that he could show her his fighting skills firsthand. She still refused to remove her chastity belt, treating him like the enemy and she his captive, anxious to flee at any moment.

"Have you ever seen the *wasicu?* The hairy-faces?" he asked, hoping to impress her with his knowledge of the white man.

Star Dancer did not reply immediately, and he thought she might not answer him at all, but finally she spoke up. "No, but I am told that some have eyes the color of the sky. Is this true?"

"It is. I have seen and traded with them," Stalking Wolf said proudly.

"Do they truly have hairy faces?"

"*Aye.* And most of them smell bad, but they have good things for trade. Still, I have not decided if they can be trusted." Stalking Wolf halted his horse. "They come from the land where the sun rises. Some say there are many more there, that they might even be more in number than the Lakota."

Star Dancer moved Sotaju beside him, and Stalking Wolf felt pleased she was joining him in a conversation, no matter how mundane.

"Do you think it is true that there are more of them than us?"

Stalking Wolf studied her delicate beauty. He wanted her. "I only know that I am not afraid of them, no matter how many there are. Those I met when they came to our land hunting beaver have a look in their eyes that tells me they do not always speak true, but there are few of them in Lakota lands. I do not think they are an enemy to be feared."

"Surely there cannot be more of them than the great numbers of the Lakota."

Stalking Wolf took pleasure in her worry and wonder. Finally she seemed at least somewhat impressed by his superior experience and knowledge. "I suppose not." He turned and pointed to a thick stand of pine. "We will make camp there." He looked over at Star Dancer. "I make no judgment yet about the *wasicu,* but you are right. So far, their numbers seem to be few, and the Lakota are many and strong. I see little harm that can come to us from the white man. In time, you will see them for yourself."

He started toward the place where they would make camp, and Star Dancer rode beside him. "Tell me, my husband. Is it true there is a place in the country of the Oglala that is called *Mako Sica?*"

Stalking Wolf smiled at her curiosity. "It is true. We call it bad land because much of it is only clay and sand. It drops below the earth rather than rising up like the mountains, yet when you go into it, you find there are deep canyons with rocky walls as high as mountains. It is a bad land for most of life, but it is very sacred for it is full of mystery, and when you go there, you are close to the heart of Mother Earth. Only the Oglala know how to find their way in and out of our Mother's heart, and it is a good place to hide from the enemy. Others are easily lost and sometimes die there. Once a hairy-face was lost there, and he became crazy from fear and helplessness."

"What happened to him?"

"It was long ago, when there were only one or two *wasicus* anywhere near Oglala country. My father told me about it. He said no one would go near the hairy-face because evil spirits possessed him. Finally, he fell from a cliff and died. No one buried him for fear evil spirits would also possess them. Vultures ate his flesh, and his bones rotted and disappeared into the clay." Stalking Wolf noticed Star Dancer shiver.

"I do not think I would like such a place," she said.

Stalking Wolf shrugged. "You will like my homeland soon enough. Most of it is hilly, and covered with sweet pine to shade you, but there is also open grassland where the buffalo roam freely, so many that a man could walk on their backs." He faced her, and for a moment, he saw something in her eyes that told him she was beginning to warm to him, at least a little, but she quickly turned away, obviously determined to keep a distance between them.

They reached their destination, and Stalking Wolf eased off his horse, his wounds still giving him pain. "Your mother told me she packed in our supplies *c'anli icahiye,* the root found in the mountains of the bighorn sheep," he told Star Dancer. "She had no moss left and will have to search for more, but she had a little of this root. If you boil it and soften it, you can rub it on my wounds. She said this would help."

"I know about *c'anli icahiye,*" Star Dancer answered. "My grandmother taught me how to use it when my father was cut by a Crow warrior's tomahawk."

Stalking Wolf noted that she spoke defensively, proudly letting him know he did not need to teach her about such things.

"You should have told me sooner that some of the wounds still bring you pain," she continued. "My grandmother always says you should not let such things go too long without treating them."

Now her words came with great authority, and Stalking Wolf had to smile. "I thought they would heal after treating them with moss," he told her. He sat down on a log and watched his wife tether the horses and search their supplies for the *c'anli icahiye.* Once she found it, she gathered wood and added to it some buffalo chips she had picked up as they traveled. She soon started a fire, and into a deep stone bowl she poured water from a buffalo bladder.

Stalking Wolf considered her well-trained in cooking and other duties, taking stock of her every good point, glad to find her energetic and ambitious. Still, every chore she performed brought with it a hint of resentment, and he did not doubt that he was the source. She would have done these things gladly for Kicking Bear, but for him, it was strictly duty.

"We have pemmican and dried meat to eat," she

told him. She put the healing root into the bowl of water, which she set over the fire's flames. "If your wounds still hurt you, it is not necessary to hunt with your bow. Such movement will only bring more pain."

The words held no particular concern. They were simply a statement of fact. She went about other chores silently: unloading the horses, preparing places to sleep, getting out the pemmican and dried meat, setting his weapons beside him so they would be handy.

Stalking Wolf watched her every move with an inward sigh. He could already tell that tonight he would again sleep restlessly because of the ache in his loins, and he could not help wondering if this new wife of his would ever show him the sexual passion he had known with Fall Leaf Woman, who had so willingly given herself to him.

When the root was properly boiled and softened, Star Dancer scooped it from the bowl and dropped it into a smaller wooden bowl, then began smashing it with a wooden spoon and working it into a thick paste. She let it cool for a few minutes, then brought it to Stalking Wolf.

"Remove your shirt. After I apply the paste, you should put the shirt back on so the salve does not rub off."

Stalking Wolf obeyed, suspecting that this woman would turn out to be quite something to handle within the confines of the tepee. Not only had she been stubborn and forthright, but she showed a tendency to be bossy. He wrapped his arms around his knees as she gently applied the paste to his back. He gritted his teeth against the heat and the sting. The wounds hurt more when someone touched and pressed on them, but he made no sound while she worked.

"How many more days before we reach your homeland?" she asked.

"Many more. My people will hunt along the way,

so we might come upon them before they reach *Paha-Sapa*." Stalking Wolf heard only a sigh, no verbal reply. "I promised you I would take you back to your own people after winter," he reminded her.

"I know. But it seems so far away. I worry about not seeing *Uncheedah* again."

"And each time I leave my own mother and sister, I worry about not seeing *them* again. Not because of old age, but because of sickness, or an attack from our enemies. It is natural to worry about those for whom you have deep feelings."

More silence. Stalking Wolf groped for something more to say, and since Star Dancer seemed curious about white men, he decided to bring up the subject again.

"It is said that people like us who lived in the land of the rising sun all died from sicknesses the white man brings wherever he goes. I have not seen such sickness, but it is the only thing that worries me about the *wasicus*."

Star Dancer finished with the salve and moved away from him. She set the wooden bowl aside, then picked up a stick and stirred the fire. Finally, she met his gaze, deep concern in her eyes. "It is like fighting something you cannot see. Maybe sickness is the weapon the white man uses against his enemy."

"Perhaps. We can fight such a thing only by being strong spiritually, by willing ourselves not to die."

"And do you believe we can do that? Just will it?"

"Yes. It is how I felt no pain during the Sun Dance, how I survive when I fast and let blood when seeking a vision. I will myself not to feel, and not to die." Stalking Wolf watched her eyes. Did he see a little hint of respect and wonder there? He put his shirt back on, wincing with awakened pain. "Thank you for making the salve."

"You are my husband. It was my duty."

He longed to hear her say she had tended him out

of feelings more than from duty, but she went about her chores with no further comment. He turned away, gingerly lying down on his right side to avoid putting any pressure on his aching left shoulder. "I am not hungry," he told her. "I will sleep while there is a little light left, and you can sleep later when I wake up to watch the night." . . . *And to watch you,* he wanted to add. This journey was going to be much longer for him than for her.

MID-OCTOBER
1832

Moon of Falling Leaves

CHAPTER THIRTEEN

STAR DANCER FOLLOWED her husband through a constantly changing landscape, from open flatland surrounded by the outline of mountains in every direction, to rocky canyons, majestic in their beauty. The seemingly endless vastness through which they rode during the first several days became rolling green hills peppered with tumbles of rocks. Star Dancer could imagine the Great Spirit playing with the rocks, throwing handfuls of boulders across the wide land to see where they would settle.

After twenty days they saw smoke in the distance, several small plumes that curled skyward.

"I think we have found my people," Stalking Wolf said, riding a little faster.

Star Dancer followed him to a grassy ridge from where they saw a large camp of tepees spread out below.

"I can see they are Oglala," Stalking Wolf told her, "those who left after the Sun Dance and said they would hunt along the way home. Look at all the buffalo hides staked out to dry! And see the meat hanging over smoking fires." He breathed deeply, obvious pride and joy in his eyes when he turned to Star Dancer. "Standing Hawk and the others have had a successful hunt. The people will eat well this coming season."

Star Dancer followed his gaze back to the camp. "Who is Standing Hawk?"

"My best friend, for as long as I can remember. Now he is a Pipe Owner, probably the one who chose this place to camp." He grinned. "I think that perhaps he has camped longer than necessary, waiting for me to reach them before our clan joins the rest of the Oglala."

Star Dancer felt her heart beat harder at the thought of meeting those below, especially her new mother-in-law and sister-in-law. "Do you think your family will like me?" she asked.

"Of course they will. You are my chosen, and so they will accept you as one of their own. They will be pleased because *I* am pleased."

Star Dancer faced him squarely. "*Are* you truly pleased?"

His gaze forbade her to look away. "Why would I not be? You have been blessed by the sacred white buffalo, and you have danced on the stars. You are beautiful to a man's eye. Others will try to steal you from me."

Star Dancer caught a glimmer of warning in his eyes. Woe to the man who might try to run off with his wife! "I belong only to you," she answered. "I would not shame you or my father by taking another man, nor do I want my nose cut off."

His eyes raked her body, and he met her gaze with a frown. "I would not bring such harm to a holy woman." He looked back then at the camp below. "I should remind you, however, that you have taken *no* man yet, not even your own husband," he added, with a strong hint of sarcasm.

At a loss for a proper reply, Star Dancer said nothing.

"Come and meet my family."

Stalking Wolf spoke the words in a flat command and headed down the hill. A nervous Star Dancer followed, strong memories of her own family suddenly vivid in her mind. Only now did the fact she had to accept—and be adopted into—an entirely new family become real for her.

This would be her first meeting with Stalking Wolf's family. During the earlier Lakota Council meeting on Medicine Mountain, most of his clan had remained camped below because of the lack of room. After Stalking Wolf had left to hunt for the grizzly, Looking Horse had decided not to let the rest of the Oglala look upon his very special daughter until one or both of the two young suitors returned with the required prize to win her hand. He had kept Star Dancer in the confines of the Sichangu camps, away from the Oglala.

Star Dancer jumped when Stalking Wolf let out a shrill signal cry and waved a blanket to announce their arrival. A warm wind carried the scent of cook fires, and several dogs ran out to greet them, barking in a chorus of tones, tails wagging. They darted under and around the horses' hooves, and as husband and wife came closer to the village, children scurried to greet them. Two men mounted horses and rode out to welcome them. Others rose from cook fires and other duties to watch.

One of the riders rode hard to reach them first, and he gave out a clipped cry of glad greeting. "My friend returns with his new wife! You must have found and killed the humpback! I am glad for you, Stalking Wolf. Your father's spirit protected you."

Stalking Wolf grinned and sat a little straighter. "I gave the hide to my wife's family, along with antelope meat and even more horses. I stole the horses from the Crow, and the one my wife rides, I took from before a Crow warrior's tepee!"

The other young man let out a piercing whoop of celebration, and the two men grasped wrists and laughed. The other man then trotted his horse beside Star Dancer. "I am Standing Hawk. Your husband and I are like brothers. Welcome to the Oglala clan. Soon we will be home, *Paha-Sapa,* and you can meet all of us. Those camped here are just a handful compared to the numbers of Oglala in our homeland!"

Star Dancer nodded in greeting, considering Standing Hawk pleasant-looking but plain, neither handsome nor ugly. His eyes danced with near childlike joy, and she could see that though he sat much shorter than Stalking Wolf, he was stocky and muscular. His puffy eyelids made his eyes appear partially closed, but his round face beamed with gladness to see his friend again. He exuded a kind of wild excitement, a young man who loved the hunt, loved a challenge, and truly loved his close friendship with Stalking Wolf.

"Now that you have arrived, my friend, we will leave at sunrise for our sacred home," Standing Hawk told Stalking Wolf. "We have had a good hunt. There is much meat and many robes to take home with us!" He turned his horse and rode off, yipping and whooping, yelling that the clan's "mystic warrior" had returned with his new wife. The second rider also gave a shrill cry and rode back to camp, both men weaving in and out among the tepees to announce the arrival of one of their own.

Several women gathered to watch, and Star Dancer felt a renewed loneliness, that of a stranger among strangers. As they rode into the midst of camp, men and women alike congratulated Stalking Wolf on taking a new wife. Star Dancer could see that the young boys were in awe of her husband, several of them vying for his permission to take care of his horses.

Stalking Wolf halted his horse, and the prized war pony snorted and scuffled sideways. Stalking Wolf dismounted and stood before a tall, heavyset woman with dark-gray hair. She immediately touched his arm, deep concern in her eyes. "The bear harmed you," she said, studying the still-pink scars on his arm and shoulder.

"I am well, Mother," he replied. He turned and

lifted Star Dancer from her mount. "This is my new wife. She is called Star Dancer." He looked down at his wife. "My mother is called Red Sun Woman."

Star Dancer nodded to the woman, who stood nearly as tall as her son. At first she felt intimidated by the woman's size, but a warm glitter in Red Sun Woman's eyes made her feel welcome. The woman's smile revealed one front tooth missing, but it did not distract from an inner beauty that shone in her friendly face.

"My new daughter," she said, reaching out and touching Star Dancer's shoulders. "You are welcome here. It is good that my son has finally taken a wife, and one so beautiful and so blessed."

Star Dancer felt warmed by the words, which brought some relief to her homesick heart. That relief was spoiled when she turned to the younger woman standing beside Red Sun Woman. Stalking Wolf introduced his sister, Many Robes Woman. She stood as tall as her mother, a stocky, big-boned girl with a round face and chubby cheeks. Star Dancer shivered under Many Robes Woman's critical glare. The girl barely smiled as she handed a leather pouch to Star Dancer.

"Quills," she said. "My mother and I chased three different porcupine with our blankets and collected many quills while we waited for Stalking Wolf to return. We knew you would want to begin making something special for your new husband. The quills have been washed clean and only need to be dyed and sorted by size. I will help you."

Star Dancer took the bag of quills, deeply grateful for the gift, a sign of true welcome. Gathering quills was not an easy task, as a woman had to be very patient, waiting for the porcupine to show itself, then throwing a blanket over the animal, frightening it so that it released its quills, which then became stuck in the blanket. The quills had to be removed by hand and washed, often leaving a woman with sore fingers.

"This is a wonderful gift," Star Dancer told Many Robes Woman. "I thank you. Perhaps when we dye them, you can explain to me your brother's favorite colors."

Many Robes Woman shrugged. "Perhaps."

The girl's aloofness disappointed Star Dancer. Many Robes Woman's eyes betrayed resentment and dislike, and Star Dancer could not imagine why. Red Sun Woman put an arm around Star Dancer then and led her to a large, airy tepee with red suns painted on the outside skins. She showed Star Dancer a pile of bleached buffalo skins.

"I saved these over many months, hoping that my son would take a wife. The quills are a gift from my daughter. These robes are a gift from me. When we are home at last, you can begin sewing these skins together to make a dwelling of your own where you and your husband can be alone." She smiled eagerly. "I am sure you are anxious to be alone with my son. He is handsome, is he not?"

Star Dancer felt an ache in the pit of her stomach. "Yes. He is indeed handsome."

"And he is a very honored man, a Shirt Wearer now. I believe one day he will be a part of *Naca Ominicia*. You will not regret taking him for a husband."

Was there not anyone who understood what it was like to marry a complete stranger, no matter how important he might be? She looked around the tepee, a neat and tidy dwelling, with lovely paintings on the inner side of the skins. "I am glad to know I will still have a mother."

"Of course. The Lakota are all one family, are they not? The Sichangu, the Oglala, the Minniconjou, Hunkpapa, Sihasapa. We are all Lakota, and we all take care of each other. I am sure Stalking Wolf will arrange for you to see your real mother again."

"He has promised to take me after the winter."

Many Robes Woman joined them, and Red Sun

Woman turned to her daughter. "Take your new sister outside and show her where we wash. Introduce her to our friends. I think that tomorrow we will leave for *Paha-Sapa.* Then she can finally make a home for herself and her new husband." The woman actually giggled like a young girl as she touched Star Dancer's cheek. "Surely my son pleases you, does he not?"

Star Dancer realized what the woman meant. She had to convince her that things were fine between herself and Stalking Wolf, or Red Sun Woman might think she was not happy to have her son for a husband; that would offend her.

"Yes," she answered. "He is very pleasing. I am a happy woman."

Red Sun Woman nodded, patting her cheek. "And he is a gentle man, I am sure. I can see happiness and pride in his eyes." She turned to Many Robes Woman.

"Take your new sister out and introduce her to the others." She took the bag of quills from Star Dancer, and Many Robes Woman took her sister-in-law's arm with a sigh, clearly resenting her duty. She led Star Dancer outside and down to a creek, where several women scrubbed children and clothing with sand. Before introducing her, Many Robes Woman folded her arms and faced Star Dancer.

"I am not happy about your union with my brother. It is not because I do not like you, or that I think you unworthy of Stalking Wolf. I know that it is important he marry a woman of great gifts. He has, after all, seen the Feathered One."

Star Dancer frowned. "Then why are you not happy?"

"It is because there is another who has loved Stalking Wolf since she was sixteen. Now she is eighteen and has never wed. She thought Stalking Wolf would take her for a wife. Her name is Fall Leaf Woman, and she is my best friend."

Star Dancer blinked back tears at the unwelcome news. "Does Stalking Wolf love her?"

"I do not know. He has never said. Stalking Wolf never thinks of himself or what he wants. He does only what the Great Spirit tells him when he prays and has visions. Only the People matter to Stalking Wolf. My brother is a very unselfish man, devoted to the Lakota. That is why he is so blessed, why the gods have made him a visionary."

The words convinced Star Dancer that Stalking Wolf had absolutely no special feelings for her. Perhaps he resented her as much as she resented him. Perhaps his heart longed for Fall Leaf Woman. If Many Robes Woman spoke the rude words in hopes of hurting her feelings, she had succeeded.

"Is Fall Leaf Woman here?" Star Dancer asked.

"No. She waits at the main camp. She could not bear to follow us to Medicine Mountain and watch Stalking Wolf take a wife. She knows of his vision, and that he left to look for the woman the black wolf told him to claim. It is only because you are my sister now that I warn you she will not be happy to see you. I also warn you that I will not give up my friendship with her."

Star Dancer thought about her own good friend, Little Fox, and how much she missed her. "I would not ask that you give up your friendship. I would only ask that you understand me. I would never steal a man from anyone. I, too, am expected to do only what is best for the Lakota."

Many Robes Woman shrugged. "But you are not only special. You are very beautiful. I can see why my brother would want you for a wife. I am big-boned and tall, like my mother, not beautiful like you and Fall Leaf Woman."

So, Fall Leaf Woman was beautiful. Star Dancer felt surprising twinges of jealousy. It angered her that she faced more obstacles to her happiness, especially the possibility that her new husband might be pining for someone else. She needed a friend among these people. It would be wise to win Many Robes Woman to her side.

"I think you are quite beautiful, Many Robes Woman, just as Stalking Wolf is most handsome. Your size makes no difference." She noticed a hint of a smile cross the young woman's otherwise stern face. "I would like to befriend Fall Leaf Woman, if it is possible."

Many Robes Woman shook her head. "You never will. You did not yearn for my brother the way Fall Leaf Woman did. I assure you, she will be jealous and very angry." She turned and walked up to one of the other women, and Star Dancer followed, wondering if Stalking Wolf loved Fall Leaf Woman. She had not thought about having to vie for her own husband's love and devotion. This was indeed an odd situation, having to win the love of a man she did not even want.

LATE OCTOBER
1832

CHAPTER FOURTEEN

STALKING WOLF'S CLAN moved quietly on its journey to the Black Hills. Experience had taught the people that an enemy war party could be lurking in the surrounding hills and that all migrations required complete cooperation and order. Even the dogs sensed they must be still, and babies riding comfortably in cradleboards worn on their mothers' backs did not cry.

Along the way Star Dancer noticed wild berries beginning to dry, and saw that the leaves of hardwood trees had begun changing color, some of them already falling to the ground, a forecast of colder weather soon to come. Already nearly three months had passed since Stalking Wolf first came to Medicine Mountain to speak for her hand.

The early morning air felt cold, but by afternoon, a pleasant warmth embraced them. The rich scent of pine filled the air as they made their way through thick forests. Star Dancer guided Sotaju behind her husband, feeling uncomfortable riding when most of the women walked. She would have preferred walking with the other women so she could get to know them better, and so they would not think she considered herself more special than they, but Stalking Wolf insisted she ride.

As a Shirt Wearer, Stalking Wolf had organized the move. They migrated for ten days, not even putting up tepees at night to sleep. When they arrived near home, Standing Hawk rode ahead to signal the main camp. Star Dancer felt the excitement of the others when he came riding back toward them at a gallop, the hooves of his horse digging into the soft, needle-covered dirt. "Only a half day's ride," he said. "We will be there before the sun goes to sleep!"

His prediction proved correct, and by evening Star Dancer could smell the smoke of many cook fires, always the first sign of a big camp. They arrived at a clearing surrounded by mountains and more heavy forest, and Star Dancer drew in her breath at the sight of a camp larger than any Sichangu camp she had ever known. Circles of tepees stretched as far as she could see, each circle made up of more tepees than the fingers of her hands. As was custom, the opening of each circle faced in the direction of the rising sun.

Several warriors galloped out to meet them, and men and women within the arriving clan shouted joyful greetings in reply. Their entrance caused quite a stir, since they not only brought with them an abundance of hides and meat, but also a new wife for Stalking Wolf. Apparently the scouts had told the Oglala that she was coming, for many came from neighboring circles to welcome them. Star Dancer felt as though she was receiving a warm, emotional embrace from the whole camp. But then Many Robes Woman ran up to one young woman in particular and pointed to Star Dancer. In that moment, all feelings of a warm welcome left Star Dancer. The other woman, tall and beautiful, came closer, and Star Dancer saw obvious hatred gleaming in her dark eyes.

Fall Leaf Woman! It could be none other. Her hair hung in a dark profusion of tangles, and she turned lust-filled eyes to Stalking Wolf, looking him over with blatant desire. Star Dancer glanced at him to see if he returned the look, but he ignored it. Star Dancer wondered if it was only for her benefit . . . whether deep inside, Stalking Wolf yearned to leap from his horse and take Fall Leaf Woman into his arms. To her relief, he paid the woman no heed.

A more friendly group of women quickly gathered around Star Dancer and nearly pulled her off Sotaju, inundating her with greetings and questions. They carried on about helping her sew a tepee of her own so she could be alone with her new husband as soon as possible. Already they teased her about Stalking Wolf's looks and abilities.

"He is a prophet," one woman claimed.

"My son is indeed blessed with special powers," Red Sun Woman bragged. She kept an arm around Star Dancer, who was feeling overwhelmed.

Many of the other women unloaded hides and meat brought by the arriving hunting party, for all would share in the bounty. They sorted through various sizes of bones, making ready to turn them into useful utensils, as well as breastplates, necklaces, even weapons. Not one part of an animal would be wasted. Everything had its purpose—bones, gristle, membrane, hair, teeth, hooves, bladder, intestines, hides, fat, meat, and more. Buffalo represented life, and nearly every sacred dance and ritual centered around this most blessed and splendid animal that roamed Mother Earth. Each successful hunt meant a reason to celebrate.

Star Dancer knew that the night would bring a good deal of dancing, eating, and laughter. All would take part in the celebration—all, she supposed, except Fall Leaf Woman, who still stared at her as though she would rather spend the night torturing her. Star Dancer decided to remain close to her mother-in-law.

CHAPTER FIFTEEN

THE NIGHT AIR resounded with drumming and songs of thanksgiving. All evening a central fire burned brightly, while Stalking Wolf spoke to a group of Big Bellies, telling them about his experience in hunting and killing the great humpbacked bear. All eagerly listened as he recounted the adventure, exclaiming their awe and approval when Stalking Wolf held out a leather pouch and took from it one of the huge claws removed from the bear's feet. He turned to Star Dancer. "My wife will make a necklace from the claws, and I will wear it proudly," he finished.

Murmurs of praise and honor came from the captivated crowd. Then Stalking Wolf brought Star Dancer into their presence, asking all to treat her with courtesy and welcome. He handed her the pouch filled with claws, and she took it with a smile, wondering what all these Big Bellies would think if they knew her true feelings toward their favorite son.

The time came for the men to speak alone, and Star Dancer gladly took leave of their stares and attention. She headed back to a tepee friends had offered for her and Stalking Wolf to share until completing their own dwelling. She decided she would begin work on the bear-claw necklace tonight. She owed Stalking Wolf that much. Perhaps making the necklace would diminish her neglect of his husbandly desires.

"You will never please him!" a harsh voice called from the darkness.

Star Dancer jolted. *Fall Leaf Woman!* Did she mean to harm her? She faced her antagonist, holding her head high and feigning bravery. It took a moment to focus on the figure looming in the shadows of the moonlight. Fall Leaf Woman exuded a menacing air as she came closer.

"What do you want?" Star Dancer asked.

"I should *kill* you!" Fall Leaf Woman answered. "But the Oglala would cast me out for such a thing, and Stalking Wolf would kill *me* in return. The people would expect it of him, but it would not be in his heart to do so. Always remember that he loves only *me!* You will never be as important to him. He took you for a wife only because of a vision."

"And it is the same for *me!*" Star Dancer answered firmly. "Because I have seen the white buffalo, I have had to marry a stranger!"

Fall Leaf Woman tossed her hair behind her shoulders. "And how could you not be pleased with a man like Stalking Wolf? If you consider it a sacrifice to marry him, then you are a fool! There are a hundred other young women in this camp who would *gladly* go to his bed. But *I* am the only one who shared him that way . . . and I will share him that way again!"

She turned and stalked away, and Star Dancer felt achingly alone. She wished she could talk to her grandmother. Shivering at the surprise visit, she hurried to her own tepee, where she set aside the leather pouch that held the bear claws. She would *not* begin making Stalking Wolf's necklace tonight. Why should she go out of her way for a husband who did not truly love or want her, who apparently desired another? He wanted only to mate with her so that she could give him sons.

She removed her tunic belt with its sacred medicine bag, elkhorn scraper, and small knife attached. She carefully laid the belt beside her bed, deciding to keep the knife handy in case Fall Leaf Woman attacked her.

She removed her tunic and crawled under the robes.

The fire inside barely glowed with dying embers, but Star Dancer did not feel like getting up to add wood and buffalo chips to it. This first day among a new people left her weary and depressed. Her encounter with Fall Leaf Woman only made things worse. She couldn't care less now if she never spoke to Stalking Wolf again.

She turned over, pouting. By the time her bragging husband returned to the tepee tonight, he would be puffed up with pride and arrogance. Perhaps if he found her asleep, he would turn to Fall Leaf Woman, the one he truly loved. She hoped he would. Then she could accuse him of being unfaithful, throw him out, and dissolve the marriage without shame.

CHAPTER SIXTEEN

STALKING WOLF ENTERED his tepee and found Star Dancer sleeping. He built up the central fire for warmth, and he saw that in her sleep, Star Dancer's robe had fallen away, revealing most of her bare back and her slender shoulders. Stalking Wolf longed to see the round, firm bottom still hidden by the robe, ached to touch and taste her ripe breasts.

And why shouldn't I? he thought. The praises and attention he had received from the Big Bellies tonight filled him with pride. He relished the love his people held for him, the honor they showed him. Why couldn't this young woman afford him the same feelings? Why did she not yearn for him as did other Oglala women . . . like Fall Leaf Woman? Surely he could entice Star Dancer with the pleasure of making love.

He sighed with resignation, fighting the urge to take her whether she liked it or not. He removed his clothing, his penis swelling with desire for his beautiful wife. Perhaps if he crawled under her robe while she slept, he could enter her before she realized his intentions. Then she would know such pleasure that she would not be angry with him.

He moved around to crouch in front of her, finding it ridiculous that he could bravely stand against any enemy, even the humpbacked bear, yet feel apprehension and intimidation at facing this small bit of woman. He must not allow her to continue to reject him. He lifted her robe and crawled in beside her, grasping a firm virgin breast and bending his head to taste her nipple.

Star Dancer started awake with a gasp. "No!" she protested, pushing at him.

"It is time!"

"I still am not ready!"

"It has been too long!" Stalking Wolf retorted, his whole body on fire for her. "I said I would never bring you harm, but this is not harm. It is a simple act of mating so that you are truly my wife, and so that my life can flow into you and create sons. I ask you to remove the bindings that keep me from claiming you."

"Please, Stalking Wolf! I am frightened, and I am alone."

"More reason to cling to your husband."

"I would be clinging to a stranger!"

He moved on top of her. "How can you still think of me in that way?"

"I will not remove my chastity belt!" Star Dancer struck at him, but Stalking Wolf pushed her arms down, unaffected by her flailing. Quickly he forced his legs between her own, then spread his knees to shove her legs apart. He let go of one arm to pull at her chastity belt, feeling a rush of ecstasy at the thought of finally bedding this young beauty; but instantly his passion vanished when he felt a sharp prick at his neck. He jerked away in surprise.

The wife he had considered small and helpless sat up, pointing a knife at him. "If you try to force me to submit, I will *cut* you, and all will know that the honorable Stalking Wolf is not so honorable in his own tepee!"

Stalking Wolf wanted to hit her. *And how easy it would be,* he thought, *to jerk the knife right out of her hand!* Did she really think she could stave him off if he decided to take what belonged to him? Still, her threat to make him look bad before the elders made him hesitate. He glared at her in heated challenge, but her vulnerability appealed to his pity for her. *Such a small thing, alone among strangers.* He realized he cared for her in a way he never thought possible, but the frustration she caused him seemed unbearable. Disappointed with her refusal, and in pain from the thwarted lovemaking, he rose, wrapping himself in a buffalo robe.

"You are a stubborn and ungrateful woman!" he snarled. "How do you expect to give me children when you behave this way!"

"I will give you children when I am ready, and when you truly *want* me, *all* of me, not just to use me for your pleasure."

"I *do* want you!"

"Not in the way that a man should truly want his wife."

Stalking Wolf breathed deeply, so angry with her and with himself that he wondered if he might beat her if he didn't get away from her. "I do not understand what more you want of me!" Still naked, he threw the robe at her and stalked out.

EARLY NOVEMBER
1832

Beaver Moon

CHAPTER SEVENTEEN

STAR DANCER LICKED her sore fingers before inserting another wooden peg through holes arduously poked into the overlapping tepee skins.

"It is a fine dwelling," Red Sun Woman told her, stepping back to study her son's new home.

Star Dancer finished the final tie, then joined her mother-in-law in observing her work. Blue and yellow stars decorated the outer skins. Beneath the stars on three sides, Star Dancer had painted three wolves, one stalking a buffalo, another stalking a bear, the third stalking a deer. The exterior of a tepee should tell something about those who lived inside, and so she had done her best to show that this dwelling belonged to her and Stalking Wolf.

"I used twenty-four buffalo hides. It is one of the biggest tepees in the camp," she bragged to Red Sun Woman. "I hope your son will be pleased."

"Um-hum." Red Sun Woman folded her thick, muscled arms, looking at Star Dancer rather slyly as she spoke. "First he must come home."

Star Dancer felt heat fill her cheeks. She had no doubt others must wonder why Stalking Wolf had left on a hunting trip. He had, at least, taken Buffalo Calf with him, providing an excuse that the young man needed more training in the hunt. "He will be here soon, I am sure. Then I will present him with the bear-claw necklace. It will be a gift from the heart," she lied. "We do not like to be long apart. Perhaps he will also bring me a gift."

"Oh?" Red Sun Woman laughed in a simple low grunt. "Look over there, Star Dancer." She pointed to where her daughter stood in the distance with Fall Leaf Woman.

Star Dancer frowned, only too aware of Fall Leaf Woman's venomous attitude, the main reason she could not feel happy here among the Oglala. "I . . . do not understand what you mean," she stammered, nervous under Red Sun Woman's scrutiny.

"You say you do not like to be apart from my son, but you have not behaved as one who misses her new husband. I have not seen that longing look in your eyes. And Fall Leaf Woman, she has been saying bad things about you. Because my son is a most honorable man among the Oglala, I think it is time you did something to make sure he keeps that honor."

Star Dancer felt sick inside, her happiness over finishing the tepee dashed by Red Sun Woman's apparent displeasure. "What does Fall Leaf Woman say about me?" she asked.

Red Sun Woman took her arm and led her inside the new tepee. "We will speak alone." She motioned for Star Dancer to sit down on the grassy floor, then sat down facing her. "You have not yet mated with my son."

The words were spoken as a statement rather than a question, and Star Dancer quickly looked away, lost for words, aware that her reaction was all the answer Red Sun Woman needed to know she spoke the truth. "He is a stranger to you."

Star Dancer nodded.

"And *we* are all strangers to you. You are afraid. I think perhaps you have angered my son. Perhaps not so much angered as made him anxious with the painful need of you. He has left because he wants to mate with you, but you are not ready."

Star Dancer drew a deep breath and wiped at a tear. "I am sorry. I have disappointed you."

Red Sun Woman shook her head. "No, my daughter. You are as much my child now as if I had borne you, and a woman can feel only love for a child. I brought you in here to tell you that Fall Leaf Woman says bad things about you. She says that perhaps my son discovered you were not a virgin and is ashamed that he married you. Perhaps he wants to throw you away. She says that since he has left his new wife so soon to go and hunt, he is surely displeased with you. She also says that twice her brother, Gray Owl, has found himself alone with you, that perhaps Gray Owl mated with you."

Star Dancer's eyes widened with horror. "That is not true!"

"I do not believe it, my daughter. But a few others are beginning to wonder. Fall Leaf Woman tells a good story."

"She is *lying!* And if her brother says he has been with me, *he* is lying! Twice he came to the creek uninvited while I was there alone. Surely Fall Leaf Woman asked him to do this, so that I would look bad to others. He tried to talk to me both times, but I sent him away. I did not like the look in his eyes."

"Gray Owl is jealous of Stalking Wolf. If he can disparage him or you, he will do it. And he is loyal to his sister. Their mother and father died, and Gray Owl watches out for his sister. Fall Leaf Woman in turn is a teaser of men. She uses them to survive. My son is her favorite, and I always feared he would take her for a wife. I am glad he chose you. You are the perfect mate for my son. Fall Leaf Woman knows this, and she is jealous. When you first arrived, I thought there would be no trouble; but with Stalking Wolf gone, it gives Fall Leaf Woman time to try to ruin your honor."

Star Dancer put a hand to her head, again longing

for her grandmother. "What can I do? How can I stop her lies?"

Red Sun Woman touched her arm. "I think you should hold a feast, celebrating your new tepee. You should act like the happy wife, even if my son is still not back. I will help you with the feast. At the feast, you will challenge Fall Leaf Woman. You will call her out for her lies, declare to all that you are the loyal wife of Stalking Wolf, that there has never been another. You should offer to bite the knife."

Star Dancer sat a little straighter. "I should not have to prove myself that way."

"No, you should not. But I feel it is necessary to stop Fall Leaf Woman's lies. She, too, should be challenged to bite the knife as a sign her words are true. She knows she risks the anger of *Wakan-Tanka* if she bites the knife falsely. Even Fall Leaf Woman would not take such a chance."

Star Dancer held her gaze. "What if she *does* risk it? It would be her word against mine, and she is Oglala. She has many friends among your people."

"And you are the wife of Stalking Wolf. This is your advantage. He did not marry Fall Leaf Woman. He married *you*."

Star Dancer sighed, getting to her feet. "I am sorry this brings trouble for you and your son."

"And I am sorry Fall Leaf Woman hurt you. She has no right. This is not your fault. It is hers." Red Sun Woman also rose. "Shall I announce the feast?"

Star Dancer dreaded the challenge, but she knew it had to be met, in order to make sure that Stalking Wolf's honor remained untarnished. "Yes. I will hold a feast and bite the knife." She faced Red Sun Woman. "I have no fear, for I tell you the truth. I belong only to your son. I think of it in no other way."

Red Sun Woman nodded. "My son should be here for the feast. I will send Standing Hawk to find him. He knows the places my son likes to hunt."

"Yes. Tell Standing Hawk to bring him quickly."
Star Dancer worried lest this only increased Stalking
Wolf's anger with her. His new wife caused him much
trouble.

Both women stepped outside. Many Robes Woman
and Fall Leaf Woman stood closer to the tepee. Star
Dancer suspected they had tried to listen to her conversation with Red Sun Woman. Fall Leaf Woman
studied the tepee, then sniffed. "Stalking Wolf will not
like it. You are not a good painter. Once Stalking Wolf
allowed *me* to paint a war shield for him."

"Then you should feel very honored," Star Dancer
answered, deciding not to fall into the trap of returning
hate for hate. She did not blame the woman for loving
Stalking Wolf, for she had also loved someone she
could not have. Yet the lies angered her. "You are
welcome to come to the feast I will hold in three
days," she added.

Fall Leaf Woman lost her arrogant stance and
frowned. "A feast?"

"Yes. I will hold a feast celebrating my marriage to
Stalking Wolf and the completion of our tepee. At the
feast, I will bite the knife." Star Dancer took great joy
at the fearful look in Fall Leaf Woman's eyes.

"You would dare to do this?"

"Of course. I have nothing to hide, nor would I bite
the knife falsely. As one who has touched the sacred
white buffalo, to lie would bring the wrath of *Wakan-
Tanka*. Perhaps the entire Lakota Nation would be
punished."

Fall Leaf Woman's ashen face surprised Star Dancer. Fall Leaf Woman straightened then, drawing a
deep breath. "I will come to your feast, just to see you
dare *Wakan-Tanka*'s anger! I hope Stalking Wolf *is*
here, for surely only he knows the truth about you. He
must not be pleased with you, for no newly married
warrior leaves his wife so soon."

She turned and walked away, and Star Dancer

watched the sway of her hips. The woman knew how to please a man. Star Dancer wondered how Fall Leaf Woman had managed not to have the end of her nose cut off for her loose ways. Most likely she had not yet been called "wife" by any of the young, unmarried men who, Star Dancer had noticed, usually watched her with great pleasure. She felt a sudden tug deep inside, a curiosity to know how to make a man happy in that way.

She glanced at Red Sun Woman, who smiled and went her way. Star Dancer turned to again survey the tepee. Sewing the skins together had been accomplished with the help of Red Sun Woman and Many Robes Woman, along with Yellow Turtle Woman, sister to Stalking Wolf's deceased father. All those who had helped now had tender, callused fingers from the project, but the task had brought Star Dancer closer to Stalking Wolf's family. They had shared in cutting just the right branches for support poles, helped tie the poles together and drape and tie the skins that covered the poles, securing the bottom of the skins with stakes in the ground.

Now she must sew skins for an inner lining of insulation for when the weather turned cold and the nights lengthened. Such a lining would also help eliminate shadows seen from outside, created by the central tepee fire after dark. Her first task in preparing the inner lining would be to paint the tanned skins with colorful designs that would bring a warm, happy feeling inside . . . if indeed there could be happiness in her home.

At least she had grown closer to Red Sun Woman and Yellow Turtle Woman and her daughter, Sweet Root Woman, who was the same age as Star Dancer. Sweet Root Woman's eighteen-year-old brother, Standing Rock, had taken part in the Sun Dance ritual for the first time this past summer at Medicine Mountain. Another brother of twelve summers was named

Little Black Horse; and Yellow Turtle Woman had given birth to yet another son late in life, an active six-month-old called Two Feet Dancing.

Bold Fox, Stalking Wolf's fraternal uncle, had trained Stalking Wolf in the hunt and in warrior ways. Among the Lakota, it was the custom for uncles to do such things, since fathers were too close to their sons to be proper disciplinarians. Bold Fox and his wife, Running Elk Woman, boasted two sons, Little Whirlwind, only six summers, and Buffalo Calf, thirteen summers. Buffalo Calf had no uncle to teach him the warrior ways, so Stalking Wolf had become the boy's mentor.

Indeed, Stalking Wolf enjoyed a loving, close family. Star Dancer realized that her acceptance by them and all of the Oglala would help Stalking Wolf see her as a true wife and perhaps curb some of his anger and irritation with her. And now that she had talked with Red Sun Woman and won her confidence, she felt stronger, more determined. She looked forward to Fall Leaf Woman's reaction when she bit the knife. Then Fall Leaf Woman would be proved a liar, and lying was forbidden among the Lakota.

CHAPTER EIGHTEEN

STAR DANCER JOINED the other women and men who lined up to greet Stalking Wolf as he rode through camp with his young cousin Buffalo Calf, leading a packhorse loaded down with four deer carcasses.

"A good hunt!" Bold Fox boasted. "Now we have even more to celebrate at the feast!"

Stalking Wolf galloped his mount closer to his uncle. "Your son killed one of the deer himself!"

"Aaahhee!" Bold Fox looked at Buffalo Calf proudly, and the young man sat straighter on his black-and-gray gelding, enjoying the first fruits of manhood. "You have done well, my son!" his father told him.

"I have a good teacher," Buffalo Calf answered, nodding toward Stalking Wolf.

"This is true." Bold Fox smiled at Stalking Wolf. "You have brought my son home safely."

"I told you that I would." Stalking Wolf tossed his hair behind his shoulders, and Star Dancer noticed that he appeared freshly bathed. He wore a fetching hairpiece, and a brightly quilled vest.

A very young boy ran up to the deer carcasses and pierced at them with a toy arrow, emitting shrill cries as though at war. Other children joined him, and older ones laughed at their game.

Stalking Wolf dismounted and greeted Star Dancer with a smile. She touched his arm, not sure if the smile was genuine or only for show. "Welcome home, my husband. I am glad you have returned unhurt, and that your hunt was successful."

Stalking Wolf looked past her to see the finished tepee with stars and wolves painted on the outside. Star Dancer followed his gaze. "I spent many days sewing the skins and painting them," she told him. "I hope you are pleased."

Stalking Wolf left her and walked around the dwelling while she waited nervously, hoping he would say something complimentary. She knew that Fall Leaf Woman, who stood nearby, watched and listened.

"You are a fine painter," Stalking Wolf finally told her. "I am very pleased."

Star Dancer sighed with relief. Stalking Wolf took her hand then, and she pretended great joy as she followed him inside the tepee, casting a quick look of smugness toward Fall Leaf Woman.

Once inside the spacious interior of the tepee, Stalking Wolf looked all around, saying nothing at first. Star Dancer had furnished the inside with two backrests made of wood and reeds. Some of Stalking Wolf's belongings, as well as brightly quilled parfleches, a water bag, some of his weapons, his feather headdress, and most of their clothing hung from stubs of branches sticking out from the tepee poles. A circle of warm stones surrounded the hot embers of the central fire, and buffalo meat wrapped in fat lay simmering on the coals.

"I prepared the meat for you, in case you returned early and might be hungry," Star Dancer explained, still feeling nervous over what he might say. "Your mother and aunt are roasting a deer your uncle killed for us to use for the feast. You are just in time, Stalking Wolf. The feast is tonight."

She watched him move to the right of the tepee, as was custom. Star Dancer walked to the left, anxious to know his feelings about the feast. He glanced around the tepee again, moving his gaze to his war shield. Star Dancer had made sure to hang it high on a tall tripod of branches, as was custom, so it would not be contaminated by any earthly beings and thus have its powers weakened. Stalking Wolf had left it behind, intending only to hunt when he departed with Buffalo Calf.

A painting of a black wolf with red stripes dripping downward from its mouth, representing the blood of Stalking Wolf's enemies, decorated the shield. Star Dancer bristled with anger because Fall Leaf Woman had painted the shield. Did Stalking Wolf treasure it because of that?

"I took good care of it for you," she spoke up, holding her chin proudly. "And I know Fall Leaf Woman painted it for you."

Stalking Wolf folded his arms and faced her. "Fall Leaf Woman wants to make trouble, to hurt you. That is not the war shield she painted for me. It was another, one that was destroyed by stampeding buffalo once on a hunt. You know it is not the custom to allow a mere woman friend to paint something as sacred as as a war shield. Bold Fox, my esteemed uncle, painted this one."

Star Dancer felt a wave of relief, but his next words dispelled it. "Is it true you have spent time alone with Fall Leaf Woman's brother, as Standing Hawk told me?"

Star Dancer swallowed, imagining how ugly she would be with her nose cut off. "It is true, but it was his doing. I knew Gray Owl was trying to make trouble. Whenever he came into my presence alone, I quickly left without speaking to him." Her chest swelled with a deep breath of determination. "Standing Hawk told you I am holding a feast tonight. There I will bite the knife!"

Stalking Wolf slowly nodded, his dark eyes penetrating. "To bite the knife means that you are faithful to your husband."

"I *have* been faithful! And that is more than I can say for my *husband!* Perhaps *I* should throw *you* out!"

Stalking Wolf pulled off his vest and threw it aside. "You think *I* have been unfaithful?"

"Fall Leaf Woman would have me believe so." Instantly, Star Dancer realized how jealous her words made her sound, and she saw the surprise in her husband's eyes.

"And does that upset you?"

Flustered, Star Dancer grappled for a fitting reply. "Only because people will wonder about my honor if my new husband is already sniffing up the skirt of another woman!" she retorted.

"I will remind you that you have not allowed me to sniff up *your* skirt yet!" Stalking Wolf replied angrily. "And how can you bite the knife as a sign of loyalty when you have not allowed your own husband to claim you? How do I know you are only mine and can truthfully bite the knife? You are *not* my wife, and so you cannot bite the knife!"

Their gazes held in defiant stubbornness. "Then *make* me your wife!" Star Dancer spit at him without thinking. "Then you will know just how loyal I am! You will know *no* other man has touched me, and we can honestly stand before the others later as husband and wife! If it must be done, then *do* it!"

Once said, she could not take back her offer.

"This is truly your wish?" Stalking Wolf asked.

Star Dancer heard the blood rushing in her ears. "I have said it," she replied, her own stubbornness helping her survive the traumatic moment. What had she done!

Anger still blazed in Stalking Wolf's eyes. "I do not wish to have my throat slit by a *woman!*"

Star Dancer flinched. All her senses came alive, and panic made her heart pound harder. She had let her own stubborn pride lead her into a place she had never planned to go. "I will not try to stop you," she promised.

Stalking Wolf looked down his nose at her with a haughty stance. "Fine." He unlaced his leggings and stepped out of them. As he walked over to close the tepee flap, Star Dancer untied the shoulders of her tunic and let it fall. She felt numb under Stalking Wolf's stare, summoning all her courage to surmount her terror and embarrassment. For the first time in two months of marriage, her husband saw her fully naked. She looked down, removing her chastity cords and dropping them aside.

Stalking Wolf approached her and lightly touched her breast, toying with a nipple taut from her unaccustomed exposure to a man's eyes. Star Dancer hardly felt the touch, but rather was filled with a rush of dread.

Stalking Wolf untied his breechcloth and the medicine bundle he wore strapped to the inside of his thigh. His swollen penis reminded Star Dancer of a stallion, and she wanted to cry at the wonder of how he could fit it inside of her. She stood frozen in place while he hung his breechcloth and medicine bundle near his war shield. He took her arm and abruptly led her to his bed of robes. She could feel a lingering anger in his touch. He knelt in front of her and took her hands, forcing her to kneel facing him.

"Someday you will not look at this as some kind of torture," he told her, obvious irritation in his voice. "You will know the pleasure of it, and I will see desire in your eyes."

He seemed unaffected by the tears that trickled down her cheeks. He pushed her onto her back and maneuvered himself between her legs.

Star Dancer closed her eyes.

"It is you who makes this painful and unwanted," he told her. "Do not forget that I had no more choice in this than you."

With that, he rammed himself into her, and the quick invasion so startled Star Dancer that she gasped, her eyes instantly opening to see the look of a conqueror in Stalking Wolf's dark eyes. Hot, searing pain tore through her, and she whimpered with each jab of his manpart. She wondered how many more times he would have to move in and out of her, bringing the pain over and over. She clenched her fists, wanting to hit at him, embarrassed, humiliated that this man invaded her most sacred self.

She closed her eyes again and gritted her teeth, stifling an urge to scream. He forced himself deep inside her and held himself there, and she felt an odd pulsation, thinking it must be his life pouring into her.

Life. Perhaps that life would take hold, and then she could tell him to leave her alone until long after the baby was born. She felt him relax, and she whimpered when he pulled himself out of her. Everything hurt inside, and she wondered if she would die. She curled up and pulled a robe over her nakedness.

"Look at me," Stalking Wolf commanded.

Star Dancer met his eyes, surprised at the tender look she now saw there. He stood up. "It is done. I will not touch you again until I see desire in your eyes." He looked down at himself. "The blood I see tells me you can bite the knife without fear. I will attend your feast, and we will pretend to be the happy husband and wife."

He turned, and Star Dancer watched him tie his medicine bundle to the inside of his thigh. An Oglala warrior never went anywhere without his sacred medicine bundle. He then tied on his breechcloth and took a clean one from his supplies. He started out. "Wait!" she called out to him.

Stalking Wolf turned, saying nothing.

"Tell me you have not slept with Fall Leaf Woman since our marriage."

She watched his jaw flex with irritation. "You

should not have to ask. I am a man of *honor*!"

With that, he left, and Star Dancer pressed a hand to her belly, groaning at the soreness there. She lifted the robe and looked down to see blood on her thighs, and she longed to talk to *Uncheedah* about this. How could this ever be pleasurable? Still, older women sometimes joked about enjoying themselves under the robes with their husbands.

She grimaced with pain as she stood and slipped into her tunic, deciding that sitting in the creek might help cool the fire deep inside her. She took up a piece of softened deer hide for drying herself and headed for the wooded area of a nearby stream, glad that the day was unusually warm for this time of year. Sometimes *Wakan-Tanka* played tricks in autumn, bringing lovely warm weather just before the first snowstorm of winter.

Before she reached the edge of the woods, she met Stalking Wolf, returning from his own bathing. They both stopped, and Star Dancer looked away, feeling embarrassed. The only thing this man still did not own was her soul. *How long before that, too, belongs to him*? she thought. And why was it suddenly important to her that they *should* share souls? She started past him, but he grasped her arm to stop her.

"I am sorry that you hurt. And I want you to know that I am proud of our tepee. In front of others, you have brought me only pride and honor, and you are a fitting wife for the most honored of warriors. You will never again suffer pain at my hands."

Star Dancer suddenly felt like crying again, but she forced back the urge, taking a deep breath before replying, still avoiding his eyes. "I made the bear-claw necklace for you, as you requested. I will present it to you tonight as a symbol of our . . ." *Love?* ". . . marriage," she finished.

He released her arm and breathed a long sigh before speaking again. "I thank you for the necklace."

He left her, and she turned to watch him go, startled by the pleasure she took at the sight of his muscled back and firm hips and thighs. She ran to the creek to wash, reminding herself she had much to do yet for the feast tonight.

CHAPTER NINETEEN

STAR DANCER, WEARING her wedding dress, and a grandly dressed Stalking Wolf graciously accepted gifts and good wishes from all who joined the celebration of their marriage. Their guests feasted on roasted venison, served by Red Sun Woman. Bold Fox had furnished the meat as a demonstration of the family's acceptance of Star Dancer into its fold.

Stalking Wolf proudly wore his bear-claw necklace, and Star Dancer felt keenly aware of his masculine presence.

Fall Leaf Woman did not show herself until after the feasting and gift-giving. When she did arrive, Star Dancer felt a rush of jealousy. Fall Leaf Woman wore a soft doeskin dress that moved enticingly over her voluptuous body as she approached, an obvious attempt at making Stalking Wolf sorry he had given her up. Onlookers quieted as she moved through the crowd. Leather ties wrapped in colorful quills decorated her hair, so that her thick tresses fell in a cascade of color. She carried no gift, but rather, handed a flaying knife to Star Dancer.

"This knife has been blessed by Moon Painter, our Oglala priest," she sneered. "Its handle is made from the jawbone of the sacred buffalo." She glanced at Stalking Wolf, boldly looking him over with hunger in her eyes. She returned a menacing gaze to Star Dancer. "To bite this knife falsely means bad luck for the Oglala. I dare you, Star Dancer, to bite this knife and swear that Stalking Wolf is the only man who has touched you. Swear that you have never lain with my brother, Gray Owl. It is also said that among the Sichangu, you fancied another man, who died trying to kill the humpbacked bear to win your hand. Swear that he, too, never touched you. Swear you are as pure as you claim to be, and that Stalking Wolf is pleased with his wife!"

Red Sun Woman moved behind Star Dancer, placing a hand at her waist. "Do not fear, Daughter. The truth is never to be feared."

Men and women alike watched in silence. Star Dancer took the knife from Fall Leaf Woman. Slowly she put the blade to her teeth, then bit down, staring defiantly at Fall Leaf Woman, who flinched but retained her air of confidence as she turned to her brother.

"Step forward, Gray Owl, if Star Dancer lies!" she ordered.

Star Dancer turned a daring look to Gray Owl. A handsome young man, but not as tall and commanding as Stalking Wolf, Gray Owl wore plain buckskins, with one feather in his straight, black hair. Star Dancer waited, seeing apprehension in the young man's eyes. He swallowed nervously from obvious indecision. Although Gray Owl was not above stealing another man's wife, he apparently could not bring himself to lie. He said nothing. Instead, he turned and walked away.

"Gray Owl!" Fall Leaf Woman shouted. "You know what is right!"

Gray Owl stopped and turned, putting his hands on his hips and facing his sister. "The *truth* is what is right! It is the same for *you!*"

Tension filled the air. Fall Leaf Woman began to tremble, her eyes tearing with rage. Stalking Wolf stepped forward. "Take the knife from your mouth," he ordered Star Dancer.

She obeyed, and Stalking Wolf took the knife and

held it toward Fall Leaf Woman. Star Dancer felt the heat of his anger.

"A man knows when the woman he beds is a virgin," he told Fall Leaf Woman. "Star Dancer has never been with anyone but *me*! How dare you suggest otherwise? You, however, are *no* man's wife. Let us see *you* bite the knife and swear your own virginity."

Others gasped, and Fall Leaf Woman looked as though she had been struck. Gray Owl walked back beside his sister, fists clenched. "This is a cruel insult to my sister, who has *loved* you!" he raged at Stalking Wolf.

Star Dancer glanced at Stalking Wolf and noticed his jaw flex with his own deserved rage. "Your sister has loved *many* young men. And if you dare to speak to me once more, I will *kill* you for trying to steal my wife."

At first Gray Owl appeared ready to fight, but he suddenly withered under Stalking Wolf's fiery stance. He turned to leave, and Fall Leaf Woman stepped back, shaking her head. She glared at Stalking Wolf in silence, a few tears trickling down her cheeks. Saying nothing more, she, too, turned and ran off.

Stalking Wolf threw the knife so that it stuck in the ground. "I thank all of you for your gifts," he announced. "Let us continue the feasting and the celebration of my marriage."

Onlookers moved slowly and quietly at first, but when the drummers resumed their rhythmic beat and again sang songs of thanksgiving, faces brightened and all returned to feasting and celebrating. The drummers sang:

> *Great Father, thank you for our meat.*
> *Great Father, thank you for good hunts.*
> *Great Father, thank you for our wives.*
> *Continue to bless us.*

Stalking Wolf turned to Star Dancer, looking her over with a new respect in his eyes.

"Thank you for defending me," Star Dancer told him.

"It was my duty. I will not have my wife embarrassed and insulted."

"But you did just that to Fall Leaf Woman, who apparently loves you, probably the same way that I loved Kicking Bear."

"She is a loose woman. I am not the only man who has shared her favors."

Star Dancer again experienced a surprisingly intense jealousy. Still, she wanted only harmony between herself and all the Oglala. "Perhaps you are right. I would not know. I only know that you meant very much to her, and that today she has been hurt and shamed. You should not be so cruel to her. Now there will be bad feelings between her family and yours. You should apologize to her, take her a gift."

Stalking Wolf's eyebrows shot up in surprise. "I owe her nothing!"

"I disagree."

Stalking Wolf rolled his eyes in aggravation. "You truly want me to do such a thing, after the way Fall Leaf Woman insulted you?"

"I want peace. I do not want my presence here to cause strife among the Oglala. To apologize would show you are a man with great abilities to forgive, a man with true leadership qualities, who thinks more of peace and unity among his people than he does of his own personal feelings and desires." Star Dancer watched him soften toward her request, and a half-smile came to his lips.

"My young wife is wiser than I thought, and she cares about my standing among the Oglala."

"You are my husband. I want my husband to be a true leader, and it is my duty to help you achieve this."

He slowly nodded. "Then I will do what you ask, but it will not be easy for me."

Star Dancer began to sense the power she truly could wield over this man of men, understanding more fully her role not only as wife, but as a woman believed to be holy and gifted. "I also think you should stay in camp for a while, so that it does not look bad for me, and so that false stories cannot be told about us." She was not so sure she had not overstepped her confidence with the remark, and she pretended not to be intimidated when Stalking Wolf folded his arms and looked down his nose at her.

"In the same tepee?" he asked.

"Of course."

"And in the same bed?"

Star Dancer quickly looked away. "No." Her insides still hurt. "Perhaps you could just . . . hold me. We need to learn to truly care about each other, as a husband and wife would care." She heard a hiss of irritation exit his lips.

"And you expect me to lie next to you and not want to touch you?"

Star Dancer bravely met his gaze. "You will have to be very strong. It will be a good test to see if you truly care about me."

"I have just shown you how much I care."

Their gazes held for several seconds while Star Dancer scrambled for words. "I feel something more is to come . . . something that will truly help us understand how we feel about each other. I want to wait until the Oglala make their final winter camp. There is much to be done before then. Once we are settled, we will have much time to spend alone."

Stalking Wolf closed his eyes and shook his head. "I will stay in camp, but I will not hold you. You ask too much of a man. Besides, I already promised I would not touch you again until you are willing."

Star Dancer nodded in agreement. "It is enough that

you stay. Will you go tomorrow to see Fall Leaf Woman?"

He dropped his arms to his sides. "I do not understand you, but I will go."

"And you will tell Gray Owl there are no hard feelings? We must set an example of harmony for the people. I want peace, Stalking Wolf, and harmony among us is as important to our survival as a good hunt is."

Stalking Wolf frowned. "I will go, but I do not trust Gray Owl, and I never will. It would be better if he and Fall Leaf Woman left us."

"Where would they go?"

"The Lakota are many. They could live with another clan."

"They have lost their honor. Others would accept them no more readily than we. We will simply have to learn to accept what has happened and open our hearts to them."

"Perhaps, but in your innocent forgiveness, you make the mistake of trusting those whom you should fear."

"And what need I fear as long as I am among the Oglala and your family?"

Stalking Wolf looked toward Fall Leaf Woman's tepee in the distance. "I am not sure, but I will keep my eye on Gray Owl, and you should be wary of Fall Leaf Woman."

"I have my brave and fierce husband here to protect me now."

Stalking Wolf turned back to her with a sly smile. "You have a way with words, Star Dancer. You truly vex me. I do not know quite what to think of you or what to expect from you."

"It is the same for me, which is why it is best we go slowly and learn about the deepest side of each other."

Stalking Wolf shrugged. "I suppose you are right,

but I tell you to always take my mother or someone with you when you go to the stream or to gather roots or buffalo chips. I can try to forgive Gray Owl, but I will never trust him."

They rejoined the celebrating, unaware that Gray Owl had sneaked around the outside of a circle of tepees to watch them, a desire for revenge burning hot in his belly.

CHAPTER TWENTY

STALKING WOLF LED two fine mares to Fall Leaf
Woman's tepee, grumbling under his breath about
having to do it. Now he understood the teasing remarks the Big Bellies had thrown at him when he first
told them he aimed to take a wife. They had told him
that all his valor and prestige would be of no help
against a wife's wishes inside the privacy of their tepee. Small as she was, Star Dancer already had a way
of making him bend to her wishes, and he did not yet
even share her bed.

Still, his wife spoke with surprising wisdom, and
much as he hated doing it, he had brought the horses
as a gift of apology to Gray Owl and Fall Leaf
Woman. As he approached, Gray Owl turned from
brushing his horse and spotted him. He stepped forward, dropping the porcupine brush and folding his
arms defensively.

"What are you doing here?" he demanded.

Stalking Wolf glanced at the tepee entrance, where
Fall Leaf Woman looked out, then emerged, her face
betraying her inner pain. He noticed a flush to her
cheeks, and he knew she still felt embarrassed and
ashamed. He moved his gaze back to Gray Owl.

"I have come to apologize, and I have brought these
horses as a gift." He looked at Fall Leaf Woman again.
"I hope you will take them as a sign of forgiveness."

Fall Leaf Woman stared at him with eyes puffy with
weeping. Her disheveled hair showed she had not slept

well, and she still wore the tunic she had worn the night before.

"This man who threw you away for another and then insulted you is here with gifts." Gray Owl addressed his sister but kept his eyes on Stalking Wolf as he spoke. "He says he is sorry for his insults."

"I have ears, Gray Owl." Fall Leaf Woman stepped closer to Stalking Wolf. "I do not want your presents. I want only you."

"Do not grovel to him, Fall Leaf Woman," Gray Owl sneered.

"I will speak for myself!" his sister retorted.

"I agree," Stalking Wolf added, his eyes blazing with renewed anger as he moved his gaze back to Gray Owl. "I could *kill* you! No one would blame me. You tried to lead others to believe my wife is unfaithful. If she *would* have been, you would have *accepted* her. You are a wife stealer, and wife stealers should *die*."

Gray Owl stiffened, his arrogance withering to obvious doubt and apprehension. "I did nothing wrong."

"So you say." Stalking Wolf drew a deep breath to hold his temper. "You are fortunate my wife has a forgiving heart. She wants only peace among the Oglala, to be friends with all of you. *She* told me to bring these gifts. You have *her* to thank for this, not me." He held out the ropes of the horses. "I have brought these for you and Fall Leaf Woman, as a token of friendship. I forgive you both because my *wife* forgives you. She is a peacemaker."

Gray Owl turned to Fall Leaf Woman. "What say you?"

Fall Leaf Woman kept her eyes on Stalking Wolf. "Take the horses and leave us," she told her brother.

Scowling, Gray Owl took the lead ropes from Stalking Wolf. "You are a fool!" he told Fall Leaf Woman. "Perhaps *you* can forgive, but I *cannot!*"

With that, he left them, and Fall Leaf Woman slithered up to Stalking Wolf, so close that her breasts nearly touched his chest. "I saw you one night, before you went away for so long. You came out of your tepee, and you were naked, and seemed very angry. Surely your wife does not please you." She touched his chest with her hands. "Not the way *I* can please you."

Stalking Wolf could almost smell her lust, and he felt the heat of her desire. "I well know the ways you can please a man." He grasped her wrists and pushed her hands away. "Star Dancer will learn. When the pain is gone, she will discover her own pleasure, and she will in turn learn how to please me in the night."

Fall Leaf Woman stepped back, her nostrils flaring as she drew a deep breath. "I can see you are truly determined it is over with us. I *curse* you, Stalking Wolf! But I will always love you. There will never be another like you."

Stalking Wolf studied her misty eyes and shook his head. "Star Dancer also loved another. She understands how you feel, and that is why she can forgive you. There is nothing that can be done about this, Fall Leaf Woman. You must accept it, and accept Star Dancer as a friend. If you truly love me, you will do this for me. Find yourself another to marry. There are many young warriors who would be glad to bed you every night. You are pleasing to the eye, and pleasing to the touch."

"And do *you* still desire to touch me?"

Stalking Wolf longed to bed a woman who would truly respond with desire, but he refused any weakness. "I desire only my wife. She is young and afraid and alone. The day will come when she looks at me the way you look at me."

Fall Leaf Woman turned away, tossing her hair with a flourish so that it swung over her shoulder. "Then go to her. Do not ever speak to me or touch me again!"

Stalking Wolf watched her for a moment, experiencing some regret. "If that is what you wish. I warn you, Fall Leaf Woman, do not be unkind to Star Dancer. She is a woman of power. One day all the Lakota Nation will speak of her as a gift from *Wakan-Tanka*. I am sorry to hurt you. But I have done what must be done."

"Just go," she said in a near whisper, her back to him.

Stalking Wolf wished he could say something that might make her feel better. He turned and walked back to his own tepee to find Star Dancer pounding berries for pemmican.

"Did they accept the horses?" she asked without looking at him.

Stalking Wolf moved to his side of the tepee. "They did." He sat down near the central fire.

"I am sorry for Fall Leaf Woman." Star Dancer finally looked at him. "And for you. You never intended to take Fall Leaf Woman for a wife, but you have lost a good friend. This is another reason to stay out of my bed for a while longer. It is *me* you should want, not Fall Leaf Woman."

Stalking Wolf shook his head. "For one so young, you have surprising patience." He studied her silently before his next remark. "I think you should change your name." He watched her eyes widen in surprise.

"Change it? Why?"

"I think you should be called Peace Maker. We will talk to Moon Painter about this. Everything you have done so far is to keep the peace. You have no mean thoughts, and you make sacrifices for the good of the People. In my vision I was told that the woman I was to wed would represent peace. Now I know you are truly that woman."

Star Dancer shrugged, returning to her grinding. "Then I will be called Peace Maker."

"You do not mind?"

She tasted the pemmican before replying. "You are a man of wisdom. Your words mean much. And you are my husband. If it is your desire to call me Peace Maker, then it will be so."

Stalking Wolf nodded. "And what if it is my desire to bed my wife?"

He watched a sly grin move over her lips. "My body and soul are something that will always belong to me. You can name me whatever you want, and you can say where we will live, where we will hunt, when we should move camp, what you wish to eat. But only I make the decision about when to take you to my bed."

Stalking Wolf silently swore at his ceaseless frustration. What made it all the more difficult to abide by her wishes was the realization that he truly was falling in love with her.

CHAPTER TWENTY-ONE

"I DO NOT trust him." Gray Owl finished eating some berries while Fall Leaf Woman mended one of his shirts. "He *could* kill me, and no one would blame him."

"Only a little while ago Stalking Wolf promised not to harm you," Fall Leaf Woman reminded her brother. "He is a man of his word."

"Maybe. But he could come up with some excuse to kill me anyway. He said himself that it is Star Dancer who is the forgiving one, not him." He spit out a berry seed. "And how can you stay here now, the way you feel about him?"

Fall Leaf Woman stopped her mending, staring at the needle she used, made from a bone sliver. "Where else would I go?"

Gray Owl leaned against his backrest. "I have seen the *wasicus*. They have fine things to trade, and some Lakota have chosen to camp near the white man's trading post at the place called Fort Pierre. They hunt meat for the white men, help trap beaver. The white men pay them for such things with horses, warm blankets and clothing, fine tobacco, and with a drink they say makes a man feel good inside and makes him stronger and braver. The white men also have the firesticks that can kill an animal from far away and makes hunting easier. I would like to know more about these things."

Fall Leaf Woman faced her brother with scorn, still

angry that he had not managed to shame Star Dancer. "The elders say there is nothing good at that place."

Gray Owl shrugged. "You have not been there, and neither have most of them. All I know is there is nothing good *here* any longer. I do not like the way the Big Bellies looked at me last night at the biting of the knife. And because of Stalking Wolf's insults, no honorable Lakota warrior will marry you now. Come away with me. I fear if we do not go now, the Council will discuss this and ban us from the Lakota Nation in shame. It would be better if we left on our own."

Fall Leaf Woman shook her head. "The season of cold is coming. We will decide when the weather warms again."

Gray Owl set the bowl of berries aside. "It will be too late then," he scoffed, "and I cannot go long without seeking revenge for Stalking Wolf's insults and the pain he's caused you."

Fall Leaf Woman resumed her sewing. "He had no choice."

Gray Owl leaned closer, glaring at her over the dim coals of a dying fire. "Where is your *pride?* Perhaps he had no choice in marrying, but he did not have to insult both of us because of it. That was an *unnecessary* choice. He cannot change it by giving us a couple of horses."

"They are fine animals. You know how valuable horses are. He has given you a chance to keep your standing among the Lakota."

"He has given me *nothing!* Nor *you.* My heart burns for revenge. And don't tell me yours *doesn't.*"

Fall Leaf Woman closed her eyes and set the sewing aside. "Of course it does. If I cannot have Stalking Wolf, then I want *no* one to have him. But there is nothing I can do about it now. He is a man of his word. The People and his vision messages come first, and he has made up his mind."

"He thinks he is so special," Gray Owl grumbled.

He reached over to pick up his war club. "I would like him and all the Oglala to see he is no more special than me or anyone else."

Fall Leaf Woman felt alarm in watching him. "Do not do something foolish, Gray Owl."

He did not reply right away, but rather, kept staring at the war club. "I think I will leave for a while."

Fall Leaf Woman frowned. "Will you go to the white man's trading post?"

"Yes."

"What about me? Who will provide for me?"

"If I like it at Fort Pierre and see that it is a good place to be, I will come for you. Until then, you have ways of getting others to provide for you. Let the young men fight over you. They will try to win your favors by bringing you anything you need."

Fall Leaf Woman felt her heart tighten. Her brother was right, but the only man she truly wanted was Stalking Wolf. "Do you promise to come back and stay if you do not like it among the *wasicus?*"

"I will return either way. Then you can decide what you want to do. I will never abandon you, Fall Leaf Woman."

Her eyes teared. "You are all I have left."

"I will not fail you. Perhaps I can even fix things so that Stalking Wolf will seek the comfort of your arms."

Fall Leaf Woman looked askance at him. "What do you mean?" Her heart raced faster when he faced her with an evil grin.

"You will see."

"Gray Owl, don't be foolish!"

"I know what I am doing. Pack some pemmican and jerked meat. I will leave in the morning."

"For Fort Pierre?" Fall Leaf Woman noticed a glimmer of sinister plotting in her brother's eyes. "Answer me, Gray Owl! Where are you really going?"

"You will know soon enough, and you will thank me."

"For what?"

"For giving Stalking Wolf back to you. At the same time, I can realize my revenge by proving Stalking Wolf no more special than anyone else."

"I beg you to do nothing about this. It is too late. What is done is done."

"Maybe it can be *un*done!" Gray Owl picked up a stick and poked at the small fire to raise the flames. "I am going out to tend to our horses and pick one out to pack."

"It is growing dark."

"I want to pack supplies yet tonight. I will leave at sunrise."

Fall Leaf Woman could see there was no arguing with him. "Why are you in such a hurry? What can you find or do at Fort Pierre that will help you get revenge?"

"I told you that you will know soon enough."

He would not meet her gaze, and Fall Leaf Woman felt alarm.

"You are *lying* to me! You are not going to Fort Pierre."

He only shrugged. "Where I go is my business. I only know I cannot stay here, at least not for a while. You can keep yourself busy preparing for the cold season, and soon the entire camp will move again for its winter refuge." He finally glanced at her. "For all you know, I may be closer than you think."

"What does that mean? You speak in circles, Gray Owl, and make no sense."

"Shut up and prepare my supplies!" He rose and threw the stick at her. "And say nothing to the others about my thoughts of revenge. Just tell them I have gone to Fort Pierre."

He stormed out. Fall Leaf Woman grabbed the stick and shoved it back into the flames. "I wish it were *you* burning in the fire, Star Dancer!" she growled.

LATE NOVEMBER
1832

Moon When the Hair
Grows Long

CHAPTER TWENTY-TWO

PEACE MAKER FOLLOWED Stalking Wolf's gaze, surveying the valley ahead of them. A light dusting of snow carpeted a vast expanse of yellowed grass, and on either side of the peaceful setting, heavily wooded hills rose in splendid colors of deep green pine, the white bark of aspens, and the yellow of aspen leaves lying on top of the snow. A stream snaked through the center of the valley, providing ample water for drinking and cooking, as well as for the horses. If the stream remained deep and rapid, the Oglala need not worry much about the water freezing over solid, but if it did, they could still break through the ice to get water.

"Hollow Horn has chosen well," Peace Maker told Stalking Wolf. "The surrounding forest should yield plenty of dry, dead firewood for our winter camp."

Stalking Wolf said nothing in reply, but only sniffed the air. "Something is wrong. I sense danger."

Peace Maker shivered, but not from the cold November air. Sometimes Stalking Wolf reminded her of the wolf after which he was named . . . alert, cunning, wary. He even physically resembled the wolf today, wearing a cape of wolfskins around his shoulders, a wolf's head crowning his own head, the skin of the front legs covering his ears for warmth.

A stiff wind buffeted the ridge where they sat side by side on horseback, and Peace Maker pulled her bearskin cloak closer around her neck. Today was a

sharp reminder of much harsher weather to come.
Their entire camp of five thousand people needed to
find a new place to settle for winter, since their herd
of over two thousand horses had depleted the grass
around the summer camp. They had started their move
later than usual this autumn, and time was growing
short. They must get settled into this new location.

Stalking Wolf had brought Peace Maker and his
mother ahead with him to learn their opinion of the
site, for the location of winter camp meant a great deal
to the women, who needed easy access to water and
firewood. Seeking a new place to settle required the
opinion of many; but Hollow Horn, a Pipe Bearer and
one who chooses campsites, had made the initial decision, and had led them to this place, south and west
of their former camp. Buffalo Calf, Stalking Wolf's
young cousin, also rode with them.

As Shirt Wearer, Stalking Wolf had organized the
actual camp move. Now he turned his horse in a circle,
scanning the surroundings. Leading a packhorse, Red
Sun Woman walked behind her son and daughter-in-
law, frowning with irritation at Stalking Wolf's mis-
givings. "I see a beautiful valley for making camp,"
she told him. "And I am tired. There is no more time
to search farther before much colder weather comes.
Why do you hesitate, Stalking Wolf?"

He turned his horse to again scan the valley. "It is
not something I can say for certain. I do not know
why I feel this way."

"There are more Oglala than any other tribe in this
land, including all the Crow Nation, if that is what
worries you," his mother answered. "If we wish to
camp here, we will camp here." Red Sun Woman
stuck out her lower lip in a determined pout.

Stalking Wolf smirked at her reply, and Peace
Maker could not help smiling at his irritation. The
three of them had accompanied Hollow Horn, Standing Hawk, Buffalo Calf, and a few scouts at the head

of the migrating band. Most of the others remained stretched out in a long line in the distance, waiting to discover whether Hollow Horn finally knew where their winter home should be.

"I agree it is a good place for grazing and wintering," Stalking Wolf told his mother. He turned to Buffalo Calf, who rode faithfully beside his mentor. "Go back and tell Runs With The Deer, Bold Fox, and other *Wicasa Itakans* to come ahead. We must talk before making a final decision. They have first choice of campsites, as do the other *akicitas* and *wakincuzas*. I do not wish to be the only one who doubts Hollow Horn's decision. I am not worthy to overrule him, but I feel uneasy."

Buffalo Calf nodded. "I will tell them." The young man whirled his mount and rode off.

"We will go down this ridge and speak with Hollow Horn," Stalking Wolf told Peace Maker. The wind blew his cape and hair sideways, and Peace Maker felt an unexpected rush of attraction to him. For weeks now, Stalking Wolf had kept his promise not to touch her, and her respect for him, as well as her secret need of him, became more intense with the passing of every day.

She followed her husband down the ridge. "The cold season will soon be upon us," she told him. "We must decide quickly."

"My mother has already reminded me of that," Stalking Wolf answered wryly.

"I like the cold season," Red Sun Woman spoke up. "It is a quiet time of mending garments, repairing war shields and moccasins, making new arrows, doing quill work and sharing tepees for warmth, telling stories of ghosts and war and the hunt." She followed Stalking Wolf and Peace Maker down the ridge as she spoke, yelling the words when they gained distance on her.

Peace Maker slowed Sotaju and turned the horse,

riding back to her mother-in-law while Stalking Wolf went on down to the bottom of the ridge. He rode to the forest's edge to speak with Hollow Horn and Standing Hawk.

"Go ahead," Red Sun Woman told Peace Maker. "I will catch up."

"I will walk with you," Peace Maker told her. She dismounted, walking at the right side of Red Sun Woman. "I, too, like the time of storytelling," she said, feeling happy inside, more relaxed. She felt glad that Fall Leaf Woman had left her and Stalking Wolf alone since the biting of the knife and Stalking Wolf's request for forgiveness. Peace Maker felt even more relieved that Gray Owl had departed their camp, although Stalking Wolf doubted Fall Leaf Woman's explanation for her brother's absence. Every night before going to sleep, Stalking Wolf voiced his distrust of Gray Owl.

"My grandmother told wonderful stories of her childhood," Peace Maker said aloud to Red Sun Woman. "She—"

A whirring sound. A thud. The unexpected sounds stole the rest of Peace Maker's words from her mouth. She heard a grunt, and abruptly she knew that something was horribly wrong. Everything happened within a second or two of the grunt. Peace Maker turned to see Red Sun Woman fall, an arrow in her side. Terror, and a need to warn Stalking Wolf, assaulted every nerve end.

Although her throat constricted with fear, Peace Maker drew on a deeper instinct that brought forth the courage needed to face whatever lay waiting for her and the others. "Stalking Wolf!" she screamed from the depths of her being. Physically numb, she was propelled by terror to hastily climb onto Sotaju's back and charge the rest of the way down the ridge, shrieking Stalking Wolf's name as her horse galloped toward him and Hollow Horn.

Before she reached either man, Peace Maker saw a band of warriors surge from the heavy forest and clamor around Stalking Wolf and Hollow Horn, most of the raiders on foot. That was how they had hidden so well in the underbrush. By the time she reached the ensuing melee, Hollow Horn had fallen to the ground, several warriors hacking at his body with tomahawks.

"Run!" she heard Stalking Wolf shout. She could not obey. Farther away, two Oglala scouts lay riddled with arrows, and Standing Hawk was nowhere in sight. Too stunned to think clearly, Peace Maker sat frozen on Sotaju, while Stalking Wolf's horse whirled in circles. Stalking Wolf swung his buffalo-horn war club wildly as more attackers descended upon him and two remaining scouts. Stalking Wolf screamed blood-chilling war whoops, fighting off the assailants with a skill and viciousness Peace Maker had never before observed.

Frantically, Peace Maker yanked from its sheath a large hunting knife Stalking Wolf had given her. A Crow warrior rammed a spear through Stalking Wolf's left calf, and yet another speared his horse's shoulder. Instinctively, Peace Maker charged Sotaju into the bedlam and rammed her knife into a Crow man's back. He cried out and fell.

Stalking Wolf drove his war club into the side of another's head, burying the tip of the buffalo horn into the enemy's skull. He yanked the club out, and blood poured from the gaping wound as the warrior fell. Stalking Wolf swung the deadly weapon at yet another of his attackers, seemingly oblivious of the hideous gash in his own leg. His wounded horse began to sink to the ground, and Stalking Wolf again screamed at Peace Maker. "Run! Save yourself!"

Peace Maker knew she should obey, but something made her stay and fight at her husband's side. Never had she seen any man confront the enemy so fearlessly. She simply could not bring herself to leave him there to fight alone. She stabbed another Crow man in the neck, but then another warrior pulled her from Sotaju. She twisted around, violently plunging her knife into her captor's stomach. Two more warriors grabbed her from behind, each taking an arm, making it impossible for her to keep fighting. Something hard slammed against her right wrist, causing her to drop her knife, and then her two abductors picked her up, one man clamping her midriff against his side and gripping her tightly so that she could not move her arms, the other man running behind the first and holding her legs tightly. Peace Maker wrenched and screamed, struggling wildly to get away, but the two men were much too strong for her. She screeched Stalking Wolf's name, catching a last look at him covered with blood as he fought valiantly against the remaining Crow warriors.

He's dying! she thought with horror.

Then, from somewhere far off, she heard Oglala warriors whooping and shouting vengeance. She knew it would be the *akicitas,* who had not been far behind them. Still, they were far enough away that they could not reach the area in time to save her from being carried away . . . or to save Stalking Wolf. She had no doubt about her husband's abilities as a warrior, but there simply were too many of the enemy for him to overcome them alone.

In that one quick moment, Peace Maker realized that she loved Stalking Wolf. But she would never be able to tell him. Instead, the enemy would carry her off and make her a slave. She continued her struggle with those who ran with her into the thicker pines, where now she could see more of the enemy waiting with horses. They all shouted back and forth excitedly in their own tongue, and Peace Maker had no doubt the ones carrying her were telling the others to mount up and ride fast. Oglala warriors were surely just behind them.

Peace Maker grimaced when her abductors threw her over a horse and tied her wrists, which they yanked under the horse's belly and then secured to her ankles so she could not fall off. A warrior jumped onto the horse's back, sitting just behind her. He kicked the horse into motion, and all galloped away. Peace Maker nearly lost her breath from the jolting against her chest and stomach.

Crow were the only possible enemy in these parts, but this was much farther south than the Crow usually came, especially in the cold season, when most tribes usually settled into winter camp and did not make war. How had they known the Oglala might be here? And why had she been the only one abducted? She felt sick at the thought of what might happen to her. At best, she would become the wife of just one man, treated like a slave by his wife, or wives. She did not want to even think about the worst that could happen—used by many men, beaten by the women, tortured and killed.

Sod flew and horses panted. Peace Maker prayed to *Wakan-Tanka* that Oglala warriors were close on their heels . . . and that by some miracle only the Great Spirit could offer, Stalking Wolf lived.

CHAPTER TWENTY-THREE

PEACE MAKER'S HOPE faded as her abductors rode hard, putting many miles between themselves and the Oglala who might be tracking them. At dusk they split up, and all but the one who carried Peace Maker slung across his horse headed north.

Peace Maker struggled to keep her senses, fighting a pounding headache and the pain of bruised ribs from her excruciatingly awkward position on the galloping horse. She fought to keep aware of her surroundings, watching the sun as best she could so she would know the direction in which the warriors rode. After covering several miles, her captor urged his horse into a shallow riverbed, and icy water splashed up into Peace Maker's face and soaked her clothes. She squinted and sputtered, her discomfort enhanced when the wind cut against her wet tunic and her bare arms and legs. She had lost her warm cloak in her initial struggle, and the man who stole her away did not bother to cover her. He remained completely silent through hours of riding, even when he slowed his horse at times to rest the animal.

Peace Maker's hope for rescue dwindled when her captor traveled in the riverbed for at least two or three miles. She knew he chose the water so that any Oglala following would lose his tracks. They would most likely follow the tracks of those who broke away earlier and headed north.

Finally her abductor left the water. After covering

several more miles, he stopped to make camp when the sky became too dark for him to see. He cut the bindings at her ankles and shoved her off the horse. She landed so hard that she momentarily lost her breath. She lay there gasping while her abductor tethered his lathered horse. She finally managed to roll to her knees, but the enemy warrior kicked her in the rump before she could get to her feet, causing her to fall again. She felt herself being dragged, and she grunted when he shoved her against a tree.

"Stay!" he commanded, using the Lakota tongue.

Peace Maker thought it odd that he spoke her own language. He took a water bag from his horse and drank from it, then came over and motioned for her to open her mouth. He poured a little water on her tongue, then took the bag away.

Peace Maker leaned her head back against the tree and shivered. Her teeth chattered from the chill of the night air against her wet tunic and hair, and she wondered if she might die from sickness before the Crow could torture her to death. She remembered her grandmother's warnings that it was not wise to let cold air penetrate one's skin when it was wet. Such conditions could cause the coughing sickness that sometimes brought death.

She wondered if the Crow intended to hold her for ransom. How many horses would Stalking Wolf be willing to pay for her? If he was dead, how much would the rest of the Oglala think she was worth? Maybe they would not come for her at all.

The Crow warrior came back and strapped her securely to the tree. Her bound wrists rested in her lap, and Peace Maker never knew such pain and discomfort, but she refused to cry or beg in front of the enemy. He left her and built a small fire, then took some jerked meat from his supplies and ate it in yanking bites. With his face fully painted in a hideous black and white, Peace Maker found it impossible to imagine how he really looked.

The man finished eating, then took two robes from his supplies. He threw one at her as he walked by. When it did not land right, he bent down and opened it, covering her around the front.

"I would not mind watching you die for what you stole from my sister," he said, surprising Peace Maker by speaking a full sentence in the Lakota tongue, "but the Crow told me to bring you to them alive!"

Peace Maker's eyes widened in horror when she recognized his voice. "Gray Owl!"

He straightened, grinning. "Yes, it is I. Stalking Wolf has paid for having hurt Fall Leaf Woman. And you are paying for being the cause of it, and for treating me as though I am nothing." He tossed his tangled hair behind his shoulders and wrapped the other robe around himself. "Stalking Wolf's woman will now belong to a Crow man, or perhaps she will die slowly, whatever the Crow Council decides to do with her. I told them about the Oglala holy woman. This is a great victory for them . . . and for *me!*"

Peace Maker stared at him in astounded silence, taking a moment to gather her thoughts and overcome this stunning discovery. "How can you do this thing to your own people?" she finally cried out to him. "Traitor! Surely the god of all the earth and the skies will punish you severely. You will die a horrible death from this, and after death, your soul will *never* know peace."

"My *sister* and I are the ones who were wronged. It is you and Stalking Wolf whose souls will never be at peace." He turned away and rolled up in the robe, lying down near the fire. "Stalking Wolf is dead by now, wandering in a world of ghosts and terror," he continued. "I did not expect him to be killed, but only humiliated in defeat. However, I cannot control the Crow warriors. Fall Leaf Woman will be saddened, but she is still better off. You will die next, so enjoy your last hours. Tomorrow will be a bad day for you."

Peace Maker wiggled against the rawhide cords that held her, but to no avail. She closed her eyes in exhaustion and pain, and she prayed to *Wakan-Tanka* that by his power, Stalking Wolf would live and that she would be saved from the wrath of Gray Owl and the Crow.

"Stalking Wolf," she whispered in grief. She hoped the Oglala would not blame her for the death of Hollow Horn and Standing Hawk . . . and, most likely, for Stalking Wolf's. She could not bear to believe he could be dead. An aching weariness helped her drift into a fitful sleep, interrupted every few minutes when she jerked awake from the effects of tension and shock.

Stalking Wolf had been right in his warning not to trust Gray Owl, and in his feelings of danger when they approached their final campsite. Peace Maker held a new respect for her husband's keen instincts.

Pain tore through her heart every time she remembered how Stalking Wolf fought to save her. She prayed she would have the chance to tell him she loved him.

CHAPTER TWENTY-FOUR

See your son here,
He has served you well.
See him lying here near death.
Bless your son, Grandfather.
He has shed blood for you.
See your son here,
Who has served you well.

MOON PAINTER SANG until his throat ached. The old medicine man loved Stalking Wolf as though he were his own son. He prayed his medicine was strong enough to conquer the young man's terrible injuries, and thus become a form of victory over the enemy who had so grievously wounded a favorite son of the Oglala.

Burning sweet grass, he waved sacred smoke over Stalking Wolf, who lay naked beneath a buffalo robe next to the central fire prepared by Crow Chaser, Moon Painter's wife. Upon learning of the awful death of Red Sun Woman, Standing Hawk, Hollow Horn, and several other scouts, the Oglala had rallied in a determined effort to save Stalking Wolf and find his beloved wife.

While the women helped Crow Chasing Woman quickly erect a tepee to shelter Stalking Wolf before the warmth of a fire, Two Foxes, an old and esteemed leader, had formed a search party, and thirty warriors had ridden off to find Peace Maker.

Now came the waiting, to see if Stalking Wolf would live, to learn whether Peace Maker would be saved. Crow Chaser pulled back the robe that covered Stalking Wolf and applied cool ashes to his hideous wounds: a severe laceration on his left calf, and a gash at the front of his right shoulder so deep that many feared he might never use his right arm again. The rest of his body was a mass of cuts and bruises, his face barely recognizable. Moon Painter feared he might die from a massive loss of blood. If Stalking Wolf lived for the next few hours, that danger would lessen. Moon Painter had learned from experience that sometimes a man's blood returned, if he lived long enough for *Wakan-Tanka* to fill him with more of the precious fluid of life.

Even if Stalking Wolf did survive the next few hours, he might die days, or even weeks, later from the bad spirits the Crow had tried to instill in him with the blows of their weapons, spirits that caused wounds to fester and turn green, sometimes making limbs rot and fall away. It would be a horrible way for any man to die, but especially a man like Stalking Wolf.

The rest of the Oglala settled into the valley and made camp, while Moon Painter sang . . . all night, all the next day, taking no time for sleep. Crow Chaser worried about her husband when he stayed awake so long, but she knew he considered it his duty and privilege to serve the Oglala this way. Her husband possessed great powers of healing, and *Wakan-Tanka* usually listened to his prayers.

She drew more ashes across Stalking Wolf's forehead, sorry for the sadness he would know when he came awake to learn of his mother's death, as well as the death of his best friend. Worse, Stalking Wolf might never know the fate of Peace Maker, for sometimes captives were never found. Outside, the Big Bellies and *Wicasa Itakans* sat in Council, contemplating sending even more men after those who had already left to rescue Peace Maker.

Stalking Wolf lay unconscious, his only sound a chilling groan from the depths of his soul when Crow Chaser stitched some of his cuts with string made of buffalo gut. Young Buffalo Calf sat faithfully at his cousin's side, shedding tears at the thought that his beloved mentor might die. Indeed, for a moment, Stalking Wolf stopped breathing. Moon Painter chanted louder, shaking his medicine rattle with more vigor, begging *Wakan-Tanka* to hear his prayers and bring Stalking Wolf back to the Oglala, who loved him.

Buffalo Calf held Stalking Wolf's hand and sobbed. "Please save him, Moon Painter."

The old medicine man raised his arms and threw back his head, tears streaming down his own face. Again he cried out his prayer, and Crow Chaser again applied ashes to Stalking Wolf's wounds. She covered him, and Buffalo Calf noticed Stalking Wolf's eyes flutter open.

"He is still alive!" he exclaimed.

Stalking Wolf stared blankly at Buffalo Calf, and Crow Chaser sprinkled more sweet grass on the fire. Moon Painter wafted more smoke over Stalking Wolf, thanking *Wakan-Tanka* for breathing new life into his faithful son.

"Can you hear me, Stalking Wolf?" Buffalo Calf asked.

Stalking Wolf moved his lips, but no sound came from them. He stirred, and Crow Chaser pressed her hands against his shoulders. "You must lie still, Stalking Wolf. You are badly injured, and you lost much blood. Moon Painter and I have been praying for you."

Stalking Wolf looked around without moving his head, then whispered something. Buffalo Calf leaned closer to hear. "What did you say?" He put his ear to Stalking Wolf's mouth.

"Peace . . . Maker," Stalking Wolf said.

Buffalo Calf looked up at Moon Painter. "He asks about Peace Maker."

Wiping tears from his cheeks, Moon Painter stopped his chanting and knelt beside Stalking Wolf. "Crow dogs have stolen your wife. I am sorry, Stalking Wolf, but they killed your mother, and also Standing Hawk and Hollow Horn." Knowing the news was a terrible blow to Stalking Wolf, Moon Painter also knew that the same news might give Stalking Wolf the needed courage and determination to survive, for his heart would be filled with the desire for revenge.

A guttural moan moved from Stalking Wolf's deepest being to his throat, and he cried out a wail of agony that could be heard outside the tepee. Tears slipped out of the corners of his eyes.

Moon Painter nodded and smiled. "He will live," he predicted. "For revenge."

CHAPTER TWENTY-FIVE

ANOTHER NEARLY FULL day of riding north brought Peace Maker and Gray Owl to a large Crow camp. Peace Maker's hope for rescue dwindled even more at the sight of hundreds of tepees. Women and warriors alike already exited tepees and left campfires to watch them ride in. Gray Owl pushed Peace Maker from his horse, her hands still tied. As soon as she hit the ground women began beating her with fists and sticks as she struggled to get to her feet.

Finally, one man jerked Peace Maker up and ordered the women to back away. He whirled her around and looked her over, curling his nose at her smell, for she had been forced to urinate down her legs during the long ride here. Gray Owl did not stop for her toilet needs or give her a chance to bathe. The Crow man who held her said something now to Gray Owl, who stood watching with a grin of pleasure.

Peace Maker suspected the man who had picked her up was one of those who had attacked Stalking Wolf. The tall, commanding Crow warrior wore a white man's red flannel shirt. She remembered seeing the same shirt on one of the raiders who had bludgeoned Stalking Wolf. In spite of its color, the shirt this man wore showed darker red spots in numerous places. *Stalking Wolf's blood?* The thought caused a wave of powerful grief to wash over her, so that for a moment she could hardly breathe.

"This man is called Elk Runner," Gray Owl told her

with a haughty air. "He says you are fine to look at but that you smell bad." He laughed lightly. "I guess you do." He strutted around her, wearing a cocky grin. "You will be a new wife to Elk Runner, and a slave to his other three wives. I promised Elk Runner that he could have you if he and his warriors helped me get my revenge on Stalking Wolf. An Oglala holy woman is a fine prize for a Crow man."

His grin made Peace Maker ill. "Stalking Wolf came to you and offered forgiveness," she told him, finding strength only in her anger. "He even brought you horses! You are a traitor of the worst kind!"

He only shrugged. "These women will take you to the creek and wash you and give you a clean tunic," he told her, ignoring her comments. He came closer and curled his nose. "The way you smell, you are lucky Elk Runner wants you at all. He is an honored warrior among the Crow. Your fate could be worse." He snickered. "Elk Runner has agreed to pay four horses for you. He does not think you of such value as Stalking Wolf did, but perhaps Stalking Wolf was the fool after all."

Peace Maker managed to jerk away from Elk Runner. "*You* are the fool, Gray Owl! One day *death* will find you for what you have done. If not at the hands of Stalking Wolf, then the Great Spirit will find *another* way."

"Stalking Wolf is *dead!*" Gray Owl reminded her.

"No! He *lives,* and he will *come* for you." Pain stabbed Peace Maker's heart to think that Stalking Wolf truly *might* be dead. She must not allow such thoughts! It was too much to bear, made worse by the realization of how foolish she had been to think she could never love Stalking Wolf, and how sad that it had taken his death to awaken her true feelings.

She noticed a hint of worry in Gray Owl's eyes, and she spat at him. He lifted his arm to hit her, but Elk Runner shoved her toward a group of women, who dragged her kicking and screaming to a creek. They cut the ropes from her wrists and yanked off her tunic and knee-high moccasins. Laughing and jeering, they dunked her into water so cold it sent her into shock. She could hardly breathe, and she stopped fighting long enough for the women to rub her with sand to clean her skin. She screamed when they poured more cold water over her to rinse her off. Then they wrapped her shivering body in a large buffalo robe and led her to a tepee. There someone kicked her hard in the back, forcing her inside, where she fell near the central fire.

Peace Maker rolled to her knees and remained where she had landed, taking a moment to get her bearings and her breath. She determined that at all costs, she would not cry. She was Lakota! A Brulé! She had touched the white buffalo and married a prestigious Oglala warrior. The little girl in her wanted to cry out for her grandmother's arms, but the woman in her refused to cower before the enemy. Everything hurt, and when she looked down at one exposed ankle, she saw a swelling bruise forming from one of the blows inflicted earlier.

She looked around, noticing four women in the tepee, all staring at her. The oldest, most likely the first wife of Elk Runner, came toward her, her dark eyes glittering with hate, no doubt because tonight the woman's husband would take pleasure in a new, young wife.

The graying, overweight woman held a short, solid tree branch in her hand, and she held it up as she spat words at Peace Maker, who could not understand what she said. She guessed the woman intended to show her that she would never rule in this dwelling or hold any importance beyond a slave. The woman brought the branch down hard. Peace Maker ducked her head, and the blow landed sharply on the top of her shoulder. Several more wicked blows followed, and Peace

Maker hunched her shoulders against the cruel beating until, finally, pride and anger took over. She jumped up and threw off the buffalo robe. She lunged at the older woman, shoving her backward so hard that she fell on her rump. "Enough!" Peace Maker screamed at her.

One of the younger wives giggled. Enraged, the older woman got to her feet and turned on the one who had laughed. The younger woman's smile vanished. She made a dash for the tepee entrance, but she did not escape one good whack from the older woman before she managed to get away. The young girl shrieked with pain when the club landed on the back of her thigh.

She disappeared, and the other two wives sat quietly, not even daring to look up at the oldest wife. Only then did Peace Maker notice four small children sitting in the shadows. They made no sound, but sat in wide-eyed curiosity. Someone darkened the entranceway to the tepee then, and Peace Maker grabbed the buffalo robe and wrapped it around her nakedness.

Elk Runner stepped inside, and he noticed the stick in the older woman's hand. He grabbed it away, shouting at her and raising the stick. He slammed it across the older woman's shoulder and she screamed, then shouted something at Elk Runner before fleeing.

Elk Runner barked an obvious order at the remaining two women, and they grabbed the children and hurriedly left. He turned then to face Peace Maker, who stood holding the robe tightly around herself. He spoke to her, but she did not understand. Then, to her relief, he left.

Peace Maker cautiously approached the entrance and lifted the deerskin covering to see two warriors standing guard. She did not doubt that more watched the back side of the dwelling, so that she could not try to crawl out.

How could she escape the clutches of Elk Runner

and the painful beatings and backbreaking work his first wife would impose upon her? Death would be better than life as a Crow slave. She examined her surroundings, shivering against a wicked chill that penetrated her whole being. Her hair still wet, she walked closer to the central fire to warm herself. She noticed a small knife lying on a rock near the fire.

Not even sure whether she would use it on herself or the enemy, she picked up the knife and hid it under the robe. Hanging nearby were several women's tunics, and she chose one closest to her size and removed it from its hook. Wincing with the pain of many welts and bruises, she dropped the robe, hiding the knife under it while she quickly slipped on the tunic. She wrapped the robe around herself again, so that when Elk Runner returned, he would think her still naked beneath it. That would likely draw him closer . . . close enough to shove a knife into his heart!

She took some wood from a nearby pile and added it to the fire, then sat down near the warm flames to wait . . . not even sure for what. Elk Runner most likely had left to pay Gray Owl the promised horses.

Gray Owl! How could he have done this? Had Fall Leaf Woman known of his plans? She hoped that one day Gray Owl would suffer proper punishment at the hands of the Oglala. But for now, she needed to think only about how to keep Elk Runner from violating her. She gripped the hidden knife tightly. Elk Runner would likely come back soon, and she would be ready for him!

CHAPTER TWENTY-SIX

SINGING AND DRUMMING filled the dark night air. All the shouting and dancing told Peace Maker that the men and women outside were working themselves into a maddening frenzy, celebrating the capture of an Oglala holy woman. Elk Runner surely celebrated the most, for he had gained a new wife. Soon he would come to claim his prize.

She watched the tepee entrance for the inevitable visit, praying to the Buffalo Spirit for the strength to do whatever she must do, or to suffer bravely whatever awful fate might lie waiting for her. Too soon, the hoof rattles at the tepee entrance clattered. Elk Runner threw open the entrance flap and ducked inside, so drunk with victory that he stumbled slightly. His dark eyes glittered with desire, and the grin on his face actually looked silly to Peace Maker.

So, she thought, *he actually believes I'll lie back and let him claim me.* He would discover his error soon enough, even if it cost her her life!

Elk Runner stripped off his clothes, and the fire's eerie light cast a glow on his dark skin. If he were not the enemy, he could be considered a fine specimen of a man. She gripped the small knife tightly. She must sink it hard and deep when she stabbed the strong-muscled Elk Runner, or she might only wound him and suffer his wrath.

Elk Runner folded his arms and barked an order. Peace Maker supposed he wanted her to remove her robe. She backed away, and he shouted the order again. Still she did not obey. He came closer, and Peace Maker forced a look of daring invitation, challenging him with her eyes. She realized he surely thought himself quite handsome. After all, he already owned four wives. She tossed her hair behind her shoulders, giving him another fetching look, while under the robe, she turned the knife in such a way that she could stab with a downward motion, putting more strength into the blow.

Elk Runner reached out then and yanked off her robe, jerking her close. Just as suddenly, Peace Maker rammed the knife deep into the middle of the man's chest. Blood spurted from the wound, spraying her on the face and the front of her tunic. She held her ground through the horror, pushing the knife harder.

Elk Runner stared at her in shock, and Peace Maker feared she had not found the proper mark. Panicked, she yanked the knife from his chest and buried it in his throat. She grimaced when blood poured from the wound, ran down Elk Runner's body, and splattered her arm. Elk Runner made no sound before dropping the buffalo robe and sinking to his knees. He never took his eyes from Peace Maker's face, and she thought how odd it was that Stalking Wolf had changed her name to Peace Maker. In her heart, she truly did want peace, but she could not allow this man to take what belonged only to a proud Oglala warrior.

She jerked out the knife, then jumped out of the way when Elk Runner's body fell forward, landing facedown in the hot fire. He let out a muffled scream before falling silent. Peace Maker dropped the knife and whimpered in horror when his hair caught fire, and she curled her nose at the smell of burning hair and flesh.

Get away! She must find a way to escape! Perhaps Elk Runner had dismissed the guards when he arrived. Since it was dark, and the others were lost in their celebrating, she might be able to slip out under the back side of the tepee now. If she ran fast enough to put some distance between herself and the village . . . and if she could find a place to hide for the rest of the night . . .

Quickly she tugged on a pair of knee-high moccasins she found, then picked up the buffalo robe. She would need it for the cold night. Her injuries brought misery to her every movement, and her two-day ordeal of constant riding, abuse, and deprivation had left her weak. Only the blessings of *Wakan-Tanka* himself had given her the strength to stab Elk Runner hard enough to kill him.

Blinking back tears of terror, she gingerly picked up the bloody knife. She might need it to defend herself, or to find food. She knelt at the back of the tepee, lifting the bottom skins far enough to look out. To her disappointment, she saw the moccasined feet of a man standing guard. Her momentary hope for escape vanished, and desperation engulfed her. Guard or no guard, she had to get away! The tepee began to fill with the stench of Elk Runner's roasting flesh. Someone could come inside at any moment. She decided that if she had killed Elk Runner with the small knife, she could also kill the guard outside with it.

She tried to cut through the tepee hide but realized only then that the tip of the knife must have chipped off when she stabbed Elk Runner. It would not cut through the tough hide. She tried again, then heard a shout from outside. The guard had noticed her efforts! Before she could turn around, another man entered the tepee. He cried out in horror and called for others. He lunged for Peace Maker, who crouched at the back of the tepee, waving the knife at him. But by now, her already-weakened state betrayed her resolve to fight, and she had nothing left with which to stave off the enemy. He grabbed for her, and she managed to slash a shallow cut across his chest, but that did not stop him. He grabbed her wrist and squeezed so hard that she screamed and dropped the knife.

Two more warriors entered, followed by Elk Runner's oldest wife. The woman screeched in shock, yanking at her husband's arm and dragging him out of the fire. The other three wives hurried inside, and all four women screamed and wailed at the sight of Elk Runner's horribly burned face and chest. The youngest wife turned away and ran out, keening in despair and grief. The oldest lunged at Peace Maker, who could not fend her off because of the Crow man who still held her arm. The woman wrapped strong fingers around Peace Maker's throat and squeezed until Peace Maker felt faint from the lack of oxygen, but finally the other two warriors managed to pull the woman away, shouting at her. One of them forced her out, and then they also dragged Peace Maker outside.

The drumming stopped as news of the disaster quickly spread through the camp. Women wept and wailed, and men gathered to discuss what to do. The angry enemy shoved and kicked Peace Maker toward the central fire, where moments earlier, all had danced in victory.

The camp broke into bedlam, the air filled with the mournful sounds of keening and crying. Men and women alike pointed at Peace Maker, screaming retributions. She must die. There could be no other justification for what she had done. She only hoped her death would not be by slow torture.

CHAPTER TWENTY-SEVEN

WOMEN PUMMELED PEACE Maker with sticks, fists, and kicks, until she became only vaguely aware that she was tied firmly to an old, dead pine tree, where she sagged against her leather bonds, already longing for death. The yelling and drumming and arguing that surrounded her seemed more like a strange dream than reality. Every part of her screamed with pain, and thirst made her tongue swell.

Her abusers left her there all night. By morning, she had no feeling in her hands and feet. Through the slits of her swollen eyes she saw Elk Runner's dead body, wrapped in a buffalo robe and laid on a travois, being carried away for burial, his keening wives walking behind. Men burned the tepee where he had died, as was custom, to banish bad spirits that might lurk within.

Peace Maker struggled to move her head and look around for Gray Owl, but saw him nowhere. She wondered if he had run off during the night in fear for his own life. Convincing the Crow to help him capture her and kill Stalking Wolf had turned into disaster for one of their favored sons. The Crow surely wanted Gray Owl's life, too.

She watched Elk Runner's tepee go up in flames, followed the black smoke that trailed skyward. "Stay with me, Great Spirit," she whispered, wincing from a cut lip. "Help me to die bravely and not shame the Sichangu or Oglala people. Give me courage."

Pain, thirst, and hunger plagued her, made worse by

a cold, damp wind that penetrated her tunic and skin. No one did anything to give her warmth, and she could not help wondering what further torture the Crow had in mind for her. She studied the beautiful mountains in the distance, praying that death would take her quickly to that place where all Lakota found peace and beauty, where they were with loved ones gone before.

She waited in agony through the burial ceremony, drifting in and out of consciousness. Thunder rumbled in the west, rousing her. This was an odd time of year for a thunderstorm, but the powers of the heavens could never be predicted. One day there might be sunshine, another a wet, gray rain, the next day a blizzard.

She saw Elk Runner's wives returning from the burial, and fear gripped her belly at what they might have in mind for her. They spoke with several other women, while the men all waited in a large gathering behind them. Peace Maker realized then that her fate lay in the hands of the women alone, who must have insisted they deserved the right to punish her however they chose. Elk Runner's wives carried on loudly, pointing to her at times. Finally the women split up and headed for various tepees, returning with arms full of kindling, brush, and firewood.

The oldest wife approached Peace Maker, her eyes gleaming with hatred and arrogance. She placed a bundle of kindling at Peace Maker's feet, then spat on her. Peace Maker refused to flinch. The woman then grinned wickedly and nodded, turning to the other three wives and barking some kind of order. The others approached Peace Maker then, one by one, each of them placing more wood and brush at her feet. They also spat on her.

Still more women followed suit, bringing yet more wood and kindling, and a deep terror crept into Peace Maker's throat. They planned to burn her alive! She imagined the horror of flames slowly licking at her feet and legs, catching her dress and searing her skin, a slow torture of wretched, unspeakable pain before death finally consumed her along with the flames! How could *Wakan-Tanka* allow her to suffer so?

For several minutes, women walked back and forth, delivering wood and brush so that they created a huge pile around Peace Maker that came nearly to her waist. They spread it out in a larger circle around her, so that it would take time for the flames to reach her, allowing Peace Maker opportunity to think about the anguish that awaited her.

Thunder vibrated in the distance, and the sky darkened. The Crow women lifted their arms toward the clouds in praise and began singing and dancing. Peace Maker supposed they considered the coming storm a sign of approval from the Great Spirit for what they were doing. She longed to believe that instead, the thunder came to somehow protect her.

So, this was their revenge! Elk Runner had fallen into the fire and suffered its pain before dying. He would go to the life beyond a horribly disfigured man. Now she must suffer the same fate, except it would be worse, because they would not first plunge a knife into her heart. She would feel every inch of the agony as the flames consumed her body.

CHAPTER TWENTY-EIGHT

THE THUNDER BECAME an almost constant rumble, and Crow warriors and women alike sang and danced even louder. Drummers added to the wild frenzy celebrating Peace Maker's slow death. Elk Runner's wives set fire to the dead wood piled around Peace Maker, and as they did so, lightning split through the dark clouds above. The storm was upon them, and the excitement among the participants escalated to a keening more like screams than singing. The drama of the Crow torture ritual was heightened by the anger of the Thunder God.

Peace Maker closed her eyes, begging *Wakan-Tanka* to keep her from feeling the greed of the encroaching flames. The thunder grew louder and became a continuous rumble. Lightning bolts cut white cracks through the clouds. The earth began to shake so that Peace Maker opened her eyes in wonder. She felt a strange new power move within her, and as the ground vibrated, the Crow, warriors and women alike, stared at her as though suddenly afraid of her. Then, before any of them realized what was really happening, it was too late for most of them to save themselves.

Peace Maker saw them first . . . buffalo! Hundreds . . . no, thousands! The thundering sound and the shaking earth were caused by a herd of buffalo headed straight through the valley toward the Crow camp, in such a massive force that they resembled one long, huge, black, winding snake, filling the valley on every side.

It became impossible to tell the difference between the roar of thundering hooves and the thunder in the heavens. All came together in one great force, and the Crow began screaming and shouting, the women picking up their children and running, the men shouting orders, trying to reach their horses. Their voices became lost in the deafening tumult of the stampeding buffalo and the raging storm. In spite of a light blanket of snow on the ground, the shaggy beasts churned the dirt so that dust rose in a great cloud above them. As they came closer and people and animals scattered, the flames crept toward Peace Maker.

Now both fire and stampeding buffalo threatened her. The herd headed straight for the village, and straight for where she stood tied to the tree. Still, the mystery of the awesome event erased all fear in Peace Maker's soul and replaced it with sheer wonder and disbelief. Perhaps her pain, her lack of food and water, all combined to create a vision, and none of this was real. Still, the thunder in the sky and on the ground became so loud it hurt her ears. There was no mistaking its reality.

Men, women, and children scattered and ran. Already the buffalo had reached the camp, and tepees were falling before them, battered down and trampled. Horses and humans alike were being run down and crushed to death. At the same time, the clouds burst open with a torrent of rain that snuffed out the burning brush around Peace Maker. Then, to her further disbelief, the herd of buffalo parted around her, cutting a swath wide enough that not one hair of a buffalo touched her.

They had come to *save* her! The surging herd battered and thundered its way past her in a seemingly never-ending stream, and the morning sky turned almost black, as the storm clouds intensified. The dust stirred by the buffalo thickened. In one brilliant flash of lightning, Peace Maker thought she saw something white on the horizon. She kept her eyes fixed on the place she had noticed it, but the next flash of lightning ripped into the tree to which she was tied.

Peace Maker screamed. The tree cracked and split, and the top portion fell sideways, ripping the rest of the trunk in half and snapping the cords that bound her.

Astounded that she was still alive, Peace Maker stood in the downpour that quenched the flames that only moments ago threatened to consume her. Another crack of thunder spurred her back to reality, and she quickly wiggled out of the cords that still bound her ankles. She jumped away from the black, smoking tree trunk, but her feet were asleep from the tight bindings, and she fell into the brush piled around her. She sat there dumbfounded at the miracles taking place before her eyes.

Her tunic sagged from the drenching rain, and her hair matted against her head and face, but the strange course of events left Peace Maker oblivious to the cold and rain. The buffalo gradually thundered off to the east, and the lightning and thunder ceased, leaving behind only a soft, steady rain.

Peace Maker remained stunned, overwhelmed by the series of pure miracles that had freed her. All around lay the dead, battered bodies of women, children, warriors, horses, and dogs, as well as trampled tepees and the scattered coals of snuffed fires. She heard no voices, nor the whinny of a horse. If any Crow were left, they were nowhere in sight. Peace Maker found herself totally alone, not sure of where to turn, what to do.

She looked all around, wondering if she could find even one horse to ride. That was when she saw it again: something white on the western hillside and slowly ambling toward her. A white buffalo!

Peace Maker shivered. Perhaps the white buffalo was the Great Spirit himself! Never did she feel more blessed, or more aware of the power of *Wakan-Tanka* . . . as well as the power that apparently lay within herself. Stalking Wolf's vision of her importance became more real to her now, and she understood why she had needed to marry someone of equal importance. Still, why then had *Wakan-Tanka* allowed Stalking Wolf to die? *Perhaps the white buffalo's presence means my husband still lives!*

Weak and dizzy from hunger and her battered condition, Peace Maker stood up on shaking legs and stumbled toward the white buffalo. Its pink eyes bore into her, as if capturing her by its spell. She knew the animal had come to help her find the Oglala, to take her home. When she went closer, the beautiful beast knelt down on its front legs, as though inviting her to climb upon its back. A buffalo robe lay nearby on the ground, and Peace Maker picked it up and wrapped it around herself. She wondered if the white buffalo might disappear once she touched it, and carefully she reached out, fingering its soft, shaggy mane.

The animal was real! She gripped the thick, soft hairs, and without fear, she mounted the animal.

The rain stopped. The white buffalo began walking, and Peace Maker clung to its thick mane. She leaned forward and rested her head, deciding to let the buffalo take her wherever it would, for she had no power to control it, and no will to stop it.

EARLY DECEMBER
1832

Long Night Moon

CHAPTER TWENTY-NINE

THE OGLALA WAR party moved through a rugged canyon that opened into hilly, barren country decorated only with rocks and a few scrubby pines.

"I still say we should have followed the tracks of many horses, Two Foxes, not of just this one man," Wind In Grass complained.

Old Two Foxes, a member of the highest Council of the Oglala, held his nose proudly in the air. "And who among us has the most experience in tracking the enemy?" he asked.

Wind In Grass frowned. "I did not mean disrespect, Grandfather," he answered, using the term as a sign of honor for Two Foxes' age. "But we have been following this man's horse for five days now. You said they tried to fool us by splitting up and sending most of the men in another direction. Perhaps it was the other way around, and we should have followed them after all."

Two Foxes shook his head. As befit his high position among the Council of the Oglala, he wore a headdress of eagle feathers and proudly carried his war lance. Five days ago, he had led twenty of the best Oglala braves on a search for Peace Maker. "You can see by the tracks in the softer earth that this man carries extra weight," he said. "But now I worry the Crow have gone even deeper into their own country. I am undecided, for even though I wish to save Peace

Maker, I do not wish to lead all of you young men to
your death."

"We are not afraid!" one of them spoke up. "We
will keep going!"

Two Foxes smiled sadly, turning back to Wind In
Grass. "I am taking the chance that I have been right
about these tracks. My heart wants to give up the
search, but my instincts tell me I am right and that
Wakan-Tanka is with me. Go over that next hill, Wind
In Grass. See if there are any signs of a Crow camp,
perhaps the smoke from campfires in the distance. It
is a high hill. You should be able to see far from
there."

Wind In Grass nodded, his coup feathers blowing
in the wind. Anxious to add to those feathers by touching the enemy, he obeyed Two Foxes' order and
headed up the hill. Two Foxes turned to the others
while he waited. He pulled his fox-fur cape closer
around himself and adjusted the beaverskin hat he
wore. "This weather is hard on an old man," he said.
"It will be difficult to go on. The wind bites, hinting
of a much fiercer wind to come. The sleet stings our
faces. It is a dangerous time to be away from winter
camp." He turned his weary horse to wait for Wind In
Grass, refusing to let the aches and pains of old age
keep him from this important mission.

The younger men also waited impatiently. A few of
them pranced their horses nervously, and Two Foxes
could see they were aching for a fight. He remembered
his own impatience in his younger days.

Wind In Grass suddenly came charging down the
hill toward them, and they all readied war lances,
bows, and tomahawks, some of them beginning to yip
and whoop their war cries.

"She is there!" Wind In Grass announced breath-
lessly when he came closer. "Just over the hill! It is
Peace Maker!"

Two Foxes' horse turned in a circle and snorted, as

though sensing the excitement. "How many Crow are with her?" Two Foxes asked anxiously.

"None!" Wind In Grass answered, his face strangely ashen. The others circled closer in alarm.

"What do you mean?" Two Foxes demanded. "Surely there are—"

"She rides a white buffalo!" Wind In Grass interrupted. "She is alone, and she rides a white buffalo! It is like nothing I have ever seen!"

The others looked at each other in astonishment.

"There!" Wind In Grass pointed to the top of the grassy hill. Two Foxes raised his eyes, catching his breath when he did indeed see Peace Maker sitting there on a white buffalo. Apparently recognizing their Oglala regalia, she raised a hand in acknowledgment, then leaned down and said something to the buffalo. The beast knelt on its front legs so that she could slide off its back.

While the Oglala warriors stared, Peace Maker walked slowly toward them. As she came closer, they all noted her tangled hair, the bruises and cuts on her face and arms. Too weak to keep a tight hold on the buffalo robe she wore, she allowed it to fall open slightly, and some could see that dried blood stained her tunic.

When she reached them, she raised weary eyes in greeting. "My heart is glad that you have found me," she said through parched, swollen lips, her voice barely audible.

Two Foxes looked past her to see the white buffalo heading over the top of the ridge. "See where it goes!" he told Wind In Grass.

The young man kicked his horse's sides and galloped back up the ridge. Two Foxes dismounted and grasped Peace Maker's arms, studying her with great concern. "I am sorry we could not find you sooner. My heart is heavy with guilt. What has happened, Peace Maker?"

Peace Maker closed her eyes. "It is such . . . a long story." She bowed her head. "I am tired, Two Foxes. I must sit down."

Two Foxes held on to her arms as she nearly collapsed into the wet grass. "Watch for the enemy!" he told the others. "They might be close!"

Still astounded at finding Peace Maker, the Oglala men needed a moment to react to the order.

"No," Peace Maker spoke up before they rode away. "There is no enemy near. Do not be alarmed."

Two Foxes ordered two men to look around and make sure, worried lest Peace Maker was only confused because of her ordeal. He took a pouch of water from his horse and sat down across from her.

"Tell me, Peace Maker, why do you say there is no enemy? What has happened to you? Where are those who stole you away?"

He handed her the water, and Peace Maker took a long drink before answering. "A Crow warrior called Elk Runner tried to claim me," she told old Two Foxes. "I would have been his fifth wife . . . slave to the other four." She looked down at her bloodied dress, then pulled her buffalo robe closer around her neck against the cold. "I . . . killed Elk Runner."

Two Foxes gasped. "You are indeed brave! You are yourself a warrior, Peace Maker. Tell us, how did you kill him?"

Peace Maker shivered at the memory. "I found a small knife in his tepee, probably left by one of his wives. I hid it, and when he came close to me, I stabbed him in the chest. His blood . . ." She closed her eyes. "His blood was everywhere. It sprayed out on my face, but later a hard rain washed it off my skin. Elk Runner did not fall right away, and so I stabbed him in the neck. He fell into the central fire, and his flesh and hair burned, so that he was terribly disfigured when one of his wives pulled him out of the fire."

"A fitting way for the enemy to suffer in the hereafter!" Two Foxes celebrated. He touched her shoulder. "Surely the Crow meant to kill you after that. How did you escape them?"

Peace Maker met his eyes, seeing much wisdom behind the many wrinkles. She told him about the buffalo stampede and the storm, and Two Foxes shook his head.

"You are truly blessed, Peace Maker. You must tell this story to the *Nacas,* for it is too miraculous to keep to yourself."

Peace Maker hung her head. "Right now all I want is to go home, to be warm. The women beat me, and I am in much pain."

Before she could go on, Wind In Grass came chasing down the ridge. He leaped from his horse before it had stopped completely.

"There is nothing but open land beyond the ridge, and yet when I reached the top, the white buffalo was gone. Gone! There are not even any tracks! I rode ahead, searching everywhere. There is no sign of the white buffalo, Two Foxes."

Two Foxes shook his head. "Truly this daughter of ours is blessed. Stalking Wolf will be pleased when he hears this."

"My husband!" Peace Maker exclaimed. "He lives?"

Two Foxes met her gaze and shook his head. "I do not know. He was alive when we left him, but gravely wounded."

"You must take me back quickly! If he is still alive and I go to him, touch him, pray for him, I know he will live. I must be with him."

Two Foxes nodded. "We will take you as quickly as possible. We came to kill the Crow warriors who stole you, but the buffalo have taken vengeance for us." He patted her arm. "The story you told us is a great sign for all the Lakota. Through you, *Wakan-*

Tanka has seen fit to bless us with a sign of strength and power by showing us the white buffalo!"

Peace Maker's eyes filled with tears. "Tell me. Did Red Sun Woman live?"

Two Foxes' eyes closed at renewed grief. "No. Hollow Horn and Standing Hawk also were killed."

"Oh, no!" Peace Maker put her head in her hands and wept. "I have lost a mother and Stalking Wolf has lost a dear friend."

"We will track down the Crow dogs and avenge the death of our loved ones!" Wind In Grass declared.

Peace Maker gasped, looking up at Wind In Grass with eyes that suddenly changed from grief to hatred. "It is not the Crow who should die for this."

Two Foxes studied her in surprise. "How can you say this?"

Peace Maker managed to rise and face all of them. "It is one of our own who must pay for Red Sun Woman's death! Gray Owl planned this with our enemy. He is the one who took me away and sold me to Elk Runner—for four horses!"

Shock lit up all their faces, and Two Foxes held up his lance. "Death to Gray Owl!"

The others shouted war cries, raising their own lances and war clubs. Two Foxes turned back to Peace Maker with questioning eyes. "Perhaps Gray Owl, too, was killed by the stampeding buffalo."

"I am not sure. I did not see him before the stampede. I think that he ran away after I killed Elk Runner, afraid for his own life. I do not think he was among those killed."

"He must die!" Wind In Grass declared.

"If Stalking Wolf lives, he must sink his lance into Gray Owl," Two Foxes told the others. "He has first chance."

"Gray Owl will never go far enough away or hide himself cleverly enough to escape Stalking Wolf," one of the others shouted.

Two Foxes put an arm around Peace Maker, who looked so pale she seemed ready to faint. "First, we must take Peace Maker to our winter camp so that the women can tend to her. We will spend the winter discussing what has happened and what these signs mean." He took his medicine rattle from his waist and shook it over Peace Maker, chanting a song of healing while the others prepared a travois for her.

Two Foxes then touched Peace Maker's shoulder with his medicine rattle. "From this day forward, you shall be called Buffalo Dreamer," he declared, changing her name once again. "The magic powers gifted to you by the white buffalo will be used to guide the Oglala."

Peace Maker nodded. "Buffalo Dreamer," she said softly. "I am . . . Buffalo Dreamer."

MID-DECEMBER
1832

CHAPTER THIRTY

THE PUNGENT SMELL of burning sweet grass met Stalking Wolf's nostrils, stirring him to an awareness of Moon Painter's chanting. He breathed deeply, trying to remember why he lay here with the Oglala medicine man praying over him. At first he could remember only terrible pain in his chest and neck, and in his left leg.

Vague visions of Crow warriors attacking him became more vivid as a gradual awakening to reality pushed through his mind. He remembered Peace Maker defending him, saw her stab one of the enemy with the hunting knife he had given her. His wife had fought beside him like a warrior! He remembered his horse falling . . . and Peace Maker . . . Peace Maker . . .

Someone stole her away! The realization of her abduction alarmed him and brought him fully awake. He opened his eyes to see Moon Painter shaking a sacred turtle rattle over his body. The old man chanted a healing prayer, and again Stalking Wolf experienced deep pain without moving a muscle. Just trying to turn his head required great effort. His vision cleared, and then he saw her. *Peace Maker!* She sat to his left. When she noticed him looking at her, she leaned closer and touched his face. "It is good to see you open your eyes, my husband. I have prayed night and day with Moon Painter that you will be healed."

Stalking Wolf noticed tears in her eyes. "Your face . . . cuts . . . bruises . . ."

"Do not worry. I will explain when you are stronger. We have much to discuss when you are better."

Stalking Wolf closed his eyes again. "I . . . failed you. I am ashamed." Devastation filled his soul at the memory. Peace Maker took his hand and pressed it to her cheek.

"You did not fail me. You risked your life to defend me. I have never seen a man fight as valiantly and relentlessly as you did, Stalking Wolf."

He opened his eyes again, noticing that her hair had been shorn above her shoulders. It hung in straggly, uneven clumps. When a woman cut off her hair, it represented great sacrifice, a sign to *Wakan-Tanka* that she wanted to give something precious of her own, to destroy her beauty if need be, to show how much she cared that her prayers should be answered. "Your hair," he said, finding it an effort to speak.

"I know now that I care deeply for you," Peace Maker answered him. "I promise to be a proper wife when you are well."

Stalking Wolf squeezed her hand weakly. "Then I will try . . . to heal quickly." He managed a sly grin, but Peace Maker remained sober.

"There is something that must be done, Stalking Wolf, that I am sorry to say will bring you even more pain. Bad spirits from a Crow warrior's tomahawk have invaded your body at your right shoulder. The infection is very bad. Moon Painter is preparing to burn the wound. It is the only way to kill the bad spirits and save your life."

Stalking Wolf drew a deep breath and moved his gaze to the old medicine man. "I have . . . twice . . . suffered the Sun Dance. I am not . . . afraid." He looked back at Peace Maker. "I live . . . and suffer whatever I must . . . to avenge . . . what has happened to Peace Maker."

She leaned closer. "I am called Buffalo Dreamer

now. Two Foxes has declared that is what I should be named."

Stalking Wolf studied her closely. "Something . . . is different. I see it . . . in your eyes. What happened, Buffalo Dreamer? Why . . . did Two Foxes . . . give you this name?"

"It is a long story," she answered softly. "And you are not well enough to keep talking. First, we must rid you of the bad spirits. I will stay by your side until you are well."

Stalking Wolf winced as he drew a deep breath. "And then . . . I will ride against . . . the Crow dogs who did this!" Tears of anger and regret filled his eyes. "Standing Hawk . . . my best friend . . . and my mother . . ."

"I am sorry, Stalking Wolf. I, too, loved Red Sun Woman and will miss her dearly. Your sister also grieves deeply and has cut off her hair. She needs you, Stalking Wolf, and so you must get well."

Stalking Wolf closed his eyes again, and a tear slipped down the side of his face. "Someone . . . must die for this!" he groaned in a rough whisper.

"*Ayee,* my husband, and he *will* die, at your hands."

Stalking Wolf wondered at her words. She made it seem that only one man was responsible. He wanted to ask her, but already darkness returned to claim him. He began to drift into another world, where again he saw visions of a Crow warrior coming at him. He raised his tomahawk, but before he could bring it down, horrible pain ripped through his right shoulder, up into his neck, down through his chest, through his back, his right arm. It seemed his whole body burst into fire, and he could smell his own flesh burning. He could not help the scream that tore from his lungs, filled the tepee where he lay, and resounded throughout the Oglala camp.

All awareness left him then, except for one thing. Someone held his hand, and he felt strength and peace from the touch.

EARLY JANUARY
1833

Moon of the Blizzard Winds

CHAPTER THIRTY-ONE

FALL LEAF WOMAN jumped awake when someone clasped a strong hand over her mouth. She managed a muffled scream and flailed at her assailant, trying to scratch his eyes.

"Shut up!" came a gruff whisper. "It is *I*, Gray Owl. I just did not want to startle you and make you scream!"

A swell of emotions rushed through Fall Leaf Woman as Gray Owl released her. She jerked away and sat up to face him, barely able to make him out by the dim light of the fading central fire. Outside, a bitter winter wind howled through the vast Oglala camp, and she sheathed herself in warm robes against the unrelenting cold inside the tepee. Shaken, she studied her brother, hating him, loving him. "Gray Owl. You *traitor!*" she whispered.

"I did it for *you*. I only meant for Star Dancer to be captured, not for Stalking Wolf to be killed."

"Star Dancer is now called Buffalo Dreamer. Her name has been changed twice since you left, the second time because of a *miracle* that saved her from the Crow. Her return makes her even more precious and beloved to the Oglala. Thanks to you, now I have no hope of *ever* knowing love and respect from *any* of them."

Gray Owl sat down beside her, sighing deeply, then cursing through gritted teeth. "I saw how she was saved. I knew that once she killed Elk Runner, the

Crow would also want *my* life, so I had to flee. From a distance, I watched to see what they would do to Star . . . I mean, Buffalo Dreamer. I hoped they would kill her. When I saw how she survived, I fled."

"And *now* where will you go? To the white man's fort? You should have gone there in the *first* place. It would have been better for *both* of us."

Gray Owl rubbed at his eyes. "I promised I would not abandon you, so I have come here first. I risked my life for you, my sister, just to show you I have not forgotten you. I want you to come with me to Fort Pierre, but if you choose to stay—"

"*Stay?*" Fall Leaf Woman interrupted him. "The Oglala think *I* knew about your plans! No one speaks to me. How can I stay? I lie awake every night wondering how to escape the stares of the others, wondering when they will come and tell me I am banished forever from the Oglala camps." She started to add wood to the fire, but Gray Owl reached across and grasped her arm.

"Do not build the fire. Someone might see our shadows," he said quietly. "The Oglala cannot know I am here. I have no doubt they would enjoy torturing me to death for the death of their beloved Stalking Wolf." He sneered the last words, his voice ringing with hatred.

"It is not the rest of the Oglala who would enjoy torturing you," Fall Leaf Woman answered. "It is Stalking Wolf himself. He did not die, Gray Owl. He *lives!*"

An odd silence hung in the air, and in the near darkness, Fall Leaf Woman felt her brother's fear.

"Lives?"

"Yes. And already he speaks of nothing but killing you. You are lucky no one saw you." Fall Leaf Woman sniffed. "I should go out there and tell all of them that you are here. Then they would know I had nothing to do with this." She saw the whites of her brother's eyes widen in surprise.

"You would do this to your only brother?" he asked. "And for *what?* Stalking Wolf betrayed you, *insulted* you. Surely you realize you will never be completely accepted here again, not because of what *I* did, but because of what *you* did, challenging a holy woman. Come away with me, Fall Leaf Woman. We must go where neither of us is in danger. That is why I came for you. I would never have deserted you."

"Go to the place of the *white* man?" Fall Leaf Woman spat. "An Oglala man who has been there once told me the white man stinks like a *skunk*. I do not want to go there."

"I think he exaggerates. The Miniconjou and Hunkpapas say the white traders have things that make life easier—soft blankets, colored beads that are better than quills for sewing, iron pots, things to cook in that can be set right on the fire and not burn. They have colored cloth and a strange object called a mirror, in which you can see your own face. You can look at yourself and see how beautiful you truly are."

Fall Leaf Woman rubbed her aching head. "I do not know *what* to do. My life is lonely here now, and I fear the wrath of Stalking Wolf's relatives."

"All the more reason to leave here. We will both be safe among the white men. The Oglala seldom go there. The *wasicu* will fight over you because of your beauty. Perhaps one of the wealthy ones will marry you and make you a rich woman with an easy life."

Fall Leaf Woman looked around her tepee, remembering the times Stalking Wolf had shared her bed and the first time she seduced him in the grass beside a stream. To see him was to want him. "I thought once that I would be a wealthy Oglala woman, as the wife of Stalking Wolf," she answered wearily. "But that can never be." She faced her brother, wanting to scratch his eyes out for what he had done, yet another part of her wanting to embrace him. "I have been lonely." She sighed deeply. "I will go away with you, Gray Owl. I have no choice. To stay here is to have to look at Stalking Wolf and never be able to have him, and I have no friends here now. Even Many Robes Woman shuns me. The Crow killed her mother."

"Truly, I did not mean for that to happen. I should never have trusted the Crow to only take Buffalo Dreamer." He rose and walked over to peek out of the tepee entrance. "Pack your parfleche," he told her. "We must go quickly, and we cannot take a travois. It will slow us down and leave easy tracks. Once they know you are not here, they will realize I must have come for you. They might try to follow. We can only hope the wind will prevail so the snow drifts and hides our tracks." Gray Owl came over and put a hand on Fall Leaf Woman's shoulder. "Surely you know how much I care for you, my sister, for I have risked my life to come for you. You are all I have, and I am all *you* have."

Sadly, Fall Leaf Woman knew he was right. She turned and embraced him, tears coming to her eyes. "I am glad you are unharmed." She sniffled as she drew away. "But surely you realized I would hate you for killing Stalking Wolf. Part of me hates you now, for wounding him."

"I am not the one who wounded him. I only meant that Buffalo Dreamer should be stolen and Stalking Wolf humiliated."

Fall Leaf Woman chose to believe him, for she loved and trusted this man, her only living family. "What's done is done. I will pack some things as quickly as possible. Do you have a horse for me?"

He nodded. "Elk Runner paid me four horses for Buffalo Dreamer, but when she killed him, I was forced to abandon them. Later, I took Crow horses that were scattered by the buffalo stampede. I am rich with horses now. I have seven of them tethered a distance from here."

"Let us go, then. There is no time to pack much."

"You will not need much. I have weapons and blankets. And once we reach the white man's trading post, you will have everything you need."

Fall Leaf Woman finished packing, then took one last look around before crawling out the back of the tepee with her brother. Quietly they made their way through the darkness to the woods beyond the camp. Fall Leaf Woman stopped at the edge of the trees and looked back, wondering if she would ever see Stalking Wolf or any of the Oglala again. She missed the friendship of Many Robes Woman.

"Good-bye, Stalking Wolf," she whispered. Her eyes stinging with tears, she turned to follow Gray Owl.

MID-JANUARY
1833

CHAPTER THIRTY-TWO

"YOU WERE RIGHT, Stalking Wolf," Wind In Grass reported. "Gray Owl and Fall Leaf Woman are at the white man's trading post in the east."

Stalking Wolf's eyes narrowed to slits of hatred. "You saw them?"

Wind In Grass tossed his long, dark hair behind his shoulders, pride and vengeance gleaming in his dark eyes. "I rode into the trading post and saw both Fall Leaf Woman and Gray Owl. I shook my lance at Gray Owl and told him that someday he will die by your hand. A *wasicu* pointed his firestick at me, but I was not afraid. I wanted to kill Gray Owl myself, but I knew you should be the one to have that pleasure, so I left them."

Stalking Wolf closed his eyes and relaxed. Since the cauterization of his infected shoulder wound, his recovery had moved more swiftly. Through it all, Buffalo Dreamer remained by his side. Seven full weeks had passed since the Crow attack, and he felt stronger every day. He exercised his arm by using rocks, lifting them in various weights to force his muscles to recover. Every few days he graduated to a bigger, heavier rock, until now he had regained almost full use of the arm.

"You were right to leave him for me," he told Wind In Grass, "but now we enter the throes of winter, a bad time to travel, especially for a man not fully well." He rubbed at the white scar that ran from his neck down across his right shoulder. "I honor you and thank you for braving the dangerous snows to find Gray Owl. You will always be welcome in our tepee, Wind In Grass."

Wind In Grass nodded. "I would brave anything to find the traitor," he answered.

Stalking Wolf turned his attention to Buffalo Dreamer. "I promised you I would take you to see your family when the winds turn warm and the snow runs off the mountains. We will go there before we go to Fort Pierre. I will know when the time is right to seek out Gray Owl. The Great Spirit will not let him slip through my hands, and I do not think Gray Owl will leave the white man's stronghold. Perhaps he thinks he is safe there. He has no home now, no place left to go. He is not welcome among the Lakota, or the Crow. I need not hurry. Let him worry and wonder when I might come for him."

The sound of soft flute music outside interrupted their conversation. Stalking Wolf frowned. "Is someone being courted?" Eager anticipation lit up Buffalo Dreamer's eyes, and she looked across the fire at Many Robes Woman. Stalking Wolf followed her gaze, noticing that his sister wore her hair in greased braids, with prettily beaded strands of rawhide wrapped into the twists. His sister had fiddled and fussed all afternoon with her hair and with painting her arms. Stalking Wolf thought she did so only for the fun of it, a way to help ease her sorrow over the loss of their mother. Now he understood she had more reason to primp. Young love was helping her return to her normal boisterous self. "The music is for you?" he asked.

Many Robes Woman smiled bashfully and looked away. Stalking Wolf looked back at Buffalo Dreamer. "My sister has a suitor?"

"It is Arrow Runner. He has dreamed of your sister for many moons. You did not know?"

Stalking Wolf thought for a moment. "Arrow Runner spoke to me a full winter past, but I told him my sister was too young for his attentions."

"She is a whole year older, Stalking Wolf," Buffalo Dreamer reminded him. "Arrow Runner feared your anger if he pestered you, so he stayed away. Many Robes Woman is seventeen summers now, and she has no father or mother. Arrow Runner wishes to care and provide for her. He asked me to speak to you about it as soon as you were well enough. He loves Many Robes Woman and wants to take her for a wife."

Stalking Wolf frowned. "He should have spoken to me personally."

Buffalo Dreamer gave him a patient smile. "He is anxious, and in love. And he feels that you have carried the burden of caring for your whole family long enough. Now that Many Robes Woman is alone, and you have taken a wife—"

"Say no more," Stalking Wolf interrupted. "Arrow Runner is clever with his reasoning."

Buffalo Dreamer, Wind In Grass, and Many Robes Woman all looked at each other, not sure if Stalking Wolf was amused or angry. Finally, Many Robes Woman broke into a giggle. Wind In Grass rose, the fringes of his buckskin clothing dancing with his movements. "I will leave you alone to speak with your wife and sister about this." He left the tepee, and Stalking Wolf turned his attention to his sister. Many Robes Woman looked away, covering her mouth in an obvious effort to quell more laughter.

"Let me see your eyes, Many Robes Woman," Stalking Wolf commanded.

His sister lost her smile and moved closer, her eyes wide with wary hope.

"You are fond of Arrow Runner?"

Many Robes Woman slowly nodded. "He is easy on my eyes, and last summer he suffered the Sun Dance bravely. He has many horses, Stalking Wolf, and he told Buffalo Dreamer he would give four of them for me. That would make you even more wealthy. He would give you the fine white one with the black mane that you so admire."

Stalking Wolf turned to Buffalo Dreamer. "He told you this?"

"Yes."

Stalking Wolf stared at the fire. "The Crow killed my best horse in their attack," he said, again remembering the vicious fight. He leaned against his backrest, beginning to feel tired. "Arrow Runner is a member of the Badger Society. I remember that when he was very young, he bravely went out into the darkness when Pawnee surrounded our war party. He carried water back to us. Even now he carries the water bag in battle." He looked at Many Robes Woman. "Arrow Runner's offer of the white horse is a fine one, and his *tiyospe* is not of our clan. He is *Ochenon pa*, of the Two Kettles clan. The Oglala and Ochenon pa have always married well." He closed his eyes, and Many Robes Woman looked wide-eyed at Buffalo Dreamer.

"What does he mean? Does he approve?"

Stalking Wolf's eyes flickered open again. "Do not speak as though I am not here. I have not yet finished." He studied his sister a moment longer before continuing. "Tell me more about your feelings, Many Robes Woman."

His sister smiled excitedly. "At our Sun Dance this past summer, I threw my blanket over Arrow Runner at a Night Dance," she told him. "You did not know this because you had left to find the humpbacked bear. Mother knew I thought fondly of Arrow Runner, but because of your quest to find the bear and later your need to give attention to your new wife, Mother did not want to burden you with decisions about me. Now our mother has gone to the place in the stars, and I believe it is time for me to take a husband."

Stalking Wolf listened quietly to Arrow Runner's flute playing, then slowly nodded. "You may set a bowl of food outside. If he comes and takes it, you may lean outside and speak with him, but do not dally too long or I will think he is spoiling your honor. Make sure your legs remain inside the tepee where I can see them, as is required. Tell him to come and speak with me when the sun is high tomorrow."

"Thank you, my brother!" Quickly, Many Robes Woman took up a wooden bowl and filled it with stew left heating over the fire. She set it at the entrance and waited there, her back to them. Stalking Wolf turned to Buffalo Dreamer, seeing a longing look in her eyes as she watched his sister.

"He plays well," she commented absently. "They are pretty songs."

Stalking Wolf touched her hand, admiring and appreciating her faithful watch over him as he healed. "That is what you miss, isn't it?" he said softly.

Buffalo Dreamer looked at him in surprise. "I do not understand."

"I think you do." Stalking Wolf rubbed the back of her hand with his thumb. "Perhaps if I had properly courted you, you could find it easier to be a true wife to me." He saw tears spring into her eyes, and a flush of embarrassment colored her cheeks.

"I . . . ours is a different sort of marriage. I understand that now."

Stalking Wolf shook his head. "I think to understand is not enough, especially for one so young. I think that I should court you." He watched her eyebrows rise in astonishment.

"But I am already your wife!"

"And you have never been a willing one. I will make you willing."

Buffalo Dreamer looked down. "When I thought you had died, my heart never knew such agony. I am

. . . already willing . . . for now I know my true feelings for you."

The flute-playing stopped, and Stalking Wolf waited until his sister leaned out of the tepee before answering his wife. "I would not feel right about it until it is done by proper custom, for you are truly a woman of special blessings and powers. During my vision quest before finding you, buffalo stampeded out of the sky and thundered around me. And to save you from death by fire, buffalo stampeded around you, too, only it was not a vision. It was real. And so we know we truly share something special, for the stampeding buffalo have visited both of us." He sighed deeply. "I will allow my sister to marry Arrow Runner. They will live near us in my mother's tepee, and when I am well, I will go and stay with them for a while. That way, I will be close and can protect you and provide for you. But I will not sleep here. I will court you for one moon."

Buffalo Dreamer put a hand to her chest. "What will others say?"

"They will understand. I will tell them it is because my beautiful young wife has never been properly courted. It is something I want to do. They know that you are special. They will respect my decision."

Many Robes Woman giggled, and Stalking Wolf ordered her back inside. He turned again to Buffalo Dreamer. "Does my offer agree with you?" He felt touched at the utter joy in her eyes.

"Yes, I would be happy and honored for such a man as you to humble himself to courting his own wife. It shows me how much you truly care."

Stalking Wolf nodded. "I *do* care, Buffalo Dreamer, and I will show you how much." He would do all he could to make her want him with all her heart and soul. The next time he made love to this woman, it would be because she came to him willingly, because she was filled with love for him. He deeply desired vengeance against Gray Owl, but this woman's needs came first now. He would always put her first.

MID-FEBRUARY
1833

Moon of the Heavy Snows

CHAPTER THIRTY-THREE

"HOW I WOULD love to be courted again by *my* husband." The remark came from Stalking Wolf's aunt, Yellow Turtle Woman. Giggles and sly grins swept through Buffalo Dreamer's tepee, where twelve women sat quilling, each trying to outdo the other in the beauty of her designs.

The remark embarrassed Buffalo Dreamer, but she enjoyed the flutter Stalking Wolf created in her heart with his attentions. His courting brought fun and gossip to the long, cold, snowy days of the Moon of the Heavy Snows. For many bitterly cold nights, Stalking Wolf sat outside her tepee playing his flute. Many Robes Woman told her that Stalking Wolf had whittled the instrument from a slender tree branch, even though the work brought pain to his wounded arm and hand.

The music brightened the gray days of winter, and Stalking Wolf impressed Buffalo Dreamer with his willingness to weather the wicked winds and blowing snow just to play for her.

"I think Stalking Wolf could teach our men a lesson in how to make their wives happy," said Running Elk Woman.

"Perhaps my cousin will teach Wind In Grass the ways of a lover." Sweet Root Woman said the words shyly. Sixteen summers in age, she had eyes for Wind In Grass, and he for her.

"You should be careful," Yellow Turtle Woman

warned her daughter. "If Wind In Grass learns too much of this fancy courting, he will make your heart leap and your head spin when you throw your blanket over him at the next Night Dance. He will make you think about giving away more than your heart."

More laughter filled the tepee. Winter camp brought the need for many hours of huddling together near fires, time to relax and get to know the other women more intimately. Many Robes Woman enjoyed married life with Arrow Runner, and Yellow Turtle Woman had become the mother that both Buffalo Dreamer and Many Robes Woman yearned for. They in turn helped care for Two Feet Dancing, the baby Yellow Turtle Woman had birthed late in life. A lively, strong boy, he wore out his mother by causing her to constantly chase after him.

Today the wind howled more fiercely than at any time yet this winter. Snow came down in blinding sheets, but inside Buffalo Dreamer's tepee, the central fire burned hot. Still, most of the women wore heavy furs of bear, wolf, and buffalo. Fingers felt cold, making it difficult to work with the quills. Sometimes Buffalo Dreamer stopped to wrap her hands inside her bearskin cloak. She worried about Stalking Wolf sitting out in the cold to play for her. He kept her supplied with wood, even though such a chore was a woman's job. He considered the chore an act of humility, showing Buffalo Dreamer his willingness to stoop as low as necessary and to forget his warrior pride, just to win her love and respect.

"Stalking Wolf is making life too easy for me," Buffalo Dreamer told the others. "I will be spoiled, and then when he stops all this attention, I will not know how to fetch wood."

Several of the women nodded, and most snickered. "I would not mind *my* husband spoiling me," one spoke up.

"You are special," Yellow Turtle Woman reminded

Buffalo Dreamer. "Stalking Wolf will always spoil you."

"I am no different from the rest of you," Buffalo Dreamer answered.

Several smiled warmly, some shaking their heads. "You are too humble," one of them commented.

"Do you think we are jealous?" asked another.

Buffalo Dreamer stared at the shirt she was quilling for Stalking Wolf. "I do not know. I worry that you might be. Your friendships are important to me. All of you call me a holy woman, but inside, I feel no different from you. I am just a woman who wants what all women want."

"Does that mean you think all women want Stalking Wolf?" Yellow Turtle Woman teased.

There came roaring laughter then.

"Perhaps we all do!" joked another.

"He would be welcome in my bed if he asked," yet another woman put in.

"Ah, he is a fine, handsome man, and one of our bravest warriors," someone else added.

"Surely this courting makes you crazy with desire for my brother to come back to your bed," Many Robes Woman told her.

Buffalo Dreamer shook her head and smiled as they all laughed again. She thought of how once she had never wanted Stalking Wolf to touch her, yet now an intense desire burned deep within. He was still refusing to sleep in their tepee, and Buffalo Dreamer began to wonder if he would come back any time soon.

"I think someone should hint to Stalking Wolf that I would be pleased if he stopped courting me and began behaving as a husband again," she said softly, glancing at the others. "At first I feared and disliked him, because he was a stranger to me, but now my heart . . ." She looked down again, shy about expressing her feelings.

"Now your heart hurts for him. Longs for him," Yellow Turtle Woman suggested.

Buffalo Dreamer nodded. "Every night I set out food for him, but he does not take it. Please tell him . . . tell him to take it. I am ready for him to bring it inside."

The others did not laugh this time. They understood that Buffalo Dreamer spoke with deep feeling. They all sat quietly quilling and mending, then one of them broke the silence.

"I think perhaps the coming winter nights will not be cold at all for you and Stalking Wolf."

Again there came snickers. Buffalo Dreamer joined in the laughter, feeling excited and nervous. Yellow Turtle Woman would no doubt give Stalking Wolf her message. The friendships she had developed over the past few months made Buffalo Dreamer happier than ever.

Outside, the wind whipped into fierce gales. The tepee skins flapped inward as the bitter wind strained against them. Buffalo Dreamer noticed snow sneaking in under one side of the tepee, and it seemed to whisper to her of a coming winter storm. Just as she and the other women feared, the winds kicked up throughout the rest of the day, combined with thick, blinding snow that buried many tepees even before the sun set.

The men took turns watching the horses, which they herded into the nearby forest for protection from the howling winds. In spite of their thick coats of winter hair, many horses would freeze in this extreme cold, becoming meat for Brother Wolf. Because all wild things knew great hunger in winter, the men had to guard the surviving horses from predators. There would be no flute-playing this night.

Although her husband was mostly healed, Buffalo Dreamer worried that he might not be well enough to withstand the violent cold. Here inside her tepee, several women had gathered their children under robes to keep them warm. This was a time when all husbands brought in wood and helped in other ways to protect the women and children, the lifeblood of the Nation.

Darkness enclosed the storm, and the now-silent Oglala camp. No movement occurred outside. Even the camp dogs slept inside the tepees, invited by the women so as to keep children and old ones warm. Buffalo Dreamer put her arms around the youngest daughter of Woman Who Hurries, who had so many children she needed help with protecting all of them. Inside the filled tepee, mothers told stories to occupy restless children. Warriors took turns coming inside to get warm, and they, too, told, stories, of battle and hunting, exciting tales that caused the women to snicker, joking about how much was real and how much was exaggerated. They wryly called such storytelling "making the truth bigger."

Finally, most of the children fell asleep, but Buffalo Dreamer remained wide-awake, thinking about Stalking Wolf out in the awful cold. As though he knew she worried, he ducked inside the tepee just then, quickly re-covering the entrance with the heavy buffalo skins that protected it. Buffalo Dreamer recognized him by the wolfskin headdress he wore to protect his ears and face from the cold, and by the shaggy buffalo cape she had made for him. He removed the wolfskin from his head and looked around the tepee. Because so many women and children lay huddled inside, most of them covered heavily with animal skins, Buffalo Dreamer raised her hand to show Stalking Wolf where she lay.

Stalking Wolf carefully laid aside his outer robes, trying to keep the snow that covered them from falling onto others. He stepped around sleeping bodies until he reached Buffalo Dreamer. "You are warm?" he asked.

"Yes. What about you?"

"The cloak you made for me keeps me very warm."

He knelt down closer to her. "This is not how I planned to come to you."

Buffalo Dreamer smiled. "It does not matter. You cannot stop Father Winter from blowing his white breath across the land. He is sometimes cruel. Come and lie beside me and rest a while."

Stalking Wolf leaned closer. "Are you sure?"

Buffalo Dreamer felt a rush of pleasant desire. "I intended to set food out for you again tonight. Would you have taken it?"

He grinned, a handsome smile Buffalo Dreamer had grown to love. "Of course I would. It is too bad we must share our dwelling with so many others this night. I said that I would court you for one moon, and that time has passed."

Buffalo Dreamer felt her cheeks begin to burn. "I know. I, too, have counted the days."

Stalking Wolf touched her warm cheek with a cold hand, making her flinch and giggle. "Such cold hands!" She took his hand and moved it under her robe, against her breast. "You need to warm them."

He gently fondled her breast, bringing his face close enough to lick her cheek. "You surprise me." He looked around the tepee again. "I think it is best that I go and sleep in the tepee where the unmarried men sleep," he whispered. "The first time we truly make love, we should be alone."

Buffalo Dreamer studied him in the soft firelight. "I agree," she answered. "I hope the storm ends quickly."

Delight and desire sparkled in Stalking Wolf's eyes. "It cannot end quickly enough for me." He sighed, taking his hand away and rising. "I am sorry to leave you again." He gave her a reassuring smile before making his way back to where he had left his robes. Again he covered his head with the wolfskin, then pulled the buffalo robe around himself and ducked outside.

Buffalo Dreamer settled back under her robes, newly awakened desires making her feel restless. She cursed the storm.

CHAPTER THIRTY-FOUR

BUFFALO DREAMER TRUDGED through deep snow to the edge of the pine forest. The wind had died by midmorning, but in some places snow drifted taller than a man. Only the top half of a few tepees showed above the snow, and women busily dug pathways from their tepees to woodpiles. Others chopped ice to get to needed water, while still others built fires to melt snow.

Buffalo Dreamer took the duty of carrying wood for herself, Many Robes Woman, and Yellow Turtle Woman. She dragged a carrier Bold Fox had made for her out of split logs tied together with rawhide, creating a flat bed for stacking wood. Slender tree limbs tied to the bottom of the carrier acted as runners, but hauling anything of much weight was difficult, if not impossible, in such deep snow. Buffalo Dreamer realized she needed a horse to pull the wood-sled.

Shivering in spite of the heavy robe she wore, she dragged the sled to the edge of the trees that sheltered the horses. Snow sneaked in over the top of her knee-high moccasins and melted down her leg in a cold trickle, making her yearn for summer's warmth. She wondered how sunshine could be so hot in summer and give no warmth at all in winter.

Within the heavier stands of pine, the air felt warmer. "Stalking Wolf!" she called, trudging farther into the forest. With every step, she grunted, jerking the wood-carrier behind her and calling for Stalking

Wolf again. Finally, she heard him reply. She turned toward the voice and saw him handing fistfuls of grass to his horses. He laughed when the horses nudged him, then surrounded him, nibbling at his hand as he took more grass from the bundle he carried in his other arm. Sotaju nipped at one of the horses, then shoved another with her nose.

"So, you are stingy, huh?" Stalking Wolf shook his finger at the horse. "You must learn to share as we humans do, Sotaju. We share our meat from the hunt, and you did not even have to hunt for this."

Buffalo Dreamer laughed. "Where did you get all that grass?"

Stalking Wolf glanced at her, more happiness in his dark eyes than Buffalo Dreamer had ever noticed before. "I rode my biggest horse to the grazing land south of camp and dug for it, but after all my work, it will be gone in moments."

Sotaju whinnied and stuck her nose into the bundle in his arm, trying to take a mouthful and catching part of his winter robe with it. Another horse did the same, and yet another nudged Stalking Wolf from behind, causing him to fall into the snow. He and Buffalo Dreamer laughed as he tossed the rest of the grass at the horses and rolled away from them before they stepped on him in their eagerness to get to the food.

Buffalo Dreamer trudged closer and reached out to help Stalking Wolf get up, but he pulled her down instead. She screamed when she landed in the deep snow, and Stalking Wolf rolled on top of her. He touched her cheek with his own.

"It is much warmer with you covering me." She laughed. "But I did not come here to rest. I came to gather wood, and I need a horse to pull the sled when it is full."

Stalking Wolf looked down at her, smiling. "You are beautiful when you laugh. I hardly ever hear or see you laugh."

Buffalo Dreamer's smile faded as she studied his face. "And you are more handsome when *you* laugh." Never had she been so aware of just how handsome he was, in spite of his battle scars. "My grandmother called you a 'fine-looking' man," she told him. "She was so right."

"And Runs With The Deer said you were most beautiful. I felt greatly relieved after his visit to your family, for I knew I had to marry you. Sometimes I worried you might be fat as a buffalo, with a face to match."

Buffalo Dreamer giggled.

"I am glad my wife is finally happy," Stalking Wolf told her.

Buffalo Dreamer breathed deeply, grateful to at last feel content and at home. "I have many friends here now. I feel more like I belong."

"You do not belong just to the Oglala. You belong to Stalking Wolf. You will always belong only to me."

Fire moved through her blood, and a sweet feeling gripped her belly in a pleasant ache. "I will always belong only to you. At first, you owned only my body. Now I give you my heart, Stalking Wolf, for now I feel love for you. I truly want my husband. I only need to hear his words of love."

Stalking Wolf closed his eyes and sighed deeply, bending down to nuzzle her neck. He licked her throat and whispered softly, "I do love you, Buffalo Dreamer. You are the first and only woman for whom I have had such feelings."

Buffalo Dreamer could not stop a soft moan from escaping her lips at the feel of his tongue massaging her throat, her chin, then warming her cheeks.

"It is warm here, deep in the snow," he said softly. "I want to touch what is beneath your robe . . ."

Buffalo Dreamer looked up at the surrounding pine trees, their limbs heavy with snow. Around them, horses grazed quietly, and Buffalo Dreamer felt as though she and Stalking Wolf lay in the arms of Mother Earth, in a blanket of snow the God of the North had brought them. Stalking Wolf moved his hands beneath her robe, her tunic, gently trailing his fingers over her thigh, to the inside of her thigh. This time, she felt no urge to tell him no.

She wore nothing under the tunic. She watched Stalking Wolf's dark eyes, saw them nearly glitter with desire. He found and explored her most intimate self, and Buffalo Dreamer sucked in her breath and closed her eyes when he traced one finger inside her warm depths, moving it in and out, drawing forth an intense desire unlike anything she had known.

Her back protected by her buffalo robe, and with Stalking Wolf covering her with his body and robe, Buffalo Dreamer felt remarkably warm. She wondered if it was due to the fire Stalking Wolf had lit deep inside her. He licked her face, her lips, while he moved his fingers in a circular motion, touching a special place that drove her wild with desire. She suddenly cried out with the sheer force of a pulsation deep within that surprised her with an exquisite pleasure she could never put into words. It made her want something . . . something . . .

Stalking Wolf moved his moist hand to her lips, and together they licked his fingers. "Now you are at last ready for your husband," he said softly.

"I am," she whispered. Her next words surprised even herself. "I want you, Stalking Wolf. I want to feel you inside of me. I am not afraid anymore."

She watched his jaw flex from his own intense need, and he reached down to untie his breechcloth. He pulled it away and tossed it into the snow, then moved on top of her, pushing her tunic to her waist, resting his elbows on either side of her. Oblivious to the snow and cold around her, Buffalo Dreamer's awareness centered on Stalking Wolf's swollen penis pressing against her belly. She flinched at the memory of the pain the first time he had invaded her. Stalking Wolf traced a finger over her lips, to her ear, where he toyed with her lobe.

"Do not be afraid this time. I have already broken through the virgin barrier that brought you pain the first time. Now there is nothing to fear." He pressed his cheek to hers. "I would never hurt you, Buffalo Dreamer. I would die for you if need be, and always I will regret not being able to save you when the Crow attacked us."

"That could not be helped." She touched his face, tracing his eyebrows. "I believe now that it was all meant to be, so that I could learn my own powers from the white buffalo, and learn to be strong and brave . . . and also learn how much I love you."

Stalking Wolf licked her eyelids, then leaned down and licked her face, her lips. Buffalo Dreamer licked back, and almost by accident, their tongues touched. Enjoying the delicious desire experienced by the touch, they licked and explored their mouths, both groaning with exquisite delight. Buffalo Dreamer arched against him, eager now to feel him inside her. Stalking Wolf answered her urgent command, shifting between her legs and burying himself deep and hard.

Buffalo Dreamer cried with ecstasy. Stalking Wolf grasped her bare hips and moved in a pounding rhythm, and Buffalo Dreamer became lost in a world of pleasure and fulfillment of desire, celebrating the wonderful awareness of everything woman about herself.

She felt no pain! This act of mating was more wonderful than she ever thought it could be, and she ached to be naked, to feel her bare skin touch his. Her nipples almost pained her with a need to be touched, tasted. She wrapped her legs around Stalking Wolf, moaning with every deep thrust. Stalking Wolf groaned with his own pleasure, and Buffalo Dreamer sensed he felt the same rapture as she. Finally, she felt his life puls-

ing into her. He held himself there for several seconds
before relaxing and moving away to lie by her side,
keeping his robe over her. He sighed deeply as they
both studied the clouds.

"You felt no pain?"

"It was wonderful," Buffalo Dreamer answered
softly. She turned to face him. "And I liked tasting
your mouth."

He grinned. "I also liked it."

"I want to do it again."

"Taste my mouth?"

"Yes. But not just that."

Stalking Wolf moved on top of her again, frowning
in mock displeasure. "Do you wish that we do nothing
but this? I would soon grow weak and useless. My
beautiful young wife demands much energy from me
now. Perhaps I should not have shown you how pleasant this can be."

She put a hand to the side of his face. "I might let
you rest at times, but just as I demanded you not touch
me all this time, now I might demand you bed me
often."

"Hmmm. Perhaps I have started something I will
regret!"

Buffalo Dreamer laughed, but then her smile faded
to seriousness. "You did not touch me when I was not
ready, and you courted me when it was not necessary.
I love you for that, Stalking Wolf, and I will never
deny you when you come to me in desire."

He licked her lips again, but she put a hand to his
mouth. "Promise me you will never take another
wife."

He studied her lovingly. "Only if you are not able
to bear children. Even then, I could never love and
honor another the way I love and honor you."

"The Buffalo Spirit will bless me, I am sure. I will
give you sons, Stalking Wolf."

"Then we must make sure my seed takes hold. It must be planted deep . . . and often."

"The making of babies is a very pleasant kind of work," she said with a teasing smile.

Stalking Wolf tasted her mouth again, and she welcomed him inside once more.

EARLY JUNE 1833

Strawberries Ripening Moon

CHAPTER THIRTY-FIVE

THE OGLALA ARRIVED in a grand procession, the largest of all the Lakota bands gathered for the summer Sun Dance. The higher-ranking warriors wore their fanciest regalia, and Buffalo Dreamer felt proud of the fact she had sewn her husband's clothing herself over the winter. Fully healed, Stalking Wolf epitomized the brave, strong, handsome Oglala warrior, and she loved him with her whole being.

A conch shell decorated the bone hair-pipe choker worn around Stalking Wolf's neck, and bright yellow and blue quills accented the fringes at the sides of his leggings and shirtsleeves. A sunburst design in the same colors mixed with red highlighted the front of his shirt. He wore a round, quilled hairpiece, and added to that, Buffalo Dreamer had tied five eagle feathers into five fancy braids down the back of his head.

Excitement and joy filled Buffalo Dreamer's heart at being able to see her family again, and to tell them how happy Stalking Wolf had made her after all. She felt especially anxious to show her grandmother her talented quill work, including her own dress. Also dressing fancy for their entrance parade, she wore a bleached doeskin tunic with dyed-red quills sewn down the front in a vee design. Red quills also decorated the fringes at the hem, and Many Robes Woman had wound red quills and live flowers into a thick braid at her back.

This year the Lakota Nation, consisting of the Min-niconjou, Saones, Hunkpapa, Sihosapa, Itazipcho, Ochenon pa, and Sichangu, met at the River of Pow-dered Earth. This place of soft sands and sweet grasses was yet another of the favorite gathering places for the Lakota, where water and grazing abounded.

Buffalo Dreamer glanced back at the men, women, and children following behind her. Numbering in the thousands, the Oglala tribe stretched far beyond the hill over which she had just ridden. Beyond them, thousands of horses followed, including twelve that belonged to Stalking Wolf. Little Black Horse and Buffalo Calf tended them, and the two cousins were ready to burst with pride at being related to a Shirt Wearer.

Thousands more Lakota already were camped be-low, and Stalking Wolf waved a blanket and gave out a shrill call of greeting. From below came a chorus of yips and whoops in reply. More Oglala rode forward with more calls of greeting, and Buffalo Dreamer's heart swelled with happiness. She could see many poles cut and laid out in a circle, showing that those already here had started preparations for building the Sun Dance lodge. Soon a sacred cottonwood tree would be chosen by *Naca Ominicia,* then carried to the center of the lodge. The poles already cut would be tied horizontally to the top of the sacred tree, the other ends held up off the ground by pole supports placed in the ground, forming a circular roof. Nearby, men prepared a sweat lodge.

The first several days of the Sun Dance must be spent in prayer and sacrifice, followed by visiting and feasting. Buffalo Dreamer searched the camp below for a familiar tepee, and her heart pounded harder with excitement and joy when she saw one painted with horses that had extra-big eyes.

"There it is!" she told Stalking Wolf. "My parents' lodge!"

Stalking Wolf grinned. "Go and see them. I have much to do to help build the Sun Dance lodge. I will come and find you later."

Buffalo Dreamer kicked Sotaju's sides and rode down the hill. Before she reached her mother's tepee, she saw Tall Woman step outside and look around, surely watching for the daughter she had not seen for a whole year.

"*Ina!*" Buffalo Dreamer shouted, then also saw Looking Horse! "*Ate!*" She rode faster, leaving her packhorse and the travois it pulled behind.

Tall Woman recognized her and held out her arms, shouting her name. "Star Dancer!" Buffalo Dreamer remembered then that her mother did not know her new name. She had so much to tell her. She jumped down from Sotaju before the horse came to a full stop, and in the next moment, she felt her mother's arms wrapped tightly around her. At first, neither could speak, too filled with happiness. When Tall Woman finally let go, she looked Buffalo Dreamer over, as did Looking Horse, pride and happiness on their faces.

"You look well, Daughter! Surely your husband is very good to you," Looking Horse said.

"He is," Buffalo Dreamer answered. She saw no one looking, so she quickly embraced her father, then turned to her mother. "At first, I knew only loneliness and unhappiness. But I grew to love him, Mother. It was just as you said it would be." They grasped hands, and Buffalo Dreamer looked her mother over. "You are well?"

"We are both fine." Tall Woman put a hand to her daughter's face, touching her cheek lovingly. "I am so happy for you, Star Dancer. You look radiant, and this warms my heart. Walks Slowly will also be happy to know this." Her smile faded. "I must tell you, all is not well with your grandmother. We carried her all the way here on a travois, for she wanted so much to see you once again before . . ."

Buffalo Dreamer saw tears in her mother's eyes. "She is . . ."

Tall Woman nodded. "I believe it is only a matter of time. She stayed alive this long just to see her beloved granddaughter once more. Then she wants us to take her to her dying place."

"I must see her right away!"

Tall Woman grasped her arms. "I am so sorry for this bad news at such a happy time."

Pain stabbed Buffalo Dreamer's heart. She left her mother and ducked inside the tepee, where she knelt on a bear rug beside her grandmother. She gasped at Walks Slowly's appearance, remembering how when she was a little girl, she would compare the wrinkles on her grandmother's face to the number of stars in the sky. Now there were even more than that, and the old woman had shrunk to little but skin and bones.

Walks Slowly's eyes flickered open, and Buffalo Dreamer saw in them the filmy look of death. At first, her grandmother did not even recognize her, and Buffalo Dreamer's joy at finally seeing her family again quickly turned to grief. "I am so glad to see my beloved *Uncheedah* again," she said, taking the old woman's frail hand.

Walks Slowly brightened then with recognition, and she managed a smile that showed only three teeth. "Star Dancer," she said in a cracked voice. "At last . . . I see my sweet granddaughter again."

Buffalo Dreamer did not bother telling her that she was now called by a different name. She would always be Star Dancer to her grandmother. "I am glad, too, Grandmother. We have much to talk about." She leaned down and touched her cheek to the old woman's face. "I love you, Grandmother. I missed you most of all."

Walks Slowly breathed in labored gasps, and her grip felt weak. Buffalo Dreamer could feel every tiny bone on the back of her hand.

"You look well, Granddaughter. Tell me . . . about that fine-looking man you wed. Is he . . . good to you? Are you happy?"

Buffalo Dreamer smiled. "Yes, Stalking Wolf is good to me, and I am happy."

"Do you enjoy . . . pleasing him under your robe . . . like I said you would?"

The old woman managed a raspy cackle, and Buffalo Dreamer shook her head, amazed that in the woman's near-death condition, she could still tease about such things. "Yes, *Uncheedah.* I enjoy being a woman."

"You see? I told you. I am glad . . . you are happy. Does his life . . . grow in your belly yet?"

Buffalo Dreamer felt a renewed worry that she would not be able to bear children. Just recently she had spent four days at the back of the migration with the other women having their monthly bleeding. During these times, the men could not touch or even look upon such a woman. Because the women could not hide inside a menstrual tepee while traveling, they walked with their eyes cast down and their heads covered.

Again disappointment filled Buffalo Dreamer. After four months of passionate and frequent lovemaking, Stalking Wolf's life still did not grow in her womb. "Yes," she lied to her grandmother, wanting the old woman to die happy. "But I have not yet told Stalking Wolf, or anyone else. We will let it be our secret for now."

Walks Slowly chuckled softly, grinning again. "I am glad, Star Dancer. You are special. *Wakan-Tanka* will bless you . . . with many children."

The remark brought an ache to Buffalo Dreamer's heart. "Yes, Grandmother. I hope so."

Tall Woman came inside and knelt beside her daughter. "Do not talk too long with her, Star Dancer. She tires easily."

Already Walks Slowly's eyes fluttered shut, and she seemed hardly aware of Tall Woman's presence. Buffalo Dreamer carefully removed her hand from Walks Slowly's hand, then pulled a buffalo robe higher around her grandmother's neck. The old woman's skin felt cold and clammy in spite of the warm day. Buffalo Dreamer turned to her mother. "I can see she is very sick," she whispered. "She will not last long."

Tall Woman shook her head, and mother and daughter embraced, quietly crying. "I do not think she will survive our stay here," Tall Woman said brokenly. "She clung to life only to see you again when we all came together for Council. It is custom to leave old ones behind to die, but Looking Horse said we should bring her, for your sake."

Buffalo Dreamer nodded, hardly able to imagine life without the knowledge that her dear grandmother still walked the earth. She lowered her head and cried harder, and Tall Woman hugged her tightly.

"Walks Slowly will always be with you, my daughter . . . always. Her spirit is strong, and she will always walk beside you. Remember that. You can ask her to help you with the decisions you make in life, and she will help you. When she meets death, do not feel you have lost her, for that can never happen. One day you will join her again."

Buffalo Dreamer wiped at tears. "I did not expect this. I am so happy to see all of you, and I intended to have long talks with *Uncheedah,* to tell her some of the amazing things that have happened to me." She met her Mother's eyes, Tall Woman's face blurry because of her tears. "I must tell you the story, Mother, of how I received a new name. I am called Buffalo Dreamer. I have learned so much, and I understand that I am called to be a peacemaker among the Lakota, and that my guiding spirit truly is the white buffalo. It is such an amazing story that Stalking Wolf feels I should tell it before the entire Council."

Tall Woman's eyebrows arched in surprise and pleasure. She wiped at tears and managed a smile. "My daughter is very honored indeed! For a woman to be called before the Council to tell her own story of a vision or happening is something that brings great honor. I am happy for you, and Stalking Wolf must be very proud."

Buffalo Dreamer smiled through her own tears. "He is. I even killed three Crow warriors, in defense of my husband. Stalking Wolf says that I, too, am a warrior."

Tall Woman squeezed her hands. "I am so happy for you, and anxious to hear this wonderful story! Is Stalking Wolf's mother like a mother to you also?"

Buffalo Dreamer closed her eyes in remembered grief. "She *was* good to me, but she died at the hands of Crow warriors. I miss her deeply. Her death is part of my story."

"I am so sorry, Daughter, and also curious about this story you have to tell." Tall Woman squeezed Buffalo Dreamer's hands and smiled reassuringly. "Let's speak now of good things. Tell me about the rest of Stalking Wolf's family, his sister. I want to know if they are all like family to you."

"They are, Mother." Buffalo Dreamer turned for a moment to check on her grandmother, gently stroking the old woman's hair before continuing. "Stalking Wolf's sister, Many Robes Woman, is married now to Arrow Runner, who is the water-carrier in times of hunting and making war." She met her mother's gaze again, hoping Walks Slowly could hear her stories. She told her mother about others in Stalking Wolf's family, eager to share her happiness and all that had happened to her since leaving.

Tall Woman nodded, smiling, but her smile quickly faded as she studied Buffalo Dreamer more closely. "Your hair is shorter! What happened that made you cut it?"

"That, too, is part of my story. Red Sun Woman

died at the hands of the Crow. Stalking Wolf suffered terrible wounds fighting to protect us. I cut my hair in sacrifice when I prayed for his recovery." She sat a little straighter. "He fought so valiantly, Mother. I have never seen such courage. He is a grand warrior, and one of the best hunters among the Oglala. He truly is a good and fitting husband."

"And he is all right now?"

"Yes. He is so good to me. I never thought when I left you a year ago that I could be this happy."

"I knew, my darling daughter, that it would turn out this way for you. That is why I found it possible to let you go away with Stalking Wolf. Tell me about the land of the Black Hills, and more about life among the Oglala."

Catching up on the past year's events led to a long conversation, absorbing both women. Neither realized that, as they talked, Walks Slowly stopped breathing.

Later, when Buffalo Dreamer checked on her grandmother, she detected a smile on Walks Slowly's lips. *Uncheedah* had died happy. She had seen her beloved granddaughter once more, and learned that she was indeed happy with her fine-looking husband.

CHAPTER THIRTY-SIX

BECAUSE OF BUFFALO Dreamer's astounding story of rescue by the sacred white buffalo, the Lakota elders readily agreed to choose her to represent White Buffalo Woman at the Sun Dance ceremony. The honor helped soothe her grieving heart, for Walks Slowly surely watched proudly from above.

She wore a bleached-white buckskin tunic, a dress worn the year before by the Hunkpapa woman who then held this honor. The dress had been blessed by a Hunkpapa holy man and was still considered a sacred garment.

The days-long ceremony began with the participants, including Stalking Wolf, exiting the sweat lodge, where a Sichangu holy man had purified them. Buffalo Dreamer then led the procession of dancers, and Moon Painter, carrying a buffalo skull, walked behind her. All paraded around the outside of the lodge crying, "Oh, *Wakan-Tanka*, be merciful, that our people may live!"

Buffalo Dreamer then entered the Sun Dance lodge amid drumming and a chorus of singing. The dancers followed, taking their places at the west side of the lodge. Buffalo Dreamer waited while Moon Painter set the buffalo skull between the sacred tree at the center of the lodge and the dancers. He then set up three forked sticks, upon which Buffalo Dreamer placed the sacred pipe. She stepped back and the dancing began, lasting throughout the day and far into the night. The air inside and outside the Sun Dance lodge reverberated with sounds of rich voices and drumming, and at dawn, the dancing stopped. The dancers exited the lodge, and their relatives placed offerings outside the lodge at the four directions, north, south, east, and west. The dancers then reentered the lodge and Moon Painter purified a knife by holding it over the smoke from burning sweet grass. He prayed to Grandfather, *Wakan-Tanka,* that all creatures of the air and of the earth might rejoice. He offered a pinch of blessed earth to each of the directions, praying to the Buffalo Spirit.

Using the knife purified by the sacred smoke of sweet grass, he began piercing the breasts of those dancers wishing to make such a sacrifice. Others chose to have their calves pierced. In either case, skewers were placed into the incisions, with weights hung from the skewers. The weights helped the skewers tear away from the flesh sooner so as not to prolong the ordeal for each dancer, but the pain suffered in the process was considered an honor to suffer in sacrifice for answered prayer.

Some of the dancers chose to tie themselves to the sacred tree and hang back, forcing the skewers to pull at their skin. Rather than piercing his flesh for skewers, Stalking Wolf chose to allow Moon Painter to cut pieces of flesh from his arms and legs as his sacrifice. He then danced with the others, and Moon Painter prayed constantly to *Wakan-Tanka* amid the dancers' songs.

During the hours-long ceremony, Moon Painter made a bed of sage facing east, and he placed sage into the eyes of the buffalo skull and tied deer hide to one horn to represent a robe for the buffalo. He then painted a red line down the forehead to the nose, as well as all the way around the head, praying, "You, O Buffalo, are the earth! It is good!"

Each dancer prayed for his chosen subject, whether it be the earth, certain animals and birds, for good weather, good hunts, victory against the enemy, plentiful buffalo, or for the People themselves. Standing Rock, participating for the first time, blew on the bone whistle Stalking Wolf had gifted him for the occasion. Blowing the whistle helped keep a warrior from screaming with the pain when he leaned back to let the skewers pull at his skin. Such self-torture showed *Wakan-Tanka* how much a man willed to suffer in sacrifice for answered prayers. Many others blew fiercely on their whistles.

Buffalo Dreamer watched Standing Rock struggle bravely, blowing the whistle with nearly every breath. She knew his mother, Yellow Turtle Woman, must feel very proud of her son's bravery, and part of Buffalo Dreamer's own sung prayer was that one day she would watch her own son take part in this most beautiful and sacred ceremony.

His face painted with three stripes on each cheek in his prayer color of white, Stalking Wolf himself sang strongly. Another day and night of dancing ensued, the Sun Dance lodge ringing loudly with the songs of both men and women, rhythmic drumming, and shrill whistle-blowing. Finally, at dawn of the third morning, several participants fell when skewers at last ripped through their skin. To help end the suffering of others, relatives pulled on their bodies to add weight, and eventually all succumbed and were taken away to be treated by the medicine men of each separate tribe.

Weary, starved, and thirsty, Stalking Wolf continued dancing until Standing Rock fell away from his skewers. Then Stalking Wolf finally sank to his knees and offered a prayer to *Wakan-Tanka,* thanking him for ending his nephew's suffering, and asking that the young man's sacrifice be honored and his prayers answered.

Days of celebrating and feasting followed, including storytelling and games, gambling and horse-racing, which all helped Buffalo Dreamer bear the pain of losing her grandmother. The crowning celebration came with the Night Dance. Recovered from the Sun Dance ritual, Stalking Wolf watched Buffalo Dreamer move enticingly before his eyes. Buffalo Dreamer thought of how much had changed since the first time she had danced for him, of how much she now enjoyed teasing her husband. She threw down her blanket, and immediately Stalking Wolf picked her up in his strong arms and carried her off into the night. He laid her down in soft grass and knelt over her.

"In all the Sun Dance celebrations I have attended, never have I been prouder," he told her. "When you carried the sacred pipe into the lodge, my heart swelled with love, and I could see great wonder and respect in the eyes of others at knowing the story of how the buffalo saved you."

"And you, my Shirt Wearer, sang strong and loud, showing no pain when Moon Painter cut your flesh. And my heart raced with pride when you won many of the horse races." Buffalo Dreamer breathed deeply with happy feelings. "Tomorrow is the wedding of Wind In Grass and Sweet Root Woman. It will be a good day, a wonderful way to end the celebrations. I only wish my grandmother could have seen you one more time."

Stalking Wolf leaned down and rubbed her cheek. "Walks Slowly is in a better place, and she will always be in your heart."

"As you will be."

Stalking Wolf smiled as he pushed her tunic to her waist. "All the celebrating has made me hungry for my woman. I wish to feel myself inside of you."

Buffalo Dreamer untied her tunic and pulled the front down to expose her breasts. "And I wish to *feel* you inside of me, and to feel you taste my breasts."

Stalking Wolf licked her mouth hungrily, then moved down to taste her nipples. "One day our son will suckle here," he said softly.

"I pray it will be so, and that this time, your life will take hold, Stalking Wolf."

Stalking Wolf guided himself into her, and Mother Earth enveloped them in her arms of soft grass while he moved with the rhythm of the drums that still pounded along with the singing in the distance. All around them, crickets joined in with their own song, and a million stars twinkled above the lovers. For several minutes, husband and wife moved in delicious rhythm, reveling in the pleasure they took from this act of uniting.

Stalking Wolf rose to his knees and grasped Buffalo Dreamer's bottom, pushing deep until his life spilled into her. He remained there for a moment. "I want to be sure the life goes deep enough," he told her. Finally, he leaned down and licked her around the eyes, licked her mouth again. "Do you wish to see the hairy ones?" he asked. He rolled to his side and pulled her against him.

"The *wasicu?*"

Stalking Wolf took a deep breath and looked up at the stars. "When we leave here, we will go to Fort Pierre. It is time to find Gray Owl."

The joy of the moment changed for Buffalo Dreamer. "I am afraid for you to go there. It could be dangerous. You do not know who Gray Owl calls friend, and the *wasicu* have the fire sticks that can kill in a moment."

"I have told you many times there is nothing to fear from the white men, and you know I will never be truly happy again until I find Gray Owl and repay him for being a traitor to his own people. Only then can I feel true pride again."

Buffalo Dreamer rolled on top of him. "You must be very careful, Stalking Wolf."

The bright moonlight displayed his smile of confidence. "Do not worry so." He plied her bottom with strong fingers. "I want you to ride me like you ride Sotaju."

Buffalo Dreamer shook her head. "I try to be serious, and you can only think about making love."

Stalking Wolf reached up and massaged her breasts. "With such a beautiful wife, it is difficult to think of anything else."

Buffalo Dreamer laughed lightly and raised up, carefully guiding his hard shaft into her depths, sucking in her breath at the renewed pleasure. She threw back her head and grasped his forearms, moving in rhythm as though on horseback. Stalking Wolf fondled her breasts, toying with her nipples, and Buffalo Dreamer drank in his every touch, wanting the love they now shared to help ease her sorrow over the death of her grandmother . . . and the worry she could not banish at the thought of Stalking Wolf facing Gray Owl in the midst of the *wasicu* stronghold.

CHAPTER THIRTY-SEVEN

FALL LEAF WOMAN studied her reflection in the magic glass. Already accustomed to the conveniences of iron cook pots and wood floors, she now wore white-woman dresses. However, she refused to wear their strange undergarments. Why should a woman wear something under her dress that stifled her breath and made her ribs ache, or that had to be pulled down every time she had to relieve herself . . . and every time her man wished to bed her?

She scowled at the bruise on her cheek. John Dundee put it there. He had made her his wife many months ago by taking her to his bed. She went willingly because he offered her many wonderful things—colored ribbons, pretty beads, fancy dresses, powders and colors for her face, iron pots, and warm blankets . . . and whiskey. She had not liked the taste of the whiskey at first, but the soothing comfort she enjoyed when drinking it soon made it easy to swallow.

She liked to dress like the white women, even though the few who lived here at Fort Pierre shunned her. Most came here from outlying farms to buy supplies. They looked at her scornfully, even the dirty, ragged ones who were not at all pretty. She had decided they were only jealous of her own dark beauty. She considered herself by far more attractive than any of them, with their sickly pale skin and sour faces. Besides, John had told her himself she was much prettier. Still, her beauty would not last if John Dundee continued beating her.

The white man's firewater made him do it. She could not understand how the burning drink that made her feel so good and so happy could make John so mean. She craved whiskey now, unable to go more than a few hours without more of it.

Sighing, she turned away and poured herself another small drink, then downed it quickly. She had tried to leave John once, deciding to run off with another white man who had come here to trade. John had tracked them down and killed her companion, then beaten her into promising she would never try to leave him again. Life could be very good here if only John would treat her better. Now she was trapped, not just by John Dundee, but by her need for the whiskey and for the easier life she had come to accept.

Gray Owl proved to be no help. He, too, liked whiskey, and he became close friends with John, who gladly gave him whiskey, guns, clothes, and food in return for hunting for meat John could sell. John also sold hides and furs here at the post, but when whiskey made him lazy, which was often, he needed someone to help keep him supplied. Gray Owl gladly obliged, proud to own a firestick and relishing his free whiskey. Here at the fort, he could also gamble, and smoke the white man's cigars. He believed whiskey made him stronger, perhaps even invincible, and he swore that if Stalking Wolf ever came after him, he would easily defeat him with the power of whiskey. John promised that together they could "blow Stalking Wolf's guts out."

Fall Leaf Woman shivered at the thought. She did not want to see Stalking Wolf killed. She knew that in any ordinary hand-to-hand combat, Stalking Wolf could easily overcome her brother. Down deep inside, Gray Owl feared that Stalking Wolf would find him. But with the power of the white man's gun, Stalking

Wolf would have no chance against Gray Owl. The worst part was, she loved them both.

She put a hand to her stomach. For four moons now, she had been carrying John's child. She wished Stalking Wolf's life lived in her belly instead. He would want and love this child, but John had told her he could not love a "half-breed bastard." She knew enough English to understand what a bad name that was. The Lakota loved the children of captured enemy women the same as they did those of pure Lakota blood, but she had learned that the white man did not think the same way.

Her eyes teared as she took another swallow of whiskey; her unhappiness always eased when she drank it. This was all that remained for her—pure survival. Here she at least had food and warmth . . . and she could always get ahold of whiskey. When the baby came, she would have something to love, something to help her forget Stalking Wolf . . . and John's cruelty.

LATE JUNE 1833

Closing Days of the Sun Dance

CHAPTER THIRTY-EIGHT

STALKING WOLF HUMBLY laid his prayer pipe in front of Moon Painter, careful to be sure the stem pointed toward himself. As a sign of his respect and honor for the old priest, he had come to him wearing his finest regalia, his cheeks again painted with stripes in his white prayer color.

Both men sat near the fire in Moon Painter's tepee, and the Elder, himself shirtless, raised his hands upward, in acknowledgment of *Wakan-Tanka*. He kept his hands raised as he pointed them in the four directions; to the west, in honor of the Thunderbird Power; to the Giant of the North, purifier of the earth; to the east, the direction from which the sun and the light of wisdom come; and to the south, where the White Swan lives. He lifted Stalking Wolf's pipe and repeated the gesture, then placed the pipe on the ground to honor Mother Earth, source of all life.

"Now the whole universe has become a part of this pipe," Moon Painter said. "What is it you wish, Stalking Wolf? What is the prayer for which you come to me now and offer your pipe?"

"I wish your guidance. Here at the Sun Dance celebrations, our prayers are strong. I offer my pipe to *Wakan-Tanka,* and I ask you to help me send a voice to the powers above. The Great Spirit has blessed me in many ways, but there is one thing I would ask of him that means much to me and to Buffalo Dreamer. I prayed for this when I sacrificed my flesh at the Sun

Dance, but it seems my sacrifice was not great enough."

"And what is it you ask? For what should I pray with you?"

Stalking Wolf took a moment to answer. "It is difficult for me to say it."

Old Moon Painter nodded. "I already know what you would ask, Stalking Wolf, for I had a dream."

Stalking Wolf studied the man's wise old eyes. The bags under them sagged into a shower of wrinkles. "What did you dream, Moon Painter?"

"I waited for you to come to me, because of this dream. I wanted to be sure of its meaning, and I knew that to be sure, you would feel a need to speak with me. I think you have come to pray that your seed will be strong, that soon your life will begin to grow in Buffalo Dreamer, and that she will bless you with a son."

Stalking Wolf nodded, impressed with the old man's foresight. "For one full winter, and now another to come, my wife has not conceived. She just returned from the menstrual tepee, her heart broken, for recently she thought that at last she was with child. Before we leave to return to the Black Hills, I wanted to speak with you about this, in case you feel it is something for the *Nacas* to discuss while we are all still here together. I worry that my seed is not strong. It does not matter how brave I am, or how honored I am, how many enemy I touch, or that I am a good hunter. If my seed is not strong, I am not a true man. The only way to know this is to take another wife, but Buffalo Dreamer is still young, and we have learned to love each other in a way that would make it hard for her to have me share myself with another. Before I would take another wife, I would ask *Wakan-Tanka* to bless us with a child. I will sacrifice anything he asks of me. How do you know by your dream that this is my wish?"

Moon Painter threw a handful of sweet grass onto the fire and cupped his hands, wafting some of the smoke toward his face and breathing deeply. "In my dream, you and Buffalo Dreamer stood atop Medicine Mountain. A great light came, and it said that if you both went there and fasted, and if you let blood and then mingled your blood, your bond would be blessed and purified. Then I saw a child in Buffalo Dreamer's arms. It is good that you come to me before we leave for home, for now it will not be so far to travel to Medicine Mountain. I think that if you go there to fast and pray, and if you cut your fingers and touch them together, then when next you mate, your seed will take hold and form life. This is what I believe."

Stalking Wolf's heart filled with joy. Moon Painter's dreams held much meaning! He could hardly wait to tell Buffalo Dreamer. "I take great hope in your vision, Moon Painter."

"We must first say the proper prayers with those who would join us, and you must take part in the ceremony of prayer and purification. Then I and one other of your choosing will accompany you and Buffalo Dreamer to Medicine Mountain. You must not mate with Buffalo Dreamer until after you have received your own vision and know that the time is right. Will you do all of this?"

"I will do whatever I must do."

Moon Painter nodded. "Go then, and speak with your wife. I will have Bold Fox and Runs With The Deer again prepare a sweat lodge. Buffalo Calf will help, as it will aid him in learning the importance of these things. The Lakota will not remain here much longer. Soon the bands must separate and each go its way. The Oglala miss *Paha-Sapa*, and it is time for the buffalo hunts. The others must soon leave, but you and Buffalo Dreamer, myself and one other, will go to Medicine Mountain before we return home."

"I understand. I would choose my uncle, Runs With

The Deer, to go with us," Stalking Wolf told Moon
Painter. "He, too, is a holy man, a Big Belly, who is
wise and who has guided me well."

Moon Painter handed back Stalking Wolf's prayer
pipe. "Go then, and prepare yourself."

Stalking Wolf took the pipe and backed out of the
tepee so as not to turn his back on the old priest. The
moon was only half lit now. It would be full before
they reached Medicine Mountain, and it would take
almost until it was full again to make it back to *Paha-
Sapa,* but the trip would be worth it if it meant that
Buffalo Dreamer would conceive. He found her standing outside their dwelling, waiting anxiously for his
return so she would know what Moon Painter had said
to her husband.

"We must go to Medicine Mountain," he said upon
reaching her.

"Medicine Mountain! That is a long journey."

"Moon Painter dreamed that we must go there, both
of us. You must prepare some supplies. I will first go
through the ceremony of lamenting, and purify myself
in the sweat lodge. In Moon Painter's dream, we stood
atop Medicine Mountain, and you held a baby in your
arms. We must both go there, and fast and wait for a
vision. We must also cut our fingers and touch them
so that our blood runs together and we are fully one.
Until then, we cannot sleep under the robes as man
and wife."

Buffalo Dreamer touched his arm. "This is a good
sign. I am sorry, Stalking Wolf, that I still have not
conceived."

"We cannot know the reason for these things. Only
the Great Spirit knows." Stalking Wolf touched her
face. "I will speak with your father about returning
with my people when they leave here. Now that your
grandmother is gone, your mother will be lonely. Perhaps I can persuade Looking Horse to come to *Paha-
Sapa* to live. I am confident that if we do Moon

Painter's bidding, you will deliver a child. Your mother should be with you."

Buffalo Dreamer's eyes lit up with joy. "It is kind of you to think of her in that way, and of me. I would like nothing better than to have my own mother with me when I give birth."

"The Oglala will hunt buffalo as they journey home. Looking Horse can also hunt, and your mother can make new friends. Yellow Turtle Woman and the others will be good to her. She will find peace and happiness among the Oglala."

"Thank you, Stalking Wolf. Yellow Turtle Woman has been like a mother to me, but none can replace my real mother. I feel sure now that I will conceive. I will do whatever you say I must do."

Stalking Wolf leaned down and touched his cheek to hers. "I go now to speak with your parents, and with Runs With The Deer. He is to be my sponsor in the sweat lodge, and he will accompany us to Medicine Mountain and make the proper preparations."

Buffalo Dreamer nodded, and with mixed emotions, she watched him leave. Stalking Wolf deserved strong sons. She desperately wanted to be the one to provide them.

CHAPTER THIRTY-NINE

A NAKED STALKING Wolf stood at the center of a circle of the highest-ranking Oglala elders, his body smeared with white prayer paint. The elders wore only breechcloths covering their loins. They raised their hands in praise of *Wakan-Tanka* as Moon Painter held Stalking Wolf's prayer pipe toward the heavens and spoke.

"Grandfather, everything in the universe belongs to you. We ask that you give help to this young man. Listen, all you Powers of the universe! Bless this young man, so that his generations to come will increase."

Each in turn—Many Horses, Bold Fox, Runs With The Deer, Moon Painter, Chasing Antelope, Looking Horse, and others—offered his own prayer, after which Moon Painter again offered the pipe to the four directions, then lit it. He handed it first to Stalking Wolf, who smoked it reverently, then passed it on to the next man. When every man had smoked it, the pipe came back to Moon Painter, who cleaned it, then again handed it to Stalking Wolf.

"When do you wish to lament before going to Medicine Mountain?" The old priest asked Stalking Wolf.

"I wish to begin my lamenting as soon as the sun makes light again."

Old Moon Painter nodded. "This is good. You carry a great need for revenge in your heart, Stalking Wolf, and you had plans to go to the white man's settlement yet this summer to seek that revenge. But you understand that to produce offspring is more important, a true benefit to the People, and so you take time to pray for fertility instead of seeking revenge. *Wakan-Tanka* will recognize your unselfishness and bless you with good seed if you follow all that I tell you."

"I will do whatever you say, Grandfather," Stalking Wolf answered, using the term *Grandfather* in honor of Moon Painter's age and wisdom.

Moon Painter nodded. He thought for a moment before continuing. "You will come to me wearing only a buffalo robe, and you will sit in the sweat lodge for one full day. We will all enter with you and pray again with your prayer pipe. You will be purified there, and then I and Runs With The Deer will accompany you to Medicine Mountain. Your pipe will be blessed and purified and sealed with tallow so that nothing can contaminate it. You will take the pipe to the Medicine Wheel, and Buffalo Dreamer will go with you. There you will fast and pray until a vision comes to guide you. I will help you. You must always remember my instructions and advice."

"I will remember, Grandfather," Stalking Wolf replied.

Moon Painter raised his right hand. "Be merciful to this young man, *Wakan-Tanka,* that he may be one with all the Powers and with the winged peoples of the air. He will place his feet upon the sacred mountaintop. May he receive understanding, and may his generations multiply and become holy!"

He instructed Stalking Wolf to lie facedown for the rest of the night. When the sun appeared the next morning, Stalking Wolf rose and followed Moon Painter to the sweat lodge, where the long purification ceremony began. Afterward, Stalking Wolf again lay on his stomach all night. Moon Painter covered him with his holy buffalo robe, then instructed Buffalo Dreamer not to go near her husband. The next morning they packed supplies for their journey to Medicine Mountain. Stalking Wolf took three horses, two of them loaded with offering sticks, sacred sage, and sweet grass, all to be used in prayer rituals. He rode his spotted gray gelding, holding his prayer pipe in front of him. Buffalo Dreamer, wearing her wedding tunic, rode behind him on Sotaju, bringing with her bundles of firewood on a travois, to be used at the central fire on Medicine Mountain.

"The blessings of *Wakan-Tanka* be with you, my daughter." Tall Woman took hold of Buffalo Dreamer's hand. "I know that by the season of blossoms, I will have a grandchild."

Buffalo Dreamer squeezed her mother's hand. "I am happy that you have chosen to go back with us to the Black Hills, Mother. It will be so good to have you with me. Yellow Turtle Woman and Running Elk Woman will be good friends to you. I love you, *Ina*."

"And I love you. Remember that Medicine Mountain is *lela wakan*, very sacred. It is a good place to go to pray. Have faith, Buffalo Dreamer." Tall Woman patted her daughter's shoulder when Stalking Wolf announced they must leave. Buffalo Dreamer followed him. Behind her rode Moon Painter and Runs With The Deer. They made their way toward the wild, rocky mountains where the sheep with big horns abounded.

EARLY JULY 1833

Moon When the
Chokecherries Ripen

CHAPTER FORTY

FOR SEVERAL DAYS, Stalking Wolf, Buffalo Dreamer, Moon Painter, and Runs With The Deer rode through canyons and over open land, through forest and across rivers, most of their journey a constant climb toward Medicine Mountain.

A climb toward heaven, Buffalo Dreamer thought. It was a holy place where eagles nested, a place sometimes shrouded in clouds, close to *Wakan-Tanka.* She carried her husband's war shield secured at one side of Sotaju's neck, the same shield she had made for him herself, as he had requested. She had decorated the sturdy shield with wolves surrounding a white buffalo, and tied eight eagle feathers to the bottom half of the circular shape.

Never did she love or want her husband more than now. The Council had decided he should be appointed a part of the *Wicasa Itacans* for the Oglala. Rather than being a Shirt Wearer, he now became one of those who *appointed* the Shirt Wearers, taking the place of old Two Foxes, who had died suddenly last winter.

How excited *Uncheedah* would be to know that her granddaughter's husband now was *Wicasa Itacan.* And she could just imagine how the old woman's eyes would sparkle with mischief over their current quest, going to Medicine Mountain to find the blessing of *Wakan-Tanka* on their fertility. Walks Slowly would surely joke about how pleasant a duty it must be to bear the responsibility for giving children to such a fine-looking man.

"There!" Stalking Wolf stopped his horse and pointed. "We are close. Today the clouds embrace the Medicine Wheel, as though to hide her from us."

Buffalo Dreamer looked where he pointed, indeed seeing only clouds rather than a mountain peak. They rode one more day to reach the base of the mountain. Moon Painter declared they should make camp there.

"You and Buffalo Dreamer will begin your fast today," he told Stalking Wolf. "Runs With The Deer and I will go up the mountain and prepare a sacred place for you. It is important that while we are gone, you do not touch Buffalo Dreamer. If you do, your seed will never grow in her belly. It must first be blessed by *Wakan-Tanka* during your vision quest."

"I understand, Grandfather," Stalking Wolf answered.

Moon Painter turned to Buffalo Dreamer. "Prepare yourselves. Runs With The Deer and I will come for you when the sun rises. There is not enough time for us to go up and prepare a place and come back down before the sun sets, so we will come in the morning."

After preparing camp and gathering what they needed, Moon Painter and Runs With The Deer rode away, their supplies on a packhorse and travois. Important items included poles whittled from young trees, bags of sage and sweet grass blessed by Moon Painter, bundles of wood for a fire, and secret offerings known only to Moon Painter, all of which had to be prepared through specific prayers and rituals at the top of the mountain before Stalking Wolf and Buffalo Dreamer could go there.

Buffalo Dreamer felt much older than her sixteen summers. A year ago she never dreamed that a whole nation of Lakota would look to her for preservation.

"You must disrobe and wrap yourself in the buffalo robe Moon Painter left for you," Stalking Wolf told her. "I must do the same, but we must keep our medicine bundles with us."

Their gazes held in shared concern . . . and shared desire.

"Do not be afraid, Buffalo Dreamer. Our prayers will be answered."

Buffalo Dreamer blinked back tears of fear that she still might not conceive. What would Stalking Wolf think of her then? Would he take another wife? She hated the thought of it, glad that Fall Leaf Woman did not know of their current predicament. She would likely celebrate over it and offer herself to Stalking Wolf as a second wife, bragging that *she* could give him sons.

Stalking Wolf turned his back to her and disrobed, and Buffalo Dreamer also disrobed, wearing only her medicine bundle tied around her waist. Each took a robe left them by Moon Painter and wrapped themselves. They sat down, facing away from each other so their eyes did not meet in desire. From now on, they could not touch, except to cut their fingers and mix their blood. That would happen when they reached the summit of Medicine Mountain.

CHAPTER FORTY-ONE

BUFFALO DREAMER SHIVERED under her robe. In spite of the weather having been sweltering-hot during the Sun Dance, here in the Bighorns it had taken a strange turn. A thick bank of clouds had moved in before sunset, bringing a misty chill to the dark night that followed.

As instructed, Buffalo Dreamer sat facing away from Stalking Wolf. Neither of them spoke until late the next morning, when Moon Painter returned with Runs With The Deer. After allowing each of them to find a place to urinate, Moon Painter permitted them one drink of water, then gave them further instructions.

"From now on, neither of you should drink or eat until one of you is blessed with a vision," he told them, his aged voice cracking slightly because he raised it in an effort to stress the importance of his orders. "Once you step inside the sacred circle of stones, you must not touch each other except to cut your fingers and mix your blood."

In spite of his advanced years, Moon Painter seemed unaffected by the rigors of their journey and his trip up the mountain. The wiry, vital medicine man shook a wrinkled finger vigorously at Buffalo Dreamer.

"You, Buffalo Dreamer, must keep your husband's war shield with you at all times." He turned to Stalking Wolf. "And you both must pray constantly, until you know you have been blessed by the Great Spirit."

Buffalo Dreamer and Stalking Wolf nodded in understanding.

"Give me your lance and your war club," Moon Painter told Stalking Wolf. "You may keep only your knife and your prayer pipe with you, as well as your medicine bundle."

Buffalo Dreamer glanced at Stalking Wolf to see him hand the items to Moon Painter. "We will go now," Stalking Wolf told her. He mounted his horse.

Buffalo Dreamer tied her husband's war shield onto Sotaju. Then Runs With The Deer lifted her onto the horse.

"Be very careful," Moon Painter warned them. "It appears that no one has gone up the mountain this summer season, and the heavy snows of the past cold season caused many places along the path to wash away. The clouds are heavy, and in places so thick it is difficult to see ahead."

"*Wakan-Tanka* will be with us," Stalking Wolf replied. He headed up the base of the mountain, and Buffalo Dreamer followed, again feeling driven by destiny. Ever since she had first seen the white buffalo, others had preached to her about powers greater than any human being, powers that would pull her into pathways not always of her choosing. Now she journeyed to the very place where Stalking Wolf had first bartered for her hand. Again, Medicine Mountain beckoned her.

Husband and wife made their way up the narrow, winding path along the mountainside. Heavy clouds shrouded their way, and several times Stalking Wolf warned Buffalo Dreamer of precarious washouts along the ledge. At one point he ordered her to get down from Sotaju and lead the horse by hand. Her heart pounded harder when she stepped over a gap in the narrow path. The clouds did not have to clear for her to know what would happen if she or Sotaju lost their footing. The descent was long, and straight down. No one could survive such a fall.

Because they could not see the top and gauge the distance to get there, the climb seemed to take forever. Buffalo Dreamer drew her robe tighter around her neck against the damp cold, feeling removed from the world below.

"I am afraid, Stalking Wolf." She spoke the words softly, for the near total silence on the mountain created a sense of majesty that stilled the voice. Normally, a stiff wind howled constantly here, but today the air remained deathly still.

"Afraid of what?" Stalking Wolf's voice sounded muffled.

"I do not know. Perhaps *Wakan-Tanka* is angry with me. I was a poor wife to you in the beginning. Perhaps he will find a way to punish me while I am up here close to him."

"*Wakan-Tanka* would never allow harm to visit you," he answered. "He wants only good things for us."

Finally the ground flattened out as they reached the top of the mountain. Stalking Wolf dismounted, removing his robe and taking his prayer pipe from his horse. He wore his knife on a rawhide strap tied around his waist. That and the medicine bundle tied to his inner thigh were the only items on his otherwise naked body. Buffalo Dreamer slid down off Sotaju. She untied Stalking Wolf's war shield and walked behind him to the edge of the sacred Medicine Wheel.

"We will begin our prayer offerings," Stalking Wolf told her. "Leave the horses to graze at will."

He kept his robe with him, and still shivering, Buffalo Dreamer kept hers wrapped close around her. She took a deep breath before following her husband to the center of the sacred circle of stones, not sure of what to expect now. Anything could happen at this place. The Oglala believed that *Wakan-Tanka* had deliberately erased all memory of the beginnings of the Medicine Wheel from the minds of their ancestors, for no one really knew how and why the stone circle came to be. It simply existed, and somehow the Lakota had always known of its location, high enough that the Feathered One could find it when he returned to earth with all of the Lakota's ancestors, bringing great peace and happiness to the universe.

Buffalo Dreamer looked around, barely able to make out the sacred poles put up by Moon Painter and Bold Fox. She saw the hole they had dug nearby, filled with sacred sweet grass for Stalking Wolf to smoke in his prayer pipe. A pole set at the center of the stone circle held a leather pouch, tied to the top of the pole and filled with offerings to *Wakan-Tanka*—eagle feathers, bear claws, a buffalo horn, and smaller sacred objects. Neither Buffalo Dreamer nor Stalking Wolf knew exactly everything the bag contained. Moon Painter and Runs With The Deer had set four other sacred poles, to the north, south, east, and west of the central pole. Those, too, held bags of sacred offerings. Buffalo Dreamer noticed two beds made of sage lying near the central cairn, put there as padding for her and Stalking Wolf to sit on or lie on when they grew tired.

"I will pray first the proper prayer to open our fasting and lamenting," Stalking Wolf told her. "Then we will cut our fingers and mix our blood."

Buffalo Dreamer felt her stomach tighten as a mixture of fear and anticipation of the unknown coursed through her. Stalking Wolf built up the central fire, using wood from a pile of kindling left for them by Moon Painter and Runs With The Deer. He ordered her to sit down, and she obeyed. Stalking Wolf then sat down on his own bed of sage and stuffed the bowl of his prayer pipe with some of the sacred sweet grass left for him. He used a stick from the fire to light the pipe, and for a few minutes, he quietly smoked, then rose. Standing in naked splendor, he raised the pipe high.

"O Great Spirit, be merciful to me that my People may live!" he sang. Buffalo Dreamer watched him walk to the pole at the west, chanting the same prayer. Returning to the central pole, he sang the prayer again. "Have pity on me that my People may live!" He repeated the gesture, going to another outer pole and praying, then back to the center, out and back twice more, until he had visited all four outer poles. He then raised his pipe to the heavens, asking the winged creatures and all things of the universe to help him. Pointing the stem of the pipe toward the ground, he asked for help from Mother Earth. Then he set the pipe aside and took his knife from its sheath, turning to Buffalo Dreamer.

"The rest of the day, tonight, however long it takes, I will continue these prayers. Know that our union is sacred, for I would never ask another to accompany me on a vision quest. This vision quest we share, my wife. Because of this, our union is eternal and can never be broken, and if my seed takes hold in your belly, no other woman will be a wife to me. This I promise. Rise now, remove your robe, and put out your hand."

Buffalo Dreamer obeyed, shivering when she dropped her robe. Her knees felt weak at the thought of letting Stalking Wolf cut her fingers, but she trusted no one more than she trusted her husband. Swallowing back her hesitation, she held out her right hand. Stalking Wolf took it gently, rubbing the ends of her fingers.

"This is the last time we can touch until we receive our vision. Remember that you do this for us, and for our descendants. Do not be afraid, Buffalo Dreamer."

Buffalo Dreamer nodded, struggling to keep her legs from buckling under her. "I am ready," she whispered.

CHAPTER FORTY-TWO

BUFFALO DREAMER CLOSED her eyes and gritted her teeth, refusing to make a sound when Stalking Wolf cut into the end of her right thumb. Silent tears trickled down her cheeks as he quickly nicked the ends of her four right fingers. Although he could wield this same knife in savagery against an enemy, when she met his eyes now, she saw only concern there for her pain. He looked down then, and he deliberately cut into the ends of all five fingers of his left hand, his jaw set hard against the pain. He took a deep breath and tossed aside the knife, holding up his hand.

"Touch my fingers," he commanded.

Buffalo Dreamer reached out, touching thumb to thumb, first finger to first finger, stretching her fingers to match his. Blood flowed down her palm and forearm, as it did for Stalking Wolf, who closed his eyes and drew a deep breath, as though feeling a strange new power.

"Now we are truly one," he said. He entwined his bloody fingers between her own, holding her hand in a firm grip for a moment. Buffalo Dreamer felt a wave of heated desire sweep through her at the way his dark eyes raked over her nakedness. For a moment, she forgot the cold fog, until Stalking Wolf let go of her hand and stepped back.

"Put on your robe and sit on the bed of sage. Do not speak to me again, and do not eat or drink. Be strong, Buffalo Dreamer. We may have to sit here for two or three sunsets. It will not be easy, but because of this suffering, you will bear sons for us. Do you understand what you must do?"

Buffalo Dreamer nodded her acquiescence. She picked up her robe, gladly pulling it around her nakedness, reveling in its warmth.

"Hold my war shield close as you sit and pray," Stalking Wolf told her. "Let your blood decorate the shield."

He turned away and again took up his prayer pipe. Buffalo Dreamer sat down and took hold of the war shield as Stalking Wolf sang his prayer, that from his seed would come strong sons to continue the life circle of the Oglala.

Oh, Great Spirit, be merciful to me.
Let my People live! Bring strength to my seed.
May all the descendants of the Lakota be strong.
May the circle of life never be broken!

Hours of prayer and lamenting followed. Again Stalking Wolf raised his pipe and prayed at each of the four direction poles, walking back to the center pole after each offering and continuing to pray. Buffalo Dreamer knew he would keep up the ritual for as long as necessary, until he became so weak he could no longer stand and walk. She closed her eyes and began her own prayer song.

O Great Spirit, hear me,
That my People might live through me.
Let my body keep the circle of life whole.

This would be her prayer. Just like Stalking Wolf, she would sing it over and over, for however long it took to receive an answer. She pressed her fingers against the stretched deerskin of Stalking Wolf's war shield to help stop the bleeding.

Day moved into night, a very dark night because of the continued clouds. Morning finally brought a break in the weather, and sunshine helped relieve the chill, but the wind picked up into a constant groan, whipping Buffalo Dreamer's hair into her face. She ached for water, and her belly grumbled for food. Still, she did not complain. She drew on an inner strength achieved only from prayer, and from a deep desire to be able to give her husband sons.

By the second night, the wind calmed, but the now-clear skies heralded an even colder night than the one before. The moon cut only a sliver in the heavens, and the stars gleamed bright.

The next morning again brought relieving warmth from a bright sun. Buffalo Dreamer's mouth felt so dry she could barely utter her prayer song. She no longer needed to urinate, for her body tried to retain whatever fluid it could. She realized that Stalking Wolf, too, had not left the sacred circle to relieve himself. He continued his prayers, leaving his robe aside and dancing naked most of the time, since he danced with such frenzy it made him perspire in spite of the cool temperatures. Buffalo Dreamer wondered how he managed to stay on his feet, but this man had twice suffered the Sun Dance in full sacrifice of piercing of the flesh. He had taught himself to bear prolonged pain and suffering.

Buffalo Dreamer, however, felt herself growing weaker, and by the end of the day, she could not resist lying down. She continued singing her prayer song, so tired and hungry that the words drifted into nothingness as welcome sleep finally overcame her.

CHAPTER FORTY-THREE

STALKING WOLF PAID no heed to his sleeping wife. She might not be sleeping at all. She could be in a vision trance. He could not allow her presence to disturb his concentration. He danced and sang into the evening, finding it more and more difficult to stay on his feet. His voice became hoarse, his feet blistered and bleeding. Every muscle ached fiercely, and the rocky ground over which he danced began to feel like pointed arrows under his sore feet.

Night fell, and his legs screamed with pain. Finally, he struggled to his bed of sage and fell to his knees. Tears stung his eyes when he cried out for *Wakan-Tanka* to bring him a sign that his People would live forever, that his own sons would be a part of that assurance.

He stared at his knife, wondering if he should let more blood in sacrifice. Feeling weak and light-headed, he took up the knife with a trembling hand and placed it against his left arm, but before he cut the skin, a strange brightness surrounded him. He lowered his hand and looked around, seeing only the light, knowing that the night's sliver of a moon gave no light at this time of its travels. He rose, daring to look up. More light met his eyes, this time so brilliant that he quickly threw his arm over his face to shield himself.

In that moment he felt no pain or weakness, for the light's warmth invigorated his body. Gradually the light softened, and Stalking Wolf lowered his arm to see the light being sucked into the central fire. He watched it disappear into the flames, and then the flames shot up into a pillar of white fire that began to take the shape of a human, with straight, black hair and a powerful build.

The handsome Being slowly turned in a circle, his arms raised, flames shooting high around him. Feathers sprouted from his muscular body until finally they covered him completely. Standing at least ten feet high, he faced Stalking Wolf. An eagle's head crowned his own head, the beak draped between the Being's penetrating eyes, eyes that seemed to stare into Stalking Wolf's soul. The Being spread his arms in much the same way the mighty eagle would do when preparing for flight, displaying the magnificence of its feathers.

Stalking Wolf dropped to his knees. "Speak to me, Feathered One."

Such a glow surrounded the Being that Stalking Wolf found it impossible to distinguish between human and eagle. The Being's commanding presence held him captive, and he could not look away now, in spite of the bright light.

"Remember what I tell you," the Being spoke in thunderous tones.

"I will remember," Stalking Wolf answered, hardly able to find his voice after nearly three days of singing.

"I have heard your prayers, and I will answer them. But you must take a message to the People."

Stalking Wolf nodded.

The Feathered One folded his arms, crossing them over his chest so that he became completely enshrouded in feathers. He bowed his head, and Stalking Wolf could then see only the head of the eagle, making the Being appear to be nonhuman.

"I have come from a place in the stars where your ancestors wait for you, where one day you will join us in anticipation of the day when all the Lakota will come back to inherit Mother Earth. I came to you first as a human, the one who would save the world from evil. We are one and the same. I rose from the fire to show you that all Human Beings come from earth and fire, and I became the eagle because the eagle is sacred, and to show you that the birds and the animals are no different from Human Beings in their importance to Mother Earth. Always remember that, for a new people are coming, and they have no respect for Mother Earth, or for the winged ones, or the four-legged animals. The day will come when these new humans hunt the Lakota like the deer or the rabbit. Because of this, your future generations must be strong, and they must always remember the old ways and keep to them.

"Dark days are coming. Future generations must suffer to hold on to their land and never let go. One day, after the other humans have destroyed themselves, the Lakota will return to save Mother Earth and once again become the true Human Beings."

The Being raised his head so that Stalking Wolf could again see his human face. "You have already met these other humans. Their skin is fair, and their eyes have color. Hair covers their bodies, and they are clever. They will find ways to make you trust them, but their words are false. They will speak of peace, but for them, peace will mean putting all Lakota into one small area like tethered horses, or killing them. Only a few of these other humans will be true Human Beings who can be trusted. Be wise. Be cautious. And never give them your land."

The Being raised his arms and folded them over his head, so that feathers covered his face again. "You will not see me again until you come to me in death. From this day on, you shall be called Rising Eagle, for what you have seen here. Your children and their children will speak of you with reverence. You will be connected to them even in death. Your spirit will live on forever, Rising Eagle. Part of you will always walk this earth."

The Being turned and spread his wings, flying off into the dark sky. The glowing light left behind disappeared, and Stalking Wolf watched the fire's flames flicker down into just a few glowing embers. He looked over at Buffalo Dreamer and saw that she still lay sleeping. Apparently the Feathered One did not want her to look upon him, so he caused her to sleep through his appearance.

Stalking Wolf leaned down to touch Buffalo Dreamer, only then realizing that he felt surprisingly strong in spite of his ordeal of fasting and dancing. For the second time in his life, he had seen the Feathered One, and from within, he felt great powers of strength and wisdom that overcame his pain and hunger. The Feathered One had told him his prayers would be answered. He must waste no time now in producing the offspring who would continue the life circle of the Lakota, so that the entire Nation might live forever.

He opened Buffalo Dreamer's robe and pushed her legs apart.

CHAPTER FORTY-FOUR

BUFFALO DREAMER HEARD a baby crying, but in the darkness, she could not find it. She searched, reaching out, trying to determine the direction of the sound. Then she saw Stalking Wolf walking toward her with a baby in his arms. She ran to greet him, and the baby disappeared. Stalking Wolf stood there with arms outstretched.

"Stalking Wolf," Buffalo Dreamer whispered as he embraced her. "Where is the baby?"

"I give you a baby now," he answered.

The dream became reality when she awoke to feel Stalking Wolf licking her mouth, tasting her lips. Her robe lay open, and her husband moved between her legs. She drew in her breath when he entered her slowly, rhythmically.

"Stalking Wolf," she whispered again.

"I give you a baby now," he repeated. Buffalo Dreamer, weak and light-headed, and still confused between dream and reality, could not find the strength to respond. She only lay limp beneath Stalking Wolf's gentle thrusts. Never had she felt so keenly sensitive to his every touch, or to the exotic way his swollen penis rubbed her most private place. She grasped his muscled arms, feeling a little more strength come into her veins, her body responding in such a way that she could not help but begin moving with him. Desire overcame weakness and hunger, until finally that desire peaked in pleasant contractions deep inside, welcoming Stalking Wolf's hard shaft, wanting more.

Earnest passion consumed her, and she found the strength to arch up to her husband and meet his pulsing penetration with fiery fury. He began pounding into her with more vigor, and she cried out his name, her voice lost in the dark night. For several more minutes they mated wildly, almost as though a power beyond their control forced from them a need deeper than normal human desire.

Stalking Wolf grasped her bottom and lifted, rising to his knees and crying out like a victorious warrior as his life spilled into her. He held her against him for several seconds before pulling away. Perspiring, in spite of the chilly night air, he leaned down and recovered Buffalo Dreamer with her robe.

"Sleep more," he told her, his voice cracked from constant praying and singing. His breath came in quick pants as he recovered from the vigorous lovemaking. "It is important you lie still . . . and let my life take hold in your belly. I will also sleep. When the sun rises, we will eat and drink . . . and when we are strong enough, we will go down from the mountain."

He moved to his own bed and lay down with a groan. Buffalo Dreamer knew he suffered greatly from pain and hunger, yet he had found the strength to mate with her. She wanted to ask what had happened, for surely he'd experienced a vision, or he would not have touched her.

In time, he would tell her what happened. For now, her belly cried for food, and her dry mouth craved water. She forced herself not to think about eating or drinking. Stalking Wolf would let her know when such things were allowed. She curled into her robe and again became lost in a deep, exhausted sleep.

CHAPTER FORTY-FIVE

MORNING BROUGHT SUNSHINE and a surprising warmth, with only a light breeze instead of the usual stiff wind. Buffalo Dreamer opened her eyes, studying a nearby yellow wildflower that bobbed in the breeze. She looked over at Stalking Wolf's bed to see it empty. She struggled to sit up, then saw Stalking Wolf, still naked, walking toward her with a water bag in his hand.

"Stalking Wolf! I am sorry! I did not mean to sleep—"

"It is all right." His voice came as hardly more than a whisper. "You were supposed to sleep through my vision, until the time came for us to make love."

The words brought a sweep of desire to Buffalo Dreamer, combined with bewilderment at remembering what had happened earlier. She glanced down, feeling a warmth in her cheeks. "You mean . . . I did not dream it?"

Stalking Wolf came closer and handed her the water bag, along with a leather pouch that held dried berries and smoked meat. "Why do you think it was a dream?" He knelt down near her, and Buffalo Dreamer took the water bag from him.

"I am not sure. I only know that I slept deeply, and I dreamed. I heard a baby crying." She drank some of the water. "I looked for the baby, and then I saw you, holding a baby and walking toward me, but then the baby disappeared. You came closer and . . . and I woke up to find you making love to me." She dared to meet her husband's dark eyes, still feeling almost embarrassed at the wild lovemaking. Stalking Wolf smiled at her, looking happier than she had ever seen him.

"Never have I felt such a oneness with you," he told her. "We truly belong to each other now, Buffalo Dreamer, as never before. I know my seed will take hold this time. Now we can eat, and drink of the water. We need no longer fast. I know now that our prayers will be answered."

Buffalo Dreamer studied his eyes, hollow from his ordeal. He looked drawn and tired. "How do you know? Surely then, you experienced a vision."

He breathed deeply, renewed joy filling his eyes. "What I saw was something too wondrous to describe." He picked up his robe and sat down, facing her as he placed the robe over his lap. A true summer warmth finally visited even this high place, so that Buffalo Dreamer shed her own robe and laid it in her lap.

"First, we must both eat and rest more," Stalking Wolf told her. "Then we will talk." He took a piece of dried meat from the food pouch and bit some off. Buffalo Dreamer did the same.

"When we are rested and stronger, we will rejoin Runs With The Deer and Moon Painter," Stalking Wolf continued. "If we rest until the sun is high, there should be time to get down the mountain before the sun sets again."

"At least it will not be so dangerous. There are no clouds." Buffalo Dreamer finished the small piece of meat and lay down again. Stalking Wolf also reclined, and husband and wife lay watching each other, both filled with wonder over their experience.

"I love you," Stalking Wolf said. "You are more than my wife now. You are also my friend, and without you, I would not be the honored *Naca* that I am."

Buffalo Dreamer could not imagine a greater compliment from such a man. A lump formed in her throat. "And you are my friend, Stalking Wolf. No woman could ask for a more honored man as a husband."

Their gazes held in new understanding.

"You should know," Stalking Wolf went on, "that from here on, you are to call me Rising Eagle."

Buffalo Dreamer thought for a moment. "Rising Eagle. It is a fine name for a strong and brave warrior such as you."

Rising Eagle closed his eyes and turned onto his back. "I saw him again, Buffalo Dreamer. It is the Feathered One who named me."

Buffalo Dreamer sat up in surprise. "The Feathered One appeared to you *again?*"

Rising Eagle remained on his back, watching the clouds. "He came to me last night."

Astounded, Buffalo Dreamer sat even straighter. "How could I have slept through such a thing!"

Rising Eagle lay quietly still for a moment before replying. "He did not want you to see, or he would have caused you to wake. He gave me a message for the People. I cannot tell you the message before I deliver it to the *Nacas,* but the Winged One also told me my seed would be strong. That is how I know that this time, my life will take hold."

Buffalo Dreamer lay back down, sighing with frustration over having missed such a vision. "Tell me more, Stalking Wolf . . . I mean, Rising Eagle. I will not be able to sleep for wondering."

For several long seconds, Rising Eagle said nothing. "A light surrounded him," he finally told her, "so bright that I had to look away at first and shield my eyes. He rose out of the central fire, human at first, then slowly changing to a magnificent eagle. He told me that one day we and our ancestors will return to earth and live happily, and that my children and their children will speak of me with reverence, that I will always be connected to them, even in death. That is how I know we will be blessed with sons and daughters, Buffalo Dreamer. He otherwise would not have told me such a thing. He also said that because I saw him rise from the fire, I should be called Rising Eagle."

Buffalo Dreamer shivered. "What is he like? Is he tall? Does he have a man's face?"

"He must be ten feet high." Rising Eagle coughed, struggling to speak above a hoarse whisper, but his voice remained barely audible. Buffalo Dreamer leaned closer to hear him.

"Even when he became covered with feathers, his face was human, but an eagle's head rested on his own, and when he closed his feathered arms and bowed his head, I saw only an eagle. When he left, he flew off like an eagle. Then the flames of the fire shriveled downward to nothing but glowing embers, and I felt a desire for you like never before. I think that he meant for me to mate with you in that moment, for in spite of my own weakness, I could not stop myself."

Buffalo Dreamer lay back, enjoying the feel of the hot sun on her face and shoulders. "One day the whole Lakota Nation will have your name on their lips, Rising Eagle, because of what you have seen and heard."

"Perhaps, but I only feel humbled." He sighed. "Try to sleep. You must be stronger before we start down the mountain."

Buffalo Dreamer closed her eyes, moving a hand to her belly, praying that Rising Eagle's life already grew there. Excitement filled her, and now sleep did not come easily. She tried to imagine the Feathered One, and she opened her eyes to watch puffy white clouds dance through the blue sky. Was he up there, watching them right now? She smiled, realizing that her grandmother must also be in that mysterious land beyond the clouds, and that she was probably happier than she had ever been while on earth.

EARLY AUGUST
1833

Time of the Hot Moon

CHAPTER FORTY-SIX

BUFFALO DREAMER WATCHED proudly, and members of the highest Council of the Oglala listened in awe. Dressed in full regalia of quilled buckskins and eagle-feather headdress, Rising Eagle stood at a central fire recounting his vision.

"The Feathered One told me he lives in the stars with our ancestors," he related, slowly turning to face each man as he spoke. "One day all the Lakota will return to inherit Mother Earth. He said that the animals are no different from humans, no more or no less important. We are to remember that, because a new people are coming, who have no respect for Mother Earth or for the winged ones or the four-leggeds. One day they will hunt down the Lakota like rabbits.

"Because of this, until the day comes when the Feathered One returns with our ancestors, we must be strong, and we must teach our future generations to keep to the old ways and to remember the stories we tell them. Someday this new people will destroy themselves by their own foolish ways, and then the earth will belong to us again.

"The Feathered One said we have already seen these new humans. Their skin is fair and their eyes have color. Surely he means the *wasicus*."

Buffalo Dreamer listened as intently as the others, hearing her husband's story herself for the first time. Her mother clasped her hand, and Buffalo Dreamer took great relief in the fact that Tall Woman lived near her now. Buffalo Dreamer and Rising Eagle had spent over three weeks returning to the Black Hills, and already she knew she carried life in her womb. The time for her next visit to the menstrual lodge had passed two weeks ago. Rising Eagle's prayers had made his seed strong.

"The Feathered One told me that the *wasicus* are not to be trusted," Rising Eagle continued. "They are clever at making others believe them. They will speak of peace, but one day they will war with us, and they will try to keep us contained in one small place. He said we must be wise and cautious, and that no matter what happens, we should never give them our land."

Rising Eagle sat down then, and the rest of the Council pondered his words.

"But the white man is so weak," Arrow Runner protested. "And so few."

"We do not know how many more there might be in the land of the rising sun," Rising Eagle reminded him.

Arrow Runner nodded, but Chasing Antelope shrugged. "They tell us they come here only to hunt the beaver," he said. "They do not want our land."

"Perhaps not yet," Looking Horse told them. "But last winter, white men came to the land of the Sichangu to hunt beaver. The *wasicus* have a great desire for the beaver's fur, and although I myself have never dealt with them, I know that others have, as have the Crow. If the white men so dearly love the beaver skins, what will they want next? And if there are so many of them in the land of the rising sun, perhaps they will run out of room and will want our land next. My son-in-law only repeats what the Feathered One told him. We should listen to his warnings."

The circle of Oglala hierarchy murmured its concern.

"And do not forget that the Feathered One told me they are liars," Rising Eagle added.

Runs With The Deer sighed before speaking up. "I have heard that the white man will trade fine things for the beaver skins," he said. "They will even trade their weapons. I have heard that they have firesticks, weapons that shoot something more quickly than an arrow, and that whatever a firestick shoots, it can kill a man from a great distance. Some say that the Crow have been trading beaver skins for the firesticks. Perhaps the Pawnee also have these weapons. This could be dangerous for us. Perhaps we should go to the place called Fort Pierre and see if we can trade for some of these weapons, see how they work and if they are stronger than our arrows. Such a thing could be useful in the hunt."

Many nodded in agreement.

"We know that the Phoenix speaks only the truth," Moon Painter told them. "And so we must pay attention. We must be wary of the white man, and of the gifts he offers us."

Bold Fox frowned and took his turn to speak. "Still, they have things that might be useful to us. Perhaps we can trade for these things but never allow them to take our land. By trading with them, we can learn their ways, how they think. And we can learn to use their weapons. This could protect us someday should they decide to try to take our land, or our women and horses."

Murmurs of agreement could be heard. "It is true that to protect ourselves from the enemy, we must understand him, how he fights," Runs With The Deer offered. "We understand the Crow, and the Pawnee and Shoshoni, but we have much to learn about the *wasicus.*"

"I understand this, though," Rising Eagle told them. "I will never trust them, not after hearing the words of the Feathered One."

"We can take hope in his words that one day we will all return to inherit the earth," Bold Fox reminded them. "Because of this, we must never lose hope, no matter what happens with the coming of the *wasicus.*"

"This is true," Rising Eagle answered, "but that is far in the future. For now, we must heed his warnings about the white man. I will go to Fort Pierre and learn about the firesticks, and what other things the white man will trade for furs."

"I agree," said Runs With The Deer. "We should go to Fort Pierre."

"I cannot go until the passing of one more winter," Rising Eagle added. "My wife is young, and at last she carries a child. I do not want to risk losing the son for whom she and I prayed and fasted, nor do I want to leave her at this time. After the child is born, in the time of the melting snows and the awakening of Mother Earth, I will then make my journey to the white man's fort. The rest of you are free to do whatever you feel is right."

All sat pondering the question of visiting Fort Pierre. Then Runs With The Deer addressed the Council.

"I think we should wait and go when Rising Eagle is ready. These white men are no immediate danger to us, and if we go without Rising Eagle, one of us might be tempted to vent our rage against Gray Owl, if we find him still at the white man's settlement. Vengeance against Gray Owl must be reserved for Rising Eagle. And if we wait one more season, Gray Owl might think by then that Rising Eagle has given up and is not coming for him. He will be more careless and not watch for him."

Several nodded in agreement, and another quiet moment of consideration passed before Bold Fox spoke up. "I think we are all in agreement then," he said. "We will wait until the next warm season to go to Fort Pierre."

Rising Eagle moved his gaze around the circle of elders, his eyes taking on a look of dark anger. "It is then that I will seek out Gray Owl and make him sorry for being the traitor that he is!"

Some raised their fists in agreement, and Buffalo Dreamer felt tightness in her chest, dreading a confrontation between Rising Eagle and Gray Owl at the white man's settlement. Now that she loved her husband so, and at last carried his life in her belly, she could not bear the thought of anything happening to him.

"You must be careful, Rising Eagle," Runs With The Deer warned. "If Gray Owl is still at Fort Pierre, by now he has made friends with some of the white men. They might try to defend him."

"I fear no white man," Rising Eagle sneered. "And I have no fear of Gray Owl. He is a coward and a traitor, and if I find him at Fort Pierre, he will *die!*"

Shouts and war whoops followed. Another spell of sickness overcame Buffalo Dreamer, and she hurried away to vomit. She did not mind the sickness, because her mother told her it was the Great Spirit's way of cleansing her body of all impurities so the child in her would be perfect and pure.

She rubbed her belly, anxious for the day she would feel the first movement of life, Rising Eagle's life. Come spring, she would at last hold her baby in her arms. The only thing that spoiled her happiness was the thought of Rising Eagle going into a *wasicu* stronghold to seek out Gray Owl.

FEBRUARY 1834

Hunger Moon

CHAPTER FORTY-SEVEN

FALL LEAF WOMAN rocked her baby, a boy named Little Wolf. Outside, a stiff winter wind battered the crude cabin she shared with John Dundee. Snow sifted under the door, and she kept the rocking chair near the heating stove to help keep the baby warm while he fed at her breast.

She loved holding him close, loved this baby more than any human being ever to come into her life. Life here at Fort Pierre brought no peace or joy, leaving Little Wolf her only reason for living. Granted, she had plenty of food, and whiskey when she needed it. If she could just find a kinder husband, all would be more bearable.

None of the Indian men who hung around the trading post offered her a way out. Most of them were already married, some with more than one wife and many children to provide for. The few single Indian men here wanted nothing to do with a Lakota woman who belonged to an ornery, drunken white man. Besides, none would want to take in her child, not just because of his white blood, but because Little Wolf was deformed.

The boy's own father, who had not wanted him in the first place, refused to even look at the boy, who had two fingers missing on his left hand, only a thumb and little finger on his right hand, and several toes missing on both feet. Added to his deformities, Little Wolf was born early, a very tiny baby who at eight weeks old still looked practically newborn.

Newt Porter, the local tavern owner, claimed the child's deformities were due to his mother's consumption of whiskey, saying he had seen similar deformities on babies of whores who drank. Fall Leaf Woman refused to believe she was at fault. Her heart could not bear the thought of it. Still, John Dundee never failed to remind her daily that she shouldered all the blame.

"Ain't no seed of mine would grow into something like that," he told her often.

It hurt deeply to think how such remarks might make Little Wolf feel when he understood his father's hatred. She felt a fierce need to protect the child, afraid she might be the only one who loved him his entire life. That meant she must put up with her husband's abuse. Without John, she had no resources to provide for her son. Besides that, she had no other way to get her hands on the whiskey she needed to get through each day.

She jumped when the door suddenly burst open and John came inside. It seemed he never did anything gently or quietly. He slammed the door against the cold wind, and the noise wakened the baby, who began crying.

John hung a soiled hat on a wall hook. "Shut that brat up," he ordered.

Fall Leaf Woman raised Little Wolf to her shoulder and patted his bottom to quiet him, but the frightened infant would not be stilled. John set two bottles of whiskey on a rough-hewn, handmade table and removed his wolfskin coat.

"If he don't shut up quick, I'll throw him against the wall," he growled. "That should do it."

The baby finally calmed down, and Fall Leaf Woman rose from her rocking chair and laid him on a cot.

"Where is my supper?" John asked. "You been doting on that baby all day, haven't you? Why do you pay so much attention to that worthless little bugger? I don't think I want him around when he's bigger."

Fall Leaf Woman covered the baby, then straightened, retying her tunic to cover her breast. "I will build the fire and fix you some supper." She faced her husband, speaking in a mixture of Lakota and English that only he understood from living with her. "Do not ever again threaten to throw my baby against the wall," she told him. "If you ever hurt my son, I will *kill* you!"

John turned from the table, fierce anger in his eyes. "What did you say?"

Fall Leaf Woman faced him calmly, finding courage only from her love for her son. "You heard what I said. If you hurt my child, you had better sleep with one eye open, John Dundee!" She spoke the words in stern defiance, determined to stand her ground.

John moved closer. "Is that so?" Without warning, his fist came crashing into Fall Leaf Woman's left cheek and eye, which still showed the yellowing remains of a former bruise from a similar blow. She landed against the rocking chair, which tipped sideways. She and the rocker both fell, Fall Leaf Woman's midriff landing into one arm of the chair. Pain shot through her body as she struggled to get to her feet, and she grasped her left side, sure she must have broken a rib. She screamed in agony when John yanked her close.

"Don't you be threatenin' me again, girl!"

Fall Leaf Woman felt sick from pain, but she glared right back at him. "Then do not threaten my son again!" she answered. "Do what you will with me, but do not touch Little Wolf!"

She was surprised to actually see a hint of fear in the man's eyes. He gave her a shove. "Get that dress off, girl! You been lettin' that sorry excuse of a son suck at your tits. It's *my* turn! You oughta' be long healed by now."

Fall Leaf Woman drew a deep breath, sweat breaking out on her face because of her pain. "I do not think I can lay for you," she grimaced. "My side . . . is badly hurt."

"Too bad!" John reached out and tore at the lacings of her tunic so that the garment fell to the floor. "I won't touch your ribs. I got better things to touch!" He turned and picked up one of the whiskey bottles, uncorked it and took a swallow before handing it to Fall Leaf Woman. "Here. The firewater will dull the pain."

Fall Leaf Woman stared at the bottle. Part of her wanted to be able to say no, but she could never say no to a swallow of whiskey. Besides, John was right. Whiskey had a way of dulling pain, including the pain in a woman's heart. It hurt even more to realize that her own brother knew how her husband mistreated her, yet Gray Owl did nothing about it. He drank with John Dundee, hunted with him, gambled with him, and did anything the man asked him to do, caring about little else other than where his next bottle of firewater came from.

Fall Leaf Woman took the bottle and drank from it, a long gulp, relishing the warm burning that trickled down her throat and into her stomach. John grasped at one of her breasts, and she pulled away. "Let me drink a little more first."

John grinned. "You see? Before you know it, you won't feel a thing." His eyes raked over her. "You're still lookin' fine in spite of havin' that little half-breed." He unlaced his pants.

Fall Leaf Woman watched, wishing he would wash once in a while. She remembered how good Stalking Wolf used to smell, how gently he mated with her . . . and how magnificent he looked naked, like a fine stud horse. John's manpart looked small in comparison. He never satisfied her, but it didn't matter as long as she had a warm place for herself and the baby to stay, and there was whiskey to drink. She downed more of the firewater, walking over to the rope-spring bed that had the feather mattress John liked. She hated it. It was much too soft, but white people seemed to prefer such beds.

The whiskey began to mask the pain in her side, but her ribs still hurt enough that she had no desire to lay for a man right now. Still, she knew John Dundee would not leave her alone until he satisfied his lust. Then he would fall asleep.

Things were always this way when he drank heavily. She groaned with pain as she grudgingly lay down on the bed. Her husband moved on top of her, and she closed her eyes, pretending he was Stalking Wolf. That was the only way she could bear his mating . . . but all the imagination in the world could never erase his smell.

APRIL 1834

Moon of the Birth of Calves

CHAPTER FORTY-EIGHT

OUTSIDE, A WARM breeze caused more snow to melt. Waterfalls tumbled with burgeoning overflow, creeks and rivers rose, and spring wildflowers bloomed. The season of awakening beauty filled *Paha-Sapa,* and new sprouts showed bright green on the millions of dark pine trees that decorated the Black Hills. Still-damp pine needles that had dropped on the ground before winter brought a wonderful, fresh smell to the spring air. Burrowing animals stuck their noses out of holes in the ground, hungry bears prowled out of caves to sniff the air and look for streams with fat fish, and graceful does began foraging with their new babies, carefully guarded by wary bucks.

Spring brought new growth, new life, and a more fitting time could not have been found for the birth of Rising Eagle's first child. But giving birth did not come easily to a young woman of seventeen summers. The quiet spring air was torn with Buffalo Dreamer's screams, and Rising Eagle walked far from their tepee, climbing a high hill peppered with clusters of rocks and thick with pine. When he reached the top, he still heard faintly his wife's screams far below. He looked up at the sky, where a few puffy clouds floated on the gentle wind. He raised his arms in petition to the Great Spirit that ruled all of nature, including the birthing of human beings.

"O Great Spirit, bring me a son. Save my woman, that I might be blessed with her life, and with a new son. Bless your holy woman, who has seen the white buffalo, and take away her pain. Ruler of the Universe, my prayers are real." He repeated the prayer, determined his song would not end until someone came to tell him he had a son, and that Buffalo Dreamer still lived.

Below, a naked Buffalo Dreamer squatted on her knees on the soft deerskin that would be the birthing blanket. Legs spread, she bent over with another deep, ripping pain that seemed to consume her entire body. Many Robes Woman, who had given birth to a son only days before, supported Buffalo Dreamer on one side, and Yellow Turtle Woman held her other arm, while Tall Woman kept watch over the birth itself, massaging her daughter's back, timing the labor pains, telling Buffalo Dreamer when to push and when to wait.

Buffalo Dreamer simply wanted the baby out of her body so the pain would end. Her screams came as much from terror as from pain, for she worried something might be wrong. She did not want to disappoint Rising Eagle with a dead or deformed child. She had planned to be brave about this, to give birth with nothing more than a few groans, the way she had seen other women do. Even Many Robes Woman, young as she was, had an easier birth. It had taken only part of one morning. But Buffalo Dreamer's pains started before sunset the night before, and now the sun was almost to its highest point in the sky the next day, according to women who reported from outside the tepee. Many hours. Too many hours.

She knew that outside, most of the women of the camp waited, excitedly anxious to run and tell their husbands and others that the holy woman had finally given birth to her first child, all hoping for a son for Rising Eagle. She also knew Rising Eagle himself probably prayed even now for a son.

How can something conceived out of so much plea-

*sure and love bring so much pain when it comes into
the world? Why are women so cursed? Why can't the
men have the babies?* There came another, deeper
pain. Muscles began to act on their own, for Buffalo
Dreamer could feel her belly contracting with no effort
on her part.

"I see the head!" Tall Woman exclaimed, kneeling
in front of her now to check for the baby's long-
awaited appearance.

Buffalo Dreamer's body gleamed with sweat, and
her hair hung in damp strings. The painful contractions
consumed her again, and she could feel the baby moving through her. She screamed, one long scream of
urgent determination to pass the baby and have this
ordeal over with. She gritted her teeth and followed
her mother's instructions to push, finally expelling the
baby in a bloody little heap on the birthing blanket.

The other three women all exclaimed excitedly that
the child had finally arrived, and Tall Woman quickly
cut the cord of life. She took the baby away before
Buffalo Dreamer could even see if it was a boy or a
girl.

"Keep pushing," Yellow Turtle Woman told her. "It
is important to rid yourself of the rest of the cord and
the bed inside of you where the baby rested. The afterbirth must be saved for the baby's protection."

Beside Buffalo Dreamer lay a special deerskin
pouch in which the afterbirth would be placed for safe-
keeping, then hung high in a tree so that animals could
not get to it. It represented a thanksgiving offering to
Wakan-Tanka, so that the baby might be blessed by
the powers of the north, south, east, and west.

Buffalo Dreamer cried with relief. "Where is my
baby? Is it alive? Is it a boy?" She heard the sound of
a sharp slap, followed by an immediate squalling, a
good, healthy cry.

"It is a boy!" Tall Woman reported. "Rising Eagle
has a son!"

Buffalo Dreamer wept now with joy. The Feathered One had spoken truly. She heard the women outside cheering and laughing.

"Go and tell Rising Eagle!" someone shouted.

The child continued his wailing as Tall Woman cleaned him. Yellow Turtle Woman and Many Robes Woman helped deliver the afterbirth, then washed Buffalo Dreamer and packed her bottom with pads made from the thin skin of a young buffalo's belly and stuffed with cattail down and feathers. They tied the padding around Buffalo Dreamer with more rawhide, and then the new mother lay down on a bed of clean robes. Yellow Turtle Woman covered her with a light deerskin blanket.

"My breasts feel heavy with milk," Buffalo Dreamer told Yellow Turtle Woman. "Bring my baby and let him learn to feed at my breast and stop his crying."

Yellow Turtle Woman laughed. "Do not be so anxious. Your mother will bring him soon."

Buffalo Dreamer listened to the child's continued crying, a sign of healthy lungs.

"His body is strong and sturdy, just like his father's," Tall Woman told her daughter. She turned and brought the child to Buffalo Dreamer, placing him in his mother's arms.

Buffalo Dreamer could hardly see him at first for the tears of joy in her eyes. She quickly wiped them away and opened the soft, furry, raccoon skin wrapped around the child. She smiled when his strong legs kicked fiercely in apparent distress at being forced out of his mother's warm belly into a strange new universe.

"He is perfect," Buffalo Dreamer said joyfully, studying fingers and toes, a beautiful, unmarked face, and the child's shock of straight, black hair. She could not see his eyes, still closed tightly. "It is as you said," she told her mother. "He is truly Rising Eagle's son, strong and healthy and handsome. One day he will be a great warrior!"

"He is beautiful, Buffalo Dreamer," Many Robes Woman told her. "We will sit and nurse our sons together. They will grow up not just as cousins, but as good friends." Her own baby lay sleeping at the side of the tepee, amazingly undisturbed by all the screaming and crying that had taken place.

"He is hungry," Tall Woman told Buffalo Dreamer. She helped to properly place the child at Buffalo Dreamer's breast, giving her instructions about breastfeeding. Buffalo Dreamer hardly had time to learn anything before the baby, searching wildly for sustenance, finally found a nipple. Instantly his crying stopped. His tiny hand grasped and pinched at his mother's breast, and Buffalo Dreamer winced with pain at the first sensation of the baby's eager sucking.

"Rising Eagle will be jealous," she joked.

The other women laughed. "It is common for a man to be a little jealous," Yellow Turtle Woman told her. "But for now, your husband will be so proud there will be no controlling him. There will be much dancing and feasting this night in celebration of the birth of a son to our holy woman and our most honored *Naca*."

For the next few minutes, the women cleaned up the birthing area, while Buffalo Dreamer nursed her son.

"Soon the cord of life still attached to his belly will fall off," Tall Woman told her. "You must watch for it and keep it. We will put it in the child's medicine bag, the first holy object he will carry with him forever, just as you carry yours in your own medicine bag."

"He comes!" someone outside shouted.

"Rising Eagle is here," Yellow Turtle Woman told Buffalo Dreamer. "We will leave you alone."

All the women left the tepee, and moments later,

Rising Eagle ducked inside. Buffalo Dreamer knew instantly that she would never forget the look of sheer joy and ecstasy on his face. He knelt beside her, and Buffalo Dreamer opened the infant's wrappings to show him a whole and healthy baby.

"His lungs are strong," she told him. "I will have to keep him close so that he does not cry in times of danger, in case we must hide, for his crying is very loud."

Rising Eagle grinned widely, his eyes misty. "Of course it is loud. He is strong." He carefully placed a finger in the baby's palm, and the child's tiny fingers curled around it. "Look at how he holds my finger! He will be a great warrior someday! And he is so handsome."

"Like his father."

Rising Eagle met her eyes, then gently stroked her damp hair. "I thank you, Buffalo Dreamer."

"I need no thanks. The child brings me more joy than I can tell you."

Rising Eagle stroked the baby's soft, pudgy cheek. "He represents the continuing circle of life, the survival of the Lakota. I wish to take him outside for all to see."

Buffalo Dreamer smiled as he eagerly took the naked infant out of its wrappings and gingerly held him between his two strong hands. "He is almost small enough to hold in one hand," he said, shaking his head, "but I would be afraid I would drop him." He carried the child outside, and Buffalo Dreamer could see through the tepee opening that the waiting crowd included most of the Oglala elders, and practically all the women and children as well. Rising Eagle held his son high in the air. "A son for Rising Eagle and Buffalo Dreamer!" he shouted.

Everyone cheered, and the infant began kicking and flailing, missing its mother's breast and the warmth of her arms. Amid the trilling of women and the supportive shouts of the men, the baby renewed its squalling, its crying so loud it could be heard above the noise of all the shouting and a chorus of barking dogs.

"Tonight Tall Woman will help me give a feast in celebration. We will dance and sing and eat!" Rising Eagle announced.

Buffalo Dreamer closed her eyes and breathed deeply with happiness. She waited anxiously, knowing that Rising Eagle would take the baby to his uncle, Bold Fox, who held the duty of naming him. When Rising Eagle returned several minutes later, the boy still squalling mightily, Buffalo Dreamer quickly re-wrapped her baby and held him close. His crying immediately quieted when he found her breast.

Rising Eagle shook his head in wonder and joy. "Bold Fox named him Cries Loudly," he told her.

Buffalo Dreamer laughed. "His name will be changed many times as he grows, but for now, Cries Loudly is certainly fitting."

Rising Eagle lightly stroked the baby's head. "Cries Loudly, you are a fine son. Through you, I will live forever."

Cries Loudly poked a hand through his wrappings and waved his pudgy arm in the air, almost as though he understood.

JUNE 1834

Strawberries Ripening Moon

CHAPTER FORTY-NINE

CRIES LOUDLY REMAINED true to his name, and Buffalo Dreamer spent a good share of her time feeding the constantly hungry baby to keep him quiet.

"He can already be called a Big Belly," Tall Woman often teased.

"He is just a healthy boy," Buffalo Dreamer always answered.

These were such good times. The tribe's store of buffalo meat lasted through most of the winter, a winter of plenty of robes for clothing and blankets, bones for utensils and weapons, sinew for sewing, fat for cooking and for making pemmican. Now the warmth of summer returned, and already several warriors, including Rising Eagle, hunted buffalo.

When not feeding at her breast, Cries Loudly remained strapped in his cradleboard, usually worn on Buffalo Dreamer's back wherever she went. When he was one month of age, she began teaching her son that he would not always get attention by crying. Every time he put up an extended fuss, she asked Rising Eagle, or another man in his absence, to hang Cries Loudly in a tree, high enough that no animal could get to him, but far enough away from the tepees that he did not disturb others.

All children had to be taught from an early age to give up useless crying and temper tantrums, for sometimes complete quiet became necessary, especially when hiding from the enemy. The best method for such training was to simply ignore the wailing until the baby learned that all the noise it made did no good in getting its way. Otherwise, discipline was maintained by constant loving, and when the child was older, by the simple method of teaching the child that it was responsible for any misdeed committed, and then letting its pride take care of the rest. No Lakota child ever suffered physical abuse for misbehavior.

Buffalo Dreamer kept the cradleboard packed with dried buffalo manure pounded into a powder, a fine absorbent that could simply be thrown out and replaced when necessary. Around his neck, Cries Loudly wore a little leather pouch Tall Woman had quilled for him in bright yellow. Shaped like a turtle, the pouch held the baby's umbilical cord, a charm worn to ensure long life.

Today Cries Loudly actually did not cry at all. He sat quietly in his cradleboard, propped against his mother's tepee, while Buffalo Dreamer and Many Robes Woman worked at mending moccasins. The two sisters-in-law were growing closer through sharing mutual joys and problems in the caring of their new babies. Only one week apart in age, Cries Loudly already matched his slightly older cousin, Makes Fist, in size. Makes Fist also sat propped near his mother, sound asleep; but Cries Loudly remained alert, his dark eyes taking in the camp scene before him.

Little boys played rough war games, and in the distance, a group of young girls played kick-ball. One girl threw the leather ball, stuffed with antelope hair, high into the air. Then she and the others ran frantically about in an effort to kick the ball up in the air again before it could hit the ground. Their screams and laughter brought back memories for Buffalo Dreamer.

"Were you good at kicking the ball?" she asked Many Robes Woman.

"I used to be very good, but since taking a husband

and having Makes Fist, I no longer have time for such things."

Buffalo Dreamer felt a stab of memories. "I used to enjoy the game of racing to see which young girl could put up a tepee the fastest. I won when I was thirteen summers. I did not know then that two summers later, I would wed a stranger who would become a man of such importance."

The young girls screamed, several of them falling in the scramble to kick the ball. Buffalo Dreamer realized in that moment that all the "little girl" in her had disappeared. A mother now herself, her own mother had become *Uncheedah* to Cries Loudly.

"I hope my next baby is a girl," she said. "My mother will enjoy teaching a granddaughter, the way my grandmother taught me."

Many Robes Woman smiled. "Perhaps she can also help teach a daughter that I might have."

"She would like that. Just as your mother took me in like a daughter, so my mother feels about you. Red Sun Woman would be happy to know that her daughter now has a mother again."

Many Robes Woman nodded, then suddenly jumped up. "They come!" Men rode into camp from the north, leading several horses ahead of them. Some of the men who had remained at the main camp to protect the women and old ones mounted their horses and rode out to greet those arriving.

Buffalo Dreamer felt excitement and relief. Following Cries Loudly's birth, Rising Eagle had ridden out often to hunt. This time he had gone with Arrow Runner, Wind In Grass, Buffalo Calf, Standing Rock, Many Horses, and Bold Fox to raid Crow camps and steal horses, a much more dangerous mission. More horses were needed to replace those lost over the winter and those becoming too old and slow.

Buffalo Dreamer understood the main reason why Rising Eagle left often. He needed to find ways to be absent in order that he not sleep with his wife again too soon, but she missed him in her bed.

"Look at how many horses they have!" she remarked loudly.

"They are all good warriors, especially my brother and my husband," Many Robes woman bragged, her face beaming.

The children's games stopped, and they all ran toward the incoming herd of horses, waving their arms and shouting, helping slow down the eager, confused animals. The whole camp of nearly five thousand Oglala came alive.

Rising Eagle headed straight for Buffalo Dreamer's tepee, pride and joy in his eyes. Many Robes Woman ran off to greet her own husband.

"You are all right?" Buffalo Dreamer asked Rising Eagle, looking him over as he dismounted.

"I have yet to be harmed in stealing horses from under a Crow man's nose," he bragged, grinning.

They studied each other, each reading the other's thoughts, knowing they could not yet act on those thoughts.

"I would like you to just hold me, Rising Eagle. I have missed you so."

He came closer and wrapped his arms around her. "I also missed you." He embraced her lightly, then pulled away. Buffalo Dreamer felt the odd strain between them over not being able to make love. She ached to feel him inside her again, and she knew by his eyes that he felt the same desire for her.

"I want to see my son," he said.

Buffalo Dreamer smiled. "You will be surprised at how much he grows in a short time," she told him. She turned and unstrapped the child and held him out to Rising Eagle, who took him and held him high.

"So big and strong already!" he exclaimed. "He is such a healthy, handsome boy, Buffalo Dreamer. I could not have asked for more."

"He finally is not crying so often. I had to hang him in a tree many times. It hurts my heart to do so, but he must learn he cannot get his way by crying."

Rising Eagle laughed. "So, your mother is very strict, is she?" He nuzzled the baby's cheek and handed him back to Buffalo Dreamer. "We went on many raids. I have brought back fifteen horses of my own, and Buffalo Calf stole four. Once the Crow warriors chased us for a long way, but we outran them." His smile faded. "Now that we are back and my son is strong and well, it is time to make the trip to Fort Pierre."

Buffalo Dreamer frowned as she strapped Cries Loudly back into his cradleboard. "I do not want you to go there. There could be much trouble with the *wasicu* if you try to kill Gray Owl."

"I am not worried about Gray Owl *or* the *wasicu*. You know that I must go, Buffalo Dreamer."

She closed her eyes in resignation. "I know."

"I cannot rest until Gray Owl pays for what he did."

Buffalo Dreamer nodded. The joy of the moment became lost in concern. She feared her husband's trip to Fort Pierre more than she feared his raids on Crow and Pawnee camps. They were a familiar enemy, and he knew how to fight and outwit them. But the white man was a new enemy, with strange weapons. Still, Rising Eagle's mind was made up. There was vengeance to be had, and no stopping a proud Rising Eagle from seeking it.

JULY 1834

Moon of the Blooming Lilies

CHAPTER FIFTY

THE OGLALA ARRIVED at Fort Pierre in a grand procession of several hundred warriors in full regalia of quilled, fringed shirts, coup feathers decorating their hair, war shields strapped to their mounts. Rising Eagle had painted the rump and neck of his chestnut-colored horse with wolf faces, and on one side, a picture of a feathered human.

Buffalo Dreamer rode proudly beside her husband, Cries Loudly's cradleboard hanging at Sotaju's side. The swaying motion of the cradleboard rocked him, and he mostly slept during the three-week journey to the trading post. Buffalo Dreamer had secured the baby's head with a band around his forehead, tied at the back of the cradleboard so that he would not hurt his neck. And she had painted Sotaju's rump with white dots for stars. She painted a woman holding a baby on one side of the horse's neck. Sotaju pulled a travois loaded with furs for trade, as well as other supplies.

"I already do not like this place," she told Rising Eagle. She stared in wonder at a large, square, wooden structure, the logs surrounding it tied tightly together and whittled to points at the top. Men in strange looking clothing and hats stood in two towers at opposite corners of the fort, holding what looked like weapons. Buffalo Dreamer guessed them to be the firesticks she had heard so much about.

Tepees erected in scattered locations around the outside of the fort made it obvious that some Lakota and other Indians lived around the settlement, and Buffalo Dreamer could not imagine why. She saw only dust from horses and heard only noise from clattering wagons. Beyond the fort she saw numerous smaller log structures, which she supposed belonged to the white men.

"Many *wasicus*," Rising Eagle commented, holding up his hand to halt those who followed. "More than I thought."

Nearby, a bearded man stepped out of a cabin, carrying a bucket. He wore no shirt, and Buffalo Dreamer felt repulsed by all the hair on his face and chest. The hair on his head hung in a tangled, unwashed clump, and his eyes were bloodshot. He threw the contents of the bucket out on the ground, and almost instantly, flies gathered over it. Buffalo Dreamer curled her nose, and the man only grinned through yellowed teeth, looking her over as though she was his for the taking.

Buffalo Dreamer glanced at Rising Eagle, who looked down his nose scornfully at the man. "Our dogs are cleaner," he told Buffalo Dreamer. The man lost his smile, and Buffalo Dreamer realized he apparently had understood the comment. The *wasicu*'s hands moved into fists, but when he looked behind Rising Eagle at the huge procession of warriors who followed, he lost his arrogance. He waved Rising Eagle off and went back inside his cabin.

"So, this is how the white man lives," Rising Eagle commented.

Buffalo Dreamer looked down at the slop thrown out by the white man a moment earlier. "These *wasicus* have no respect for Mother Earth," she said. "It is just as the Feathered One told you." A stiff breeze blew her hair forward over her face, and she grabbed it and pulled it around to one side of her neck. Bold Fox rode up beside Rising Eagle then.

"Do you think Gray Owl is still here?" he asked.

"We will soon know." Rising Eagle slowly headed his horse toward the trading post. Buffalo Dreamer reluctantly followed. Indians and whites alike gathered to watch the impressive entourage, and Buffalo Dreamer heard shouting. The white men apparently took alarm at their approach.

"They must think we mean to attack them," Bold Fox commented.

"Perhaps we should," Rising Eagle answered. "Look at how many horses graze beyond the post. We could claim quite a bounty here."

"*Ayee!*" Bold Fox laughed. "But do not forget the whites have the firesticks."

As the Lakota rode closer, several men on horseback and on foot lined up outside the fort.

"Stay here," Rising Eagle asked Bold Fox. "I will go in first." He rode forward, calling out in the Lakota tongue that he came in peace. Some of the traders apparently understood him, for they lowered their weapons. They spoke to others, and everyone seemed to relax. Buffalo Dreamer looked around fearfully, but she did not see Gray Owl or Fall Leaf Woman.

A white man in fringed buckskins almost the same as those of the Lakota men stepped closer to Rising Eagle. Buffalo Dreamer stared incredulously at the man's bright red hair and beard. Even his eyebrows were red, and his pale blue eyes were set amid a sea of pale red markings that covered the part of his face not hidden by the beard. He grinned at Rising Eagle in an obvious attempt to show friendship.

"I speak your tongue," he told Rising Eagle, using some Lakota as well as sign language. "I am called James McConnel. The others want to know why you have come here."

"We come to trade," Rising Eagle answered. He made a sign for buffalo, putting both hands to his head like horns. "Buffalo hides," he indicated. "Many furs."

McConnel nodded and pointed at the gates of the fort, indicating that Rising Eagle should follow him. Rising Eagle turned to signal the others to make camp, then followed McConnel inside the walled post.

Buffalo Dreamer watched helplessly, afraid for her husband. "Already I miss home," she told Bold Fox.

"Do not worry, Buffalo Dreamer. Look at those other white men. See the fear in their eyes. There are many of us, much more in number than they. There is nothing to fear. Come. We will make camp."

Reluctantly, Buffalo Dreamer turned Sotaju and left with Bold Fox to erect her tepee and wait for Rising Eagle to come out of the fort.

CHAPTER FIFTY-ONE

RISING EAGLE, FOLLOWING McConnel, wondered why the *wasicus* barricaded themselves behind log walls. Were they afraid of wild animals? More likely, they feared the Lakota, as well they should. The thought caused him to sit a little straighter, taking great pleasure in thinking these white men must be easily intimidated. Most watched him warily, probably because he came here with so many warriors. Attacking the fort remained an interesting challenge.

He noticed a white woman walking toward them, and he stopped to study her. Her full-skirted dress, worn tight at the waist, looked uncomfortable. She wore her hair wound into a little mound at the back of her neck, hiding its beauty, and her skin looked sickly white. She stopped walking, staring at him then with wide blue eyes that showed terror. Rising Eagle could not imagine what she feared. He made no threatening moves, and he looked at her only in curiosity, but she gasped, put a hand to her chest, and hurried away as though she thought her life was in danger. She passed another woman as she fled, a woman dressed in similar attire, but the second woman did not have white skin . . . and she did not run.

Fall Leaf Woman!

She stepped back slightly, obviously startled at recognizing Rising Eagle. She looked around, as though she considered running. Rising Eagle looked her over scathingly, noticing that she wore a white woman's faded dress, frayed at the hem and too big for her. He wondered how a woman as beautiful as Fall Leaf Woman could become the sorry wreck who stood before him now. Her hollow eyes showed shame and embarrassment, and he detected bruises on one cheek.

He glanced around, watching those who walked nearby.

"If you are looking for Gray Owl, Stalking Wolf, my brother is not here," Fall Leaf Woman told him defiantly. She clutched a baby in her arms, wrapped in a blanket in spite of the heat.

"I am called Rising Eagle now," he answered. He dismounted, walking a little closer. "You have a child?"

Fall Leaf Woman stepped back again, keeping some distance between them. "A son. He is called Little Wolf, born seven months ago." Her hesitant demeanor turned to a look of challenge and pretended pride. "Has Buffalo Dreamer given *you* a son yet?"

Rising Eagle folded his arms, looking down his nose at her. "Yes. He is called Cries Loudly, and he was born three moons past. He is very strong, bigger than any other baby his size. He has strong lungs, and he keeps Buffalo Dreamer busy with feedings." He watched the disappointment in Fall Leaf Woman's eyes. "If your brother is not here, where is he?" he asked, then warning her: "Do not tell me lies, Fall Leaf Woman. You know why I am here!"

She kept her baby close. "He is hunting. But if he were here, I would not tell you where he is. I cannot betray my own brother. I know you wish to *kill* him!"

"*He* betrayed the entire Lakota *Nation*! He *deserves* to die. And now *you* betray me by hiding him."

"I do *not* hide him! Even so, he is of my own blood."

"You are *Lakota*! As am I. We are *also* of the same blood, and you know that what your brother did was the worst kind of betrayal, to lead an enemy against his own people!"

Fall Leaf Woman blinked, and Rising Eagle noticed tears in her eyes. "I had nothing to do with that," she protested.

"You do if you hide your brother from me."

"I told you. I do *not* hide him." She glanced at McConnel. "Tell him! Tell him my brother is not here," she asked in English.

"Gray Owl?" McConnel stepped closer. "Her brother is off hunting. Been gone a long time, so he should be back any day now. You got a mind to make trouble here? You'd best not do it, Rising Eagle."

Rising Eagle looked around once more, wary of trusting McConnel or Fall Leaf Woman. He glanced at the bundle in Fall Leaf Woman's arms again, ignoring McConnel. "Who is your husband? Is he Lakota?"

Fall Leaf Woman turned away. "No. I married a white man. His name is John Dundee."

"He is not good to you."

She looked back at him with a scowl. "How would *you* know?"

"Because there is no happiness in your eyes, and you look away when you speak of him. You are not the beautiful Fall Leaf Woman I once knew. I see bruises on your face."

Fall Leaf Woman held her chin high, though averting her eyes. "If my beauty is gone, it is *your* fault," she sneered. "I live how I must live." She faced him then. "Go away, Rising Eagle. You should not be in this place. And it does no good for you to be concerned about me now. You did not care before. You should not care now."

"I have always cared. Why do you stay with a man who beats you and brings you only unhappiness? You could throw him away. You have the right."

She curled her lip in disgust. "Not by *white* man's

custom, and that is the custom by which I live now. Besides, John Dundee brings me firewater, all that I need. It is something I cannot live without. Now go away! This is no place for you. It is dangerous. My brother has many friends here."

She turned and walked away, and Rising Eagle watched after her curiously. What was this firewater of which she spoke, so powerful that a person would rather live in unhappiness than be without it? She disappeared around a corner, and he looked around once more. He would wait for Gray Owl to return from his hunting, no matter how long it took.

He faced McConnel, who looked confused by the confrontation. "That's John Dundee's woman, Rising Eagle," McConnel told him in a mixture of sign language and what he knew of the Lakota tongue. "If you've come here for her, you should go away, like she said. John Dundee once killed a man who had eyes for that one. If you're here to trade, I can help you. Just go over there to that store where you see hides piled in front. The man there can assist you. Otherwise, you'd best go."

Rising Eagle took hold of his horse's rope bridle and grinned snidely. "I will come and go as I please, white man. Meet me at this place tomorrow when the sun is high enough to be warm. I have many skins to trade, and I wish to learn about the white man's firesticks. I thank you for your help, but for now, I must help my wife make camp and see to my horses. And you should know it is not Fall Leaf Woman for whom I come. I come for her brother, Gray Owl, a traitor to his own people."

He leaped onto his horse and rode out of the fort, glancing at an old Minniconjou man who held a brown bottle in his hand. He drank from it, then held up the bottle in a mock salute to Rising Eagle, showing a toothless grin. He stumbled and fell, and Rising Eagle stared at him critically as he rode past.

The Indians around here appear mostly dirty and lazy, he thought. *They show no pride. Indeed, the Feathered One spoke truly when he said these new human beings would come into Lakota lands and try to destroy the People.* From what he'd seen of Fall Leaf Woman and the Indians camped around the fort, the destruction had already begun.

He rode out to find Buffalo Dreamer in the process of erecting their tepee, noting the relieved look on her face when she saw him coming. She straightened from pounding a peg into the ground.

"I have seen Fall Leaf Woman," he told her.

The relief in her eyes turned to alarm. "And Gray Owl?" she asked.

"She says he is not here. He hunts with her husband, a white man called John Dundee." Rising Eagle slid down from his horse.

Buffalo Dreamer's eyebrows raised in surprise. "A *wasicu?*"

"She has a son, but she would not show him to me. I can see that her husband abuses her, and she is not happy. But she will not leave him because of something he gives her called firewater. She says she cannot live without it. I intend to learn about this firewater, why it has such power."

"It must be bad, Rising Eagle, if it makes Fall Leaf Woman stay with a man who is cruel to her. She has the right to throw him away."

"She said that the white man does not abide by such a custom." A young boy ran up and eagerly asked Rising Eagle if he could tend his horse for him. Rising Eagle handed the boy the horse's rope, smiling as the lad led the mount away. His smile faded when he turned back to Buffalo Dreamer. "Fall Leaf Woman looks terrible, bruised and haggard. She is far from the beautiful woman who left us."

Buffalo Dreamer sighed. "Perhaps the firewater did that to her. She should never have come here, but it was her choice. Such things frighten me and make me want to leave this place. Look over there." She pointed toward the distant river. "I have been watching it. It is like a monster."

Rising Eagle studied the strange structure floating on the river, moving toward the shore. Black smoke belched from two high funnels, and a wailing sound from it pierced the air. Buffalo Dreamer gripped Rising Eagle's arm at the startling sound.

"It must be what Wind In Grass told us about—what the white man calls a steamboat," Rising Eagle told her. "He learned about them when he tracked Gray Owl here when I was wounded. He said the boats bring trade goods to the fort, and many more *wasicus*, even wagons and horses and other animals."

They both watched curiously. A paddle-like device pushed the boat, driven by some mysterious force deep in the bowels of the river monster and kicking great splashes of water into white foam.

"I do not like it. It makes me wonder how many whites there really are in the land of the rising sun," Buffalo Dreamer told him. "And what kind of things they have, things of power and mystery." She shivered in spite of the heat. "This is a strange place, so many people, so much movement, so many new sounds."

Rising Eagle touched her hand before moving away. "The Feathered One warned us about all these things," he said, still watching the boat. "It is good that we see them for ourselves. We will have much to discuss at Council when we go home." He faced her. "Including the story of how Gray Owl suffered at my hands."

Buffalo Dreamer closed her eyes against the dread of a confrontation. The steamboat sounded another long, shrill whistle, only making her more uneasy. The sound seemed a foreboding of something menacing come to this land, a new sound to replace that of the wolf's howl.

CHAPTER FIFTY-TWO

RISING EAGLE KEPT watch as Buffalo Dreamer, Tall Woman, and Yellow Turtle Woman marveled over an array of colorful bolts of cloth, spools of ribbon, barrels of buttons, assorted boxes of colored beads, and soft blankets. The *wasicus* indeed carried an abundance of wonderful items for trade. The women hardly knew how to pick and choose.

James McConnel introduced them to a delightful edible called sugar, and showed them the heavy black pots that white women used for cooking. While the women talked and fussed over their newfound treasures, McConnel stuffed a small, corncob pipe with a wad of fresh tobacco from his pouch. He held out the pouch to Rising Eagle, indicating he should smell the tobacco. A cautious Rising Eagle took the pouch and sniffed at the brown, leafy substance inside, then lost some of his skepticism at the pleasant smell. McConnel lit his pipe and puffed on it for a moment, then handed it over to Rising Eagle. "See? It's just like the sweet grass or sage or whatever it is you put into your peace pipes."

Rising Eagle took the pipe and puffed on it himself, nodding in agreement that the tobacco indeed pleased him.

"You can have the pipe and the tobacco," McConnel explained as best he could. "Keep 'em. My token of friendship." He made the sign for friend, and Rising Eagle understood he meant the pipe and tobacco as a gift. He nodded, puffing on the pipe once again and handing the bag of tobacco to Buffalo Dreamer to put into the leather sack she had brought along for collecting trade items. She had left Cries Loudly with Many Robes Woman back at camp, not caring to bring her baby into the fort full of *wasicus,* afraid Cries Loudly might somehow be hurt or take sick.

McConnel offered Rising Eagle colored ribbons and a mirror for a fox fur, three rabbit skins and a beaver skin, adding two blankets in exchange for two deerskins and a buffalo robe.

Rising Eagle considered the exchange, all the while thinking of how repulsive white men smelled. In spite of the look of genuine friendship in McConnel's eyes, Rising Eagle's mind-set told him to trust no white man, because of the words of the Feathered One. He let McConnel know, through hand signals and whatever Lakota tongue McConnel could recognize, that he thought the trade unfair.

McConnel stepped back, folding his arms. "What do you think *is* fair?" he asked, frowning with irritation.

Rising Eagle picked up two more blankets and handed them to Buffalo Dreamer. Then he took one of the black iron pots and carried it over to the boxes of beads, buttons, and ribbons, where he promptly grabbed handfuls of every color of each and loaded them into the pot. He then filled a brown sack with sugar and handed it to Tall Woman.

"Hey, wait!" the storekeeper shouted.

"Leave him be," McConnel told him. "I'll get you a good trade, Jake. Besides, I have a feeling this is one Indian you don't mess with."

Rising Eagle handed the pot to Yellow Turtle Woman, who could hardly hang on to it for its weight. He turned to McConnel. "*That* is fair," he said flatly.

McConnel rubbed the back of his neck, sighing

deeply as he considered the deal. "All right," he finally said. "Let the women take the pretty beads and buttons and go make you a fancy shirt with it."

Rising Eagle told the women they could keep the pot full of goodies, the blankets, sugar, and mirror, and Tall Woman and Yellow Turtle Woman gleefully left with the treasure. Buffalo Dreamer stayed with Rising Eagle, feeling safer at his side, and worried over what might happen if he spotted Gray Owl. Rising Eagle turned and pointed to a musket hanging in brackets on the wall behind the counter, indicating to McConnel that he would like to see the "firestick."

"Show me," he signed. "I wish to learn how to use the white man's weapon. I have a very fine horse to trade."

McConnel asked the storekeeper to lift the gun down. "Give me some shot and powder, too, Jake," he added. "I'll go look at the man's horse and see what it's worth. If it ain't worth enough, I'll bring the musket back."

"You ought to go see Newt about some whiskey," the storekeeper answered. He took a powder horn and a small pouch of shot from under the glass counter and handed them to McConnel. "Might be the big buck here would rather have a couple bottles of firewater for the horse, instead of a weapon he could end up using against us."

He winked and grinned, and Rising Eagle watched every move and listened to every word. He understood nothing of what the man said, except the word "firewater." By the look on the storekeeper's face, the man obviously thought he could somehow fool him. His attitude only assured Rising Eagle that the strange firewater was something he should avoid.

McConnel turned to him and tried to explain the suggestion of trading for whiskey instead of a gun. Rising Eagle shook his head vigorously. "I want no firewater. Only the long gun. You show me," he repeated, indicating he wanted to learn how to use the weapon.

McConnel shrugged and looked back at the store-keeper. "Don't be concerned about what the women took, Jake. I've seen this man's furs, and they're worth what the squaws took." He turned and motioned for Rising Eagle to follow him, and Buffalo Dreamer stayed close behind, trying to avoid the smell of the white men. She followed Rising Eagle and McConnel outside the fort to an open area, where McConnel carefully demonstrated how to load the long gun. He walked over to a stump and set a tin can on it, then walked back to Rising Eagle and hoisted the heavy musket. He fired, and Buffalo Dreamer jumped at the loud boom, covering her ears. At almost the same moment the gun was fired, the tin can flew into the air and landed several feet away.

"Go take a look," McConnel told Rising Eagle, nodding toward the can. Although he spoke the words in English, Rising Eagle understood the gesture. First he handed the corncob pipe to Buffalo Dreamer, then took the musket from McConnel and felt of its weight, raised it to his shoulder to get a feel of it. He handed it back and walked over close to the stump to look at the can, paying no attention to two approaching riders. He studied the can, impressed by the big hole in it. He would gladly trade a horse for the musket. If the white man should ever use such a weapon against the Lakota, the Lakota must have the same kind of weapon to fight back with.

"Dundee!" he heard McConnel shout then. "Over here! You've been gone a hell of a long time."

Rising Eagle straightened at the name Dundee, all senses coming alert. He remained turned away for a moment. If John Dundee was riding toward them, so was Gray Owl! He waited until he could hear the horses come much closer, pretending to continue studying the can. He did not want Gray Owl to notice

him too soon and ride off. He glanced at Buffalo
Dreamer, telling her with his eyes to stay calm and
not call out.

"Got a good supply of meat this time around." The
words were spoken in the white man's tongue. Rising
Eagle guessed it must be the one called John Dundee.
He set down the can and wrapped his fingers around
his hunting knife, then slowly turned. Just as he
thought, Gray Owl sat on a horse beside a white man
in buckskins. Both men led packhorses laden with
fresh-killed game. Gray Owl stared back at him in
shock, turning his gaze then to Buffalo Dreamer, then
back to Rising Eagle.

"Afternoon, James!" Dundee greeted McConnel. He
held up a brown bottle. "How about a swallow?"

"Always thirsty for the good stuff." McConnel
looked from Dundee to Rising Eagle, then to Gray
Owl, who did not ride forward with Dundee. Mc-
Connel saw the surprise on Gray Owl's face and remembered Rising Eagle's confrontation the day before
with Fall Leaf Woman. "Shit! I think your friend's in
trouble, John." He hardly finished the sentence before
Rising Eagle charged toward Gray Owl, knife in hand.

CHAPTER FIFTY-THREE

GRAY OWL DROPPED the reins to his packhorse and turned his own horse, kicking its sides. Buffalo Dreamer knew that Rising Eagle would expect such cowardliness. Already on the run by the time Gray Owl turned his horse, Rising Eagle leaped onto the fleeing horse's rump and tackled Gray Owl, sending both men crashing to the ground.

Two white women walking nearby screamed and dropped their packages, running away. Buffalo Dreamer quickly eyed McConnel and Dundee remembering Dundee's name as the man whom Rising Eagle told her had married Fall Leaf Woman. McConnel still held the white man's long gun, and Dundee held a similar weapon. Would they try to stop the fight by shooting Rising Eagle?

"What the hell?" Dundee watched the ensuing fight dumbfounded. "Jesus, James, what's that big buck doin' tacklin' Gray Owl?"

Buffalo Dreamer could not understand any of the conversation, but she did not like the look in John Dundee's eyes: anger, surprise, wariness. He walked closer to the wrestling, tumbling pair, and several more white men gathered around.

Rising Eagle pinned Gray Owl on his back and raised his knife. Gray Owl grasped his wrist with both hands to try to stop him from plunging the weapon into his heart. At the same time, Dundee pulled out a weapon at his waist, which looked to Buffalo Dreamer like a shorter version of a firestick.

"No!" she yelled to McConnel in the Lakota tongue.

McConnel grasped Dundee's wrist and pushed up. "Leave it alone," he ordered.

Buffalo Dreamer felt great relief that McConnel apparently understood. "I wouldn't interfere, unless you want to get yourself staked out in the sun and skinned alive," McConnel warned Dundee. "Rising Eagle has a hell of a lot of friends out there."

Dundee grudgingly shoved his handgun back into its holster, glowering at the two men who struggled. "Gray Owl and I are damn good friends, drinking partners. Hell, his sister is my wife! She'll be right pissed if her brother gets killed."

"Ain't nothin' can be done about it," McConnel answered. "Must be some pretty bad blood between 'em."

Buffalo Dreamer watched the exchange. She did not like the way John Dundee looked at Rising Eagle, but now her first concern must be the struggle between her husband and Gray Owl. Rising Eagle wrapped a powerful left hand around Gray Owl's throat and pressed hard. Gray Owl held off Rising Eagle's knife hand as long as he could, but soon lack of air forced him to drop his hands. Rising Eagle's knife came down, but not into Gray Owl's heart as expected. Instead, he sliced off Gray Owl's left ear.

Various curses of surprise emanated from the gathered crowd of white men, and Buffalo Dreamer stood frozen in place, surprised herself that Rising Eagle did not kill Gray Owl. Before Gray Owl could recover his breath, Rising Eagle sliced off his other ear, and now blood poured from both sides of his head.

Gray Owl pressed his hands to his ears, regaining his breath and screaming. He tried to get up and run, but Rising Eagle forced him back to the ground, slamming his head sideways against the gravel. Onlookers stared in astonishment then when Rising Eagle swiftly whacked off Gray Owl's nose.

Grown men gasped, and some turned away at the sight.

"A traitorous wife has her nose cut off," Rising Eagle growled at Gray Owl. "Surely a man who betrays the entire Lakota Nation deserves no less! Now you are marked forever for the coward that you are!"

Rising Eagle stood up, his near-naked body covered with dirt and sweat, and with Gray Owl's blood. His dark eyes gleamed with sweet revenge. "I should tie you down and slowly peel your skin away until you are *dead,* but then you would suffer only a short while. This way, you suffer *forever!*"

Gray Owl made no reply. He only gave out a sickening gurgling sound, a mixture of weeping and groaning. Rising Eagle rammed his knife into its sheath and faced John Dundee, who fingered his handgun nervously as Rising Eagle stepped closer.

"You are John Dundee?"

Dundee knew enough Lakota to understand the question. He nodded, facing Rising Eagle squarely, built nearly as tall and broad. "What the hell do you care, Indian?"

Rising Eagle glanced at McConnel. "Interpret for him what I say now," he asked.

The look in McConnel's eyes told Rising Eagle the man was not about to argue with him. He nodded, and Rising Eagle turned back to Dundee. "You are cruel to your wife," he declared. "If you continue beating Fall Leaf Woman, I will do to you what I have just done to her brother."

Dundee stepped back as McConnel interpreted for him. A worried Buffalo Dreamer walked cautiously closer, moving among a crowd of men who reeked of perspiration and unwashed bodies. Dundee looked just as dirty, his buckskins soiled and his face covered with a stubby beard.

"Who the hell are you, that you dare talk to me that way?" Dundee demanded.

McConnel continued to help interpret.

"I am Rising Eagle. Fall Leaf Woman knew me as Stalking Wolf. I have seen her, and I know that you are cruel to her. I will come back here again, and I will know if you have continued to abuse her. If you have, you will not live another day." Rising Eagle turned to McConnel, glancing at the musket. "I wish to trade my horse for the long gun. Come with me to my camp, and I will show you the horse."

McConnel swallowed. "Well now, I'm not so sure I want to walk into a Lakota Indian camp with you in this mood," he tried to joke. He turned to Dundee. "Remember what I told you. Keep that handgun in its holster. I've got a feelin' this one is pretty important. You could start a passel of trouble if you use that thing."

"I don't like bein' threatened!" Dundee answered, still glaring at Rising Eagle.

"And I like my *scalp*," McConnel answered. "Hell, it's only an Indian he hurt, not a white man. Whatever Gray Owl did, he must deserve this punishment by Indian custom, so let it be."

Dundee glanced at Gray Owl, who still writhed on the ground, blood covering his hands, arms, chest, and mixing into the dirt. He turned then to Rising Eagle, hatred burning in his eyes. He guzzled down more whiskey. "Go trade for his horse," he grumbled to McConnel. "I'd just as soon open a hole in his belly, but I won't—not now, anyway."

The surrounding crowd of men mumbled among themselves, most gawking at Gray Owl, some looking warily at Rising Eagle, who turned to Buffalo Dreamer. "Today you are avenged, and I tell you now that never again will I allow an enemy to carry you away!"

Buffalo Dreamer knew his pride had suffered deeply

when the Crow carried her off while others took him down and nearly killed him. Rising Eagle did not take defeat lightly. Now he had found his revenge, and his face glowed with it. He turned to McConnel. "Bring the gun!" he ordered. He took Buffalo Dreamer's arm and headed back to camp.

McConnel followed. "Far be it for me to argue with an angry Lakota warrior," he muttered. He obeyed Rising Eagle's request, leaving behind a bloody, groveling Gray Owl and an infuriated John Dundee.

CHAPTER FIFTY-FOUR

THE CROWD OF white men walked about nervously, none sure of what to do for Gray Owl. From behind a wooden fence, Fall Leaf Woman had witnessed the entire event. Rising Eagle had done a terrible thing to her brother, yet she knew the Lakota way, and Gray Owl could have expected no less. Her brother had allowed himself to grow more confident over the past several moons, sure that Rising Eagle would not come for him after all, but Fall Leaf Woman always knew that he would.

She should hate Rising Eagle for leaving Gray Owl an ugly, scarred mess. But Rising Eagle also had defended her to John. That surprised and touched her. Rising Eagle was so much more man than John Dundee would ever be. She wished Little Wolf could be raised by such a man.

John walked over and offered Gray Owl the rest of the whiskey in his bottle. "Pour some on the wounds, Gray Owl, then drink the rest. We'll get you more to kill the pain."

Gray Owl eagerly took the bottle, guzzling down part of its contents, then crying out when he dashed some against his maimed nose. Fall Leaf Woman came out from hiding then and walked closer. "How can I help you, Gray Owl?"

"Get away!" Gray Owl refused to look at her. Fall Leaf Woman felt sick at the sight of the bloody holes on his head where his ears once were. He kept a hand over his nose as he drank more whiskey, and he remained turned away from her. "You should have sent someone to warn me!" he barked, already beginning to slur his words.

"I did not know you would be back this soon. If Rising Eagle did not leave tomorrow, I meant to send someone to tell you. I am sorry, Gray Owl, but you knew that this could happen. It was your own actions that caused it." She gasped when suddenly John grabbed hold of her wrist in a painful grip.

"How much have you already seen of that big buck?" he snarled.

"I only saw him for a moment when he first rode into the fort," she answered, trying to jerk her arm away.

"You had enough time to tell him I *beat* you and try to win his *sympathy*!"

"I told him nothing of the kind! He knew it just by *looking* at me, my eyes, my face! Rising Eagle is not a fool!"

"He's a fool to threaten *me*! A fool to tell me how I can treat my own *wife*!" He gave her a shove. "And just how loyal a wife *are* you, woman? Did you lay for that buck—for old times' sake, maybe?"

"I told you—"

John backhanded her and sent her sprawling to the ground. A few of the onlookers chuckled; others just frowned and shook their heads. Most were already gone.

Fall Leaf Woman put a shaky hand to her face, and tears welled in her eyes. Before she could get back to her feet on her own, Dundee jerked her up by an arm and yanked her close. "You hopin' that worthless Indian will come after me for this? Huh?"

"I told you I only spoke to him for a moment. I said nothing—"

"Stop your lies, you slut! I hope he *does* come for me. I *welcome* the chance to blow a hole in his belly.

I don't take kindly to an ignorant Indian threatenin' me, especially when it's in front of half the men of this fort."

Fall Leaf Woman finally jerked her arm away. "He is not ignorant, nor worthless! He is *Naca!* He is a high-ranking warrior, and a prophet. He is more man that you will ever be . . . in *every* way!"

She knew she would suffer for the words, but at the moment, it seemed worth it. Dundee grabbed her close.

"I'll show you how much man I am!"

Before Fall Leaf Woman could utter a sound, her husband slammed a fist into her mouth. She fell again, and dizziness overwhelmed her. She had no fight left in her as John again pulled her to her feet and half dragged her to their cabin. Onlookers shook their heads, joking about the marriage, unconcerned for Fall Leaf Woman. After all, she was only a squaw.

CHAPTER FIFTY-FIVE

BUFFALO DREAMER COULD not sleep. Accustomed to the quiet of an Indian camp at night, the constant noise here disturbed her. Strange-sounding music in the distance continued all night, a tinkling sound she did not recognize. Besides the music, loud voices, and sometimes shrieking laughter, also filled the air. Added to that, a steamboat occasionally disgorged several short whistle blasts.

Buffalo Dreamer wondered how the white man could stand so much noise. By day, it was clattering wagons, whistling steamboats, gunshots from men practicing with their weapons, oddly feathered birds that clucked and crowed and strutted about pecking at things, strange-looking mule horses that made ugly wheezing noises instead of whinnying.

She saw nothing really pretty here, except the river itself. Still, the river, the blood of earth, surely could not flow as easily or as clean and pure when clogged with those big, belching boats.

Irritated and upset, Buffalo Dreamer sat up, glad that Cries Loudly was managing to sleep through all the unfamiliar noises.

"What is wrong?" Rising Eagle also sat up. He looked at her from across a dying central fire, for they still slept apart.

"You know what is wrong. This place makes me restless and afraid, Rising Eagle. I miss the peace and quiet of home, the beauty of the Black Hills. And I

worry for you. Some of those white men will disap-
prove of what you did to Gray Owl. I did not like the
look on John Dundee's face today when you warned
him not to hurt Fall Leaf Woman anymore."

Rising Eagle rubbed his eyes. "I have no worry
about that one. I probably should have killed him then
and there, but he is a white man, and many white men
were around us. I was more afraid for you than for
myself." He sighed. "We will leave in the morning, if
that is your wish. I have the long gun, and we have
traded all our furs and skins for some fine things."

Buffalo Dreamer rose and stepped into her tunic,
tying the shoulders. "Something is not right. I feel it,"
she said softly, trying not to wake the baby. "Put
something on, Rising Eagle."

Frowning, Rising Eagle obeyed, respecting his
wife's keen instincts. He covered his nakedness with
a pair of light deerskin leggings, and just as he laced
them, someone called to them softly from outside.

"Rising Eagle. Are you there?"

Rising Eagle and Buffalo Dreamer looked at each
other in surprise. It was a woman's voice.

"We are here," Buffalo Dreamer answered. "Who is
it?"

"It is I, Fall Leaf Woman. I must speak with you.
Please, let me in quickly!"

Buffalo Dreamer pushed back the entrance flap, and
Rising Eagle marveled at his wife's intuition that they
might have a visitor.

Fall Leaf Woman stepped inside. Rising Eagle
added wood to the central fire to bring more light, and
Fall Leaf Woman sat down on the women's side of
the dwelling. In her arms she held her fully wrapped
baby close. As the fire blazed a little higher, Buffalo
Dreamer gasped at the sight of Fall Leaf Woman's
battered face—a swollen and bleeding bottom lip, a
dark purpling on her right cheek—and the bruises on

her neck. The once-proud woman bent over her baby and wept.

"Fall Leaf Woman! What has happened?" Buffalo Dreamer asked the question, going near her and putting a hand on her shoulder. "Let me take your baby and—"

"No!" She held her baby closer. "Not yet! It is soon enough when I will never hold him again."

Buffalo Dreamer moved away, looking to Rising Eagle for help.

Rising Eagle's jaw flexed with anger. "He has hurt you again! I will *kill* him!"

"No!" Fall Leaf Woman looked at him with fear and pleading in her eyes. "I did not come here for that. Please do not kill him, Rising Eagle. Not here, where there are so many white men. I do not want trouble for you. It is important that you leave here in peace, for I have something to ask of you."

Rising Eagle hesitated in confusion. "Why did he beat you?"

Fall Leaf Woman faced him squarely. "Because he—" She glanced at Buffalo Dreamer. "He would not believe that I did not lay with you while he was gone, and he is angry that you threatened him."

"I *meant* what I told him."

Fall Leaf Woman sniffled and wiped at her tears with one hand, unable to press too hard because of her injuries. "You must let it be, Rising Eagle. It is not his fault that he would think such a thing, for I mentioned you to him often. He knows what happened between you and Gray Owl in the past, and how I feel about you. He thinks that you came for me, to take me away from here."

"And I will, if that is your choice."

New tears came to her eyes. "I can never go back. You know that. Now you have angered my husband and brought shame to my brother. But because I once loved you—and still do love you—I come to ask you to do something for me, something that would be better than taking me back to the Oglala."

Rising Eagle sat back on his heels and glanced over at Buffalo Dreamer.

"You must hear her out, my husband." Buffalo Dreamer felt sorry for Fall Leaf Woman's predicament, in spite of the bad feelings they had once held for each other.

Rising Eagle frowned and faced Fall Leaf Woman, anger still burning in his heart at what a coward her husband must be to use his superior strength to beat the mother of his child. "What is it you would ask?"

Fall Leaf Woman swallowed. "Whatever my brother did to you, and in spite of the trouble I tried to cause for you and Buffalo Dreamer, my son is innocent. I know in my heart he will never carry my wildness and troublemaking ways, and he does not have his father's evil heart."

Rising Eagle nodded, still confused. "The child is always innocent."

Fall Leaf Woman took a deep breath before continuing. "Then I ask a great favor of you." She turned to Buffalo Dreamer. "I want you to take my son. I want him to be raised with pride . . . among the Oglala."

Buffalo Dreamer gasped at Fall Leaf Woman's request. For a woman to give away a child was the same as to tear out her heart.

CHAPTER FIFTY-SIX

BUFFALO DREAMER SAW in her husband's eyes the same surprise she felt. "There is no need for you to give away your son," she told Fall Leaf Woman. "It is not true that you can never come back to *Paha-Sapa*. You and your son can both come with us tomorrow when we leave. You have the right to throw away your husband. Rising Eagle is not afraid of John Dundee."

Fall Leaf Woman shook her head. She wiped at her eyes with the palm of her hand, looking forlorn in a plain gray-cotton dress worn thin in many places.

"No proper Oglala man would want me for a wife. And too much has changed. I am of no use to the Oglala anymore. I have grown accustomed to my life here, living like a white woman. I wish only to protect my son. My husband hates the child because he is . . . deformed."

Buffalo Dreamer drew in her breath at the shocking news, and she glanced at Rising Eagle, who frowned in concern.

"Being deformed does not mean he cannot be loved," Fall Leaf Woman added defensively. "If I give him away, it will be best for him. My husband is the most cruel when I give attention to the baby, and sometimes he threatens to hurt the boy because he has no love for him. I could not bear that. If he hurts him, I will kill my husband, and then the white men would kill me. My son would be left with no one to care for him. Even if that does not happen, my son will have a bad life here. My husband will be cruel to him and the other whites will look down on him also, because he is deformed and because of his Indian blood. Most of them have no respect for the Lakota."

Fall Leaf Woman spoke with great effort, the words slightly slurred because of her torn lips.

"It is a difficult thing that I ask of you," she continued, keeping her eyes on Buffalo Dreamer, "but I know now that you are special, holy. Surely a holy woman of the Oglala, and one of the Lakota's best and most blessed warriors, would raise my son to be strong and proud, a hunter and warrior, in spite of his condition. If I stay here with him, he will never prosper and be happy. With you, he will live and grow into a fine, strong man."

She turned her attention to Rising Eagle. "I can think of no one better to raise my son than he whom I would have wanted to truly be the father of my children. I am confident you can mold him into a man of respect and pride. Once a white doctor who came here told me that my Little Wolf will always be slow, that he will not learn easily. The Oglala understand that sometimes *Wakan-Tanka* gives some of us special gifts. I am confident that Little Wolf has a gift from the Great Spirit that will be known only if he is raised among those who understand this, and who would care for him lovingly, no matter how slow or clumsy he might be. Will you accept him into your family, provide for him, guide and teach him, be like a father to him?"

Rising Eagle turned to stare at the fire, giving out a long sigh. "You ask much of us." He thought for a moment before continuing. "Show us the child."

Hesitantly, Fall Leaf Woman laid the baby near Rising Eagle. She unfolded the blanket around him, and Rising Eagle and Buffalo Dreamer studied his clear and handsome little face. He opened his blue eyes and grinned, kicking his spindly legs when Rising Eagle bent over to study the missing fingers and toes.

Buffalo Dreamer's heart went out to the child, so small, his little limbs thin and frail, but he cooed and smiled as though he had not a care.

"He has a good spirit," Fall Leaf Woman said. "He seldom cries, except when John does something to startle him."

"He has eyes like the sky," Buffalo Dreamer commented.

Rising Eagle touched a finger to the baby's fist, and Little Wolf grasped it with what fingers he had, but his grip was weak. "He will need much help."

"I believe you are the one who will understand his spirit and see his gifts," Fall Leaf Woman told him. "Giving him away is the hardest thing I will ever do." Her voice broke into more sobs. "I would like him welcomed . . . the way all new babies are welcomed into the family of the Oglala," she wept. "I want him to have all the same ceremonies as any other young man. I want him to be proud . . . to be Oglala, and to understand . . . why I gave him to you."

"We will make him understand," Buffalo Dreamer answered.

Fall Leaf Woman wiped at more tears. "Does that mean you will take him?"

Buffalo Dreamer faced Rising Eagle. "I would like to take him. And I know my mother would be made happy having him to care for. What do you think, Rising Eagle?"

Rising Eagle lightly touched the baby's forehead. "We will take him, if that is your wish." He looked at Fall Leaf Woman. "I will have him blessed by old Crow Chasing Woman. She can sing over him, perhaps help affect his mind and growth. He will be passed among the *Nacas,* who will touch him and pray for him. Then I will take him to Medicine Mountain and offer him to the Feathered One for blessings."

Deeply moved, Fall Leaf Woman gasped with delight. "Then I will know there is great hope for my son! Knowing that will ease the pain and loneliness in my heart." She grasped a small flask that had been tied to her waistband and uncorked it. She took a swallow of its contents. "And this will help dry my tears, help make all the pain go away."

Rising Eagle straightened, the softness in his eyes turning to anger. "What do you drink, Fall Leaf Woman?"

She wiped at another tear and stared at the flask. "It is the white man's firewater. I cannot go long without it. It is my strength."

Frowning, Rising Eagle rose, walked over and grabbed the flask. He sniffed it, then tasted its contents. He made a face and spit out the liquid. "It is *evil!* Perhaps it is the reason your child is deformed. I have heard about this firewater, and what I know tells me it is bad!"

"No!" Fall Leaf Woman protested. "It has great powers to stop pain and bring happiness." She rose to face him. "Please, Rising Eagle, give it back to me!"

"It *controls* you and causes you to abandon your son!" He turned and threw the flask out of the tepee. "It is *bad,* Fall Leaf Woman, and if you would give it up, you could come back with us and be with your son. The *firewater* is the reason you cannot leave this place, is it not?"

Fall Leaf Woman put a hand to her mouth, crying harder again. "No. No, it is not the firewater."

"Admit it!"

Cries Loudly awoke at the sound of loud voices. He stared at his father with big, dark eyes, not sure what to think of the shouting. Buffalo Dreamer reached over and tickled his cheek to reassure him.

"You do not understand," Fall Leaf Woman told them. "The whiskey soothes my heart, and it ... it takes away pain. I need it."

"You only *think* that you need it," Rising Eagle scolded. "It takes control of your mind and makes you do foolish things, like stay here among the *wasicus* and marry one of them, a man who is cruel to you and hates his own child! Look at what the whiskey has done to *you*. You give your baby away, instead of throwing away the man who abuses you."

Fall Leaf Woman covered her face. "I need him, Rising Eagle. John Dundee gives me the whiskey." She choked in a sob and faced him. "But it is not the whiskey that makes me give away my son. It is my love for him . . . and for *you!* I give my son to the strongest, bravest, and most holy warrior of the Oglala because I love him dearly and want what I know is best for him, something I can *never* give him!"

Rising Eagle shook his head. "I am sorry for you, Fall Leaf Woman."

Fall Leaf Woman wept harder, but her tears were interrupted when she heard her name shouted from outside.

"Fall Leaf Woman! Where are you, you bitch!"

Fall Leaf Woman's eyes grew bigger, and she moved farther back. "It is John. When I left him, he was in deep sleep from drinking much whiskey. I thought that he would not wake up!"

"If you're with that stinkin' Indian savage, I'll kill him! I'll kill *both* of you!" Dundee yelled.

Fall Leaf Woman quickly interpreted for Rising Eagle as John Dundee's voice came closer. "He does not know which dwelling is yours," she added quietly, shaking with fear. "He might not find me. I found you only because I asked one of your scouts who stood guard for the night."

"You do not belong here!" Wind In Grass, who stood night guard outside, shouted the words at Dundee.

"I go wherever I damn well please," Dundee answered gruffly.

"Do not let him hurt me again, or my son," Fall Leaf Woman asked, cringing farther away.

Rising Eagle looked at Buffalo Dreamer. "Hide the boy behind the pile of robes." He turned to Fall Leaf Woman. "You choose to stay here, so go to your husband."

Buffalo Dreamer picked up the baby to hide him, and Fall Leaf Woman shivered at the sound of Dundee arguing with someone outside. "He is drunk. He will beat me again."

"Where are you, woman?" John shouted again. "Get your whorin' ass out here in front of me. Bring that wife-stealing bastard buck with you so I can blow his guts out!"

Buffalo Dreamer did not understand everything John Dundee said, but it was obviously another barrage of insults, and she feared for Rising Eagle.

"He says he will kill you," Fall Leaf Woman told them.

Rising Eagle curled his lip in disgust. "Then let him try," he answered. He ducked outside.

CHAPTER FIFTY-SEVEN

SEVERAL OGLALA MEN gathered around John Dundee, who whirled in circles, flailing a handgun and threatening to shoot any of them who came too close. Rising Eagle pushed through the gathering of warriors, and Dundee stopped short when he saw him. He grinned, the whites of his eyes red from too much whiskey.

"Well, it's about time." He spoke the words in English, but then, in the Lakota tongue, he called Rising Eagle a wife-stealing coward. He cocked his gun, but was too drunk to hold it steady, and too drunk to be able to react quickly to anything Rising Eagle might do. Before he could fire the gun, Rising Eagle kicked upward, knocking the weapon aside.

Dundee lunged for the gun, but Rising Eagle kicked his rump, so that he stumbled and fell forward. The other warriors laughed at him, and a furious Dundee rose and turned, pulling a knife from a belt at his waist. He lunged at Rising Eagle, who simply put a shoulder into the man as Dundee charged him. He grasped the man's right wrist and forced his hand outward, then shoved him onto his back and landed on top of him. Dundee grunted and dropped his knife, and Rising Eagle stood and jerked him to his feet.

"Now you will go home. I want no trouble here."

Dundee stood on wobbly legs, glaring at Rising Eagle. Fall Leaf Woman ventured outside then and approached her husband. "Come home, John," she told him. "Do not make any more trouble here."

Dundee stiffened and looked her over. "You stinkin' squaw whore! You've been with him, haven't you? Where's my son?"

"You do not want your son, so why do you ask? I have given him away, to be raised by a people who will *love* him and raise him proudly."

He grasped her arms, snarling his words. "You'd *never* give that half-breed bastard to *anybody!* You came here because you lusted after your old Indian lover! You just used the baby as an excuse. I'm sick of you moanin' over that worthless, deformed *brat!*" He drew back his fist and slammed it into Fall Leaf Woman's face. She cried out and fell, and Rising Eagle hesitated at first to help her. Lakota custom forbade interference in domestic disputes, but he had already warned Dundee about abusing Fall Leaf Woman again, and he still felt an obligation to protect her.

"I'll make sure that kid doesn't take your attention from me again!" Dundee raged. He searched for his pistol, but he could hardly stand. "I'll shoot the little bastard!" He looked around menacingly. "Hell, I'll just smash his soft little head between my hands!" He started past Rising Eagle and tried to enter the tepee. "Where is the deformed little nit?"

"No! Do not touch Little Wolf!" Fall Leaf Woman looked at Rising Eagle, screaming for him to stop Dundee from finding the baby.

Inside the tepee, both babies were crying, upset by all the commotion. Buffalo Dreamer screamed when Dundee started to enter but Rising Eagle, unable to hold back his outrage any longer, grabbed the man by his long hair and jerked him away. Buffalo Dreamer scrambled to the tepee entrance, hearing Rising Eagle's shouted words as she ran outside.

"You will not hurt Fall Leaf Woman or your son again!" Standing behind Dundee, Rising Eagle yanked the man's head backward and pulled his own knife from its sheath.

"No, Rising Eagle!" Buffalo Dreamer cried, too late.

Rising Eagle sliced the knife across Dundee's throat. He stepped back and let the man's body slump to the ground. Dundee writhed, making gurgling noises as blood poured from his jugular. His body finally went limp, and Fall Leaf Woman, still on the ground herself, put a trembling hand to where her husband had again split the skin on her left cheek. She stared wide-eyed at his dead body, tears streaming down her face and mixing with blood from her own wound. She crawled to where Dundee lay, touching his hand before looking up at Rising Eagle.

"What will I do now?" she screamed. "You have killed my husband and destroyed my brother!"

Rising Eagle stood over the body, blood still dripping from his knife. "You told me not to let him touch your son. Now he also will never hurt *you* again. I have only done your bidding, Fall Leaf Woman."

Gasping with the trauma of her ordeal, Fall Leaf Woman crawled away from the body, looking confused. She began searching the ground on hands and knees, as though she had lost something. Then her face brightened, and she got to her feet and stumbled over to where the flask of whiskey had landed after Rising Eagle threw it out earlier. She bent down and grasped it, then took a long swallow. Rising Eagle closed his eyes at the sight.

"What should we do with John Dundee?" Wind In Grass asked. "The white traders might be very angry about this."

Rising Eagle sighed. "I am not sure."

Fall Leaf Woman rose and staggered closer, tossing her hair behind her shoulders. "You must hide his body until you go away, or the white men inside the trading post will make much trouble for you," she told

Rising Eagle. "They all liked John Dundee. Tomorrow I will tell them . . . that he took our son out to the Lakota to give him away. They will believe that, for they know John did not want the boy." She took another swallow from the little bottle. "Do as I say, or there could be much trouble for you. It will be best if you do nothing to look suspicious. Tomorrow you will rise as normal, and you will leave for *Paha-Sapa*. I will wait until you are gone many hours, and then I will tell those inside the fort that after taking our son out to the Lakota, my husband never returned. They will look for him, and they will probably find his body . . . wherever you choose to put it. They will know then . . . but you will be gone. They will not follow you into Oglala country. They will be too afraid. Then, finally, my son will be away from here."

She turned to Buffalo Dreamer. "Remember this," she slurred. "The white man does not forgive when a man from any Indian tribe kills one of their own. I know. I have heard . . . from white men who know. Once there were people like us living in the land of the rising sun." She waved her arm. "Thousands of them. Most of them are gone now . . . killed or died out because of the white man and his diseases. Do not let that happen to the Lakota."

She stepped closer to Buffalo Dreamer, wavering on unsteady feet. "Take my son. Let him suckle at your breast and come to believe you are his mother. Never tell him about me. I do not want him to be ashamed. Tell him . . . his blue eyes . . . are a gift from the Great Spirit. Raise him to be strong and brave, a proud Lakota man."

"What will you do, Fall Leaf Woman, without your husband to provide for you?" Buffalo Dreamer asked.

Fall Leaf Woman smiled sadly. "I will survive. You have much to learn . . . about the white man. He readily pays in gifts and supplies for a woman in his bed, especially the trappers who come here after a long winter without even seeing a woman. Their manpart is always hungry. Remember that." She turned to Rising Eagle. "They also lie. They make promises . . . that they never keep. Never trust them." She looked him over hungrily, then staggered away.

All watched quietly until she disappeared into the darkness. Rising Eagle turned to Buffalo Dreamer. "The babies are quiet again. Keep them from crying." He turned to the warriors gathered around him, who included Buffalo Calf, Wind In Grass, and Runs With The Deer. "What should we do with Dundee's body, my uncle?" he asked Runs With The Deer.

"I think it is wise to hide it, as Fall Leaf Woman told us. Wrap it in a buffalo robe. We will find a good place."

Rising Eagle nodded in agreement. "Keep the small firestick he carried. Perhaps we can make use of it." He turned to Buffalo Dreamer. "Get a robe from inside."

Buffalo Dreamer hesitated, holding his gaze. "We will leave this place in the morning?"

Rising Eagle nodded. "We will leave." He looked down at Dundee's body again. "Already the warnings of the Feathered One can be seen to be true."

"The morning is not soon enough for me," Buffalo Dreamer told him. "I want to leave tonight."

Rising Eagle looked around at the others, seeing the same wish in their eyes. "All right then. I too miss the quiet of the Black Hills. We will go tonight. Tell the women to begin packing their tepees and supplies and to put the babies in their cradleboards. We must be as quiet as possible."

Everyone moved quickly then. Rising Eagle and Runs With The Deer wrapped Dundee's body in a buffalo robe. "Leave it to me and Bold Fox," Runs With The Deer told his nephew. "Stay here and help your wife. If we are not back by the time you leave, go without us. We will catch up."

Rising Eagle nodded. "Thank you, Uncle."

Runs With The Deer touched his arm. "This is a bad place. It is good that we go."

With hardly a sound, the huge contingent of Oglala packed up and left, and no one inside the fort or sleeping in tepees and cabins around the compound even knew they had departed until the next day, when they discovered the entire Oglala camp empty, only a few smoldering campfires left behind.

Not far away, a white woman opened the door to a dugout where she stored vegetables. A terrible smell struck her nostrils, and she thought at first it might be from rotted potatoes. When her eyes adjusted to the dark interior, she noticed a buffalo robe in one corner, and she felt a chill. Flies buzzed around the robe as the woman cautiously walked closer and leaned down. She carefully lifted a corner of the robe, and her screams could be heard for a great distance, both inside and outside the fort.

MID-AUGUST
1834

Moon of the Dry Dust Blowing

CHAPTER FIFTY-EIGHT

THE DANCING AND singing went on for days as the drums of the Oglala sounded their celebration to the spirits of earth and sky. In this season of blowing dust, the Oglala had chosen to hold their summer Sun Dance separate from the rest of the Lakota, and they combined the ritual with the celebration of welcoming new babies. Adding to their happiness at the occasion was the fact that upon returning from Fort Pierre, the men had enjoyed a successful buffalo hunt. Rising Eagle had brought down two of the shaggy beasts with his long gun.

Only days before the Sun Dance, Rising Eagle had tutored young Buffalo Calf through his first vision quest. Deep in the Black Hills, in a secret place chosen by himself, Rising Eagle had faithfully sat with the young man through three days of fasting, until Buffalo Calf suddenly began growling and prowling about before finally collapsing. When he regained consciousness, he remembered thinking he had become a bear, dancing fearlessly with the enemy. In honor of the young man's vision, Rising Eagle declared Buffalo Calf should now be called Bear Dancing.

During the week-long celebrations, Buffalo Dreamer held her own special feast to welcome her son into the Oglala fold, and also to formally introduce Little Wolf as her and Rising Eagle's new adopted son. The Sun Dance lodge surged with singing and drumming. When young Sun Dancers completed their sacrifices of flesh, the ceremony for renaming Buffalo Calf took place, followed by the men offering prayers of thanksgiving for a good hunt.

Then came the welcoming of all new babies born since the last Sun Dance. Many Robes Woman's son, Makes Fist, was among the babies to be blessed. Swaying together, mothers sang a rhythmic song of love and joy for their offspring. The fathers held their sons and daughters high over their heads and danced around a central fire.

A fast-growing Cries Loudly, now four moons old, matched the older babies in size. Arrow Runner held up Makes Fist, and in Rising Eagle's place, Runs With The Deer held up Little Wolf. Although eight moons in age, the tiny infant was smaller than Cries Loudly. Still, he seemed alert, so alert, in fact, that he seldom slept.

Buffalo Dreamer enjoyed her mother's help with both children. Tall Woman often carried Little Wolf in his cradleboard on her own back, and Buffalo Dreamer realized that her mother liked pretending that Little Wolf belonged to her. Tall Woman dismissed the boy's abnormalities, declaring they were surely given him for a reason.

According to Lakota custom, babies were renamed at their welcoming celebration. Moon Painter officially renamed Makes Fist, calling him Little Beaver. Little Wolf became Never Sleeps, and Cries Loudly became Big Little Boy.

The celebration brought a lighter note to the many days of prayers and rituals that took place during the first part of the Sun Dance. Now that the Sun Dancers had recovered from their self-inflicted wounds, the time came for pure fun. Part of the celebration included the Night Dance, now Buffalo Dreamer's favorite. Each summer since that first Night Dance, when she was forced to throw her blanket over Rising Eagle, the dance had became more important to her, more meaningful, as her feelings for her husband turned to a love deeper than she had dreamed possible.

Tonight Tall Woman watched both babies for Buffalo Dreamer, who wanted very much to join the Night Dance. The warm and beautiful night, and all the joys to be savored, made her heart happy. The little tin pieces she and some of the other women had sewn into the ends of their dress fringes tinkled rhythmically with their fancy steps and the gentle swaying of their hips. The seriousness of the other rituals now behind them, the time had come to relax and enjoy utter freedom.

Life was good. Surely it would always be this way. It became easy to believe again that the predictions of the Feathered One belonged far in the future. If the Oglala remained strong and bore many children, the Lakota Nation would always be free and proud.

Buffalo Dreamer danced with more vigor than ever before, happy to have regained her slender figure, joyful for her son, glad to be back home in the Black Hills, away from the *wasicu* stronghold. She whirled and skipped, her tunic decorated with buttons, beads, and the small pieces of tin.

Finally, she stopped before Rising Eagle, swaying seductively to the rhythm of the drums as she held her husband's gaze in deep understanding. Both realized they could not wait the year or two usually required before making love after a child is born to them. Buffalo Dreamer took secret pleasure in the knowledge that her strong, brave, principled warrior husband still could not resist her every need and request, no matter what the rules. Tonight she intended to tempt him again.

She threw her blanket over him and sat down.

"This is not a wise thing to do," Rising Eagle told her.

"Tonight I care little about being wise," she answered, "and I do not like this practice of not making love while a woman still feeds her baby at her breast."

Rising Eagle leaned close and licked her cheek. "I also do not like it. But it is the way."

Buffalo Dreamer knew he waited for an excuse to blame her for making him break a rule. She must beg him.

"I think that all our children will come to us only when the Feathered One decides it is time to make your seed strong again," she suggested. "In this way, we are free to make love as often as we wish."

Rising Eagle pretended to give the remark serious thought. "Hmmm. I never considered it in such a way."

"Oh, I think about it often, my husband, for my heart and my body miss you." Buffalo Dreamer took his hand and placed it on her breast. "I long to feel my husband, rather than my son, tasting my breast. I beg you to break the rule of lovemaking, for I cannot bear another moment without feeling you inside of me."

Rising Eagle nuzzled her neck as he massaged her breast gently. "You ask much of me," he said softly. "I am *Naca*. I am expected to be strong."

Buffalo Dreamer giggled. "I will tell you something, my husband. I am thinking that the bravest and most devoted men of the *Naca Ominicia* surely have their weak moments when lying next to their wives in the night. I do not believe that all men go without their wives' affections for very long. Perhaps only those who take second and third wives can ignore the wife who has given birth, but you promised you would never take another wife. *Wakan-Tanka* would understand your needs. I think he would say it is all right to make love to the only wife you have."

Rising Eagle fingered a nipple through the light deerskin dress she wore. "I think that we should go out into the darkness and talk about it."

Buffalo Dreamer licked his lips lightly. "Whatever

you wish." She grasped the blanket and ran off. Rising Eagle followed, laughter and suggestive remarks coming from those left behind. Buffalo Dreamer kept running, teasing Rising Eagle by darting back and forth in the darkness and calling for him. Finally she spread her blanket on the ground and lay down, calling him again when he shouted her name. "I am here."

Rising Eagle found her and fell to his knees. "You make me crazy with desire for you." He ran his hands along her legs and pushed up her tunic. Buffalo Dreamer raised up so that he could push it to her waist, and up past her breasts. He ran his hands over her belly then, and she breathed deeply with desire when he moved a thumb into the crevice between her legs, toying with the magic spot that always broke down all her defenses. She groaned his name. "Mate with me, Rising Eagle," she said softly. "I beg of you. It will be my fault if you break the rule, and so you will not be to blame."

Rising Eagle untied his apron and breechcloth and tossed them aside. He leaned over her, bending down to lick at her breasts, tasting traces of milk. "You taste sweet, my wife, and I am jealous of our son." He sucked lightly, then moved his tongue over her belly, licking her lovingly. He traced his tongue down and lightly licked her sweet juices. Buffalo Dreamer burned with heated desire and near-painful ecstasy, for it had been many months since he had touched her this way. In only moments she felt the deep, exotic pulsations that made her cry out. "Now, my husband," she moaned. "Do not make me wait one moment longer."

Rising Eagle moved his hard, hot shaft inside of her, and Buffalo Dreamer felt slight pain at first. In moments, the pain turned to pleasure, and she took great joy in giving him pleasure in return.

They mated with wild passion, quickly the first time, more slowly and for longer the second. Buffalo

Dreamer breathed deeply of her husband's familiar scent, on fire for this handsome, most honored man of the Oglala, a man of vision and power. It seemed he penetrated her very soul with his rhythmic thrusts, and she dug her nails into his muscled arms. Finally, he again released his life into her womanly depths, then lay down beside her, sighing in deep satisfaction.

"Only you can make me so weak," he said, studying the stars.

"And only you can cause me to break the rules," she answered. She settled into his shoulder, studying the stars with him. "I think that the Feathered One knows what we have done, and I think he does not mind."

"He knows everything."

They lay there quietly for several minutes before Rising Eagle spoke again. "We will leave soon for Medicine Mountain. I think that it is important to take Never Sleeps there, and to take our son and raise him up for the Feathered One to see, for it is he who granted us the gift of a son."

"I will go whenever you are ready. We will take my mother, for I need her help with two babies."

"I will have Runs With The Deer and Bear Dancing come with us, and perhaps Arrow Runner and my sister, and a few unmarried warriors for protection. It is the time of year when the Crow and Shoshoni sometimes come into Lakota land to hunt."

Buffalo Dreamer turned to nuzzle his neck. "We must teach our children to be strong and to cling to the old ways, Rising Eagle. By taking them to Medicine Mountain, perhaps the Feathered One will fill them with the strength and wisdom they will need to face whatever the future holds for us."

Rising Eagle held her close. "It is why I take them there," he answered, still watching the stars.

Buffalo Dreamer felt a sudden sadness. "It might be our last hope for Never Sleeps, for he seemed feverish today. I worry over him. He never grows bigger, and he is so frail. I fear he will die."

Rising Eagle studied the night sky. "He will not die. If I have to sacrifice blood for him, I will do it. The Feathered One will not let him die. I believe this in my heart."

SEPTEMBER 1834

When the Leaves Become
Yellow Moon

CHAPTER FIFTY-NINE

HIGH ON MEDICINE Mountain, the *Nacas* prepared a sweat lodge for Rising Eagle, who wanted to first be purified before offering prayers for his sons. Those prayers must be powerful, for his adopted son, Never Sleeps, had become very ill on their journey here. Rising Eagle and Buffalo Dreamer feared he would soon die.

Many accompanied them to the top of the mountain, most of them *Nacas,* including, as always, Runs With The Deer, who was in charge of the sacred ceremony. Buffalo Dreamer sat outside the sweat lodge with both babies, while inside, Runs With The Deer doused the heated rocks periodically with water, creating the steam that represented Mother Earth. It cleansed and purified those within.

The sun sank beyond a distant mountain range as Rising Eagle sang inside the sweat lodge. Finally, Runs With The Deer emerged, telling Buffalo Dreamer to join them at the center of the sacred circle of stones.

A baby in each arm, Buffalo Dreamer rose as Rising Eagle also exited the sweat lodge, naked but for his loincloth and the bear-claw necklace Buffalo Dreamer had made for him. Those who had accompanied them up the mountain followed Buffalo Dreamer and Rising Eagle, seating themselves around the outside of the stone circle, while Rising Eagle, Buffalo Dreamer, and

Runs With The Deer sat around the central cairn, which
blazed brightly.

All of the participants were men of the Brave Heart
Society, as well as all four Oglala Shirt Wearers, who
now included Wind In Grass; and the *wakincuzas,* or
Pipe Owners. Tall Woman and Looking Horse also
joined the prayer session.

The sun fell and darkness enveloped the mountaintop. The sky never seemed blacker, and Buffalo
Dreamer could not remember ever seeing more stars
than tonight. Like the night when she and Rising Eagle
had come here to pray for a son, the moon shone as a
tiny sliver in the black sky. Rising Eagle took Never
Sleeps from her then. He held the baby in his arms and
sang his prayer song.

> *Wakan-Tanka, I sing to you.*
> *Hear my prayer.*
> *I am your humble servant.*
> *I have shed blood in sacrifice to you.*
> *I have cleansed myself for you.*
> *Save my people, O Great Spirit,*
> *And save this child I hold.*
> *Make him strong.*

Women sat in a circle behind the men, and they
began trilling their own prayers. Bold Fox, Runs With
The Deer, and Many Horses drummed to the singing,
and Rising Eagle repeated his song. *"Hear my prayer.
Save this child. Make him strong."*

Buffalo Dreamer cuddled a sleeping Big Little Boy
in her arms, and Rising Eagle held Never Sleeps. Buffalo Dreamer joined the others in song, praying to
Wakan-Tanka to save Never Sleeps. In spite of
whatever pain the poor, deformed child might suffer,
he never cried, and he still seldom slept. Yet tonight,
he slept soundly in Rising Eagle's arms.

Buffalo Dreamer felt the Spirit of *Wakan-Tanka.*

This place was *lela wakan,* most sacred. Anything could happen here. After hours of singing and praying, clouds slowly covered the stars. Buffalo Dreamer heard thunder in those clouds, a good sign. The Thunder Spirit held much power, and it showed that power with flashing bolts of white-hot lightning. Sometimes that lightning struck a human, and the Lakota considered such a death a great blessing, for that person had been chosen by the Feathered One to immediately join him in that special place of their ancestors.

The clouds moved closer. The thunder grew louder. The drumming and singing heightened. *Wakan-Tanka* might show himself at any moment, in any form, through more thunder, through the white bolts of power, or in the form of the Feathered One. However he chose to show himself, his presence could not be denied. All in attendance sang their prayers with even more fervor, hearts pounding with anticipation. Buffalo Dreamer could not remember a more awesome moment.

Rising Eagle felt a presence, too. He stood up, holding Never Sleeps high in the air. He danced around the central fire with the boy, repeating his original prayer. It did not rain, but thunder boomed around them so loudly that it hurt Buffalo Dreamer's ears. Yet her own son still slept, and Never Sleeps gave no sign of startled fear, remaining silent as his adoptive father held him up to the gods.

The clouds suddenly lit up in blinding flashes around them, and Buffalo Dreamer felt an odd tingling, then a sensation of stunned paralysis, as though some kind of life force had embraced and paralyzed her. Then followed the loudest clap of thunder, and with it, a stupendous surge of brilliant light that enveloped the central fire, as well as Rising Eagle, Buffalo Dreamer, and the two babies. For a moment, Buffalo Dreamer heard nothing but a loud buzzing, and when she looked up at Rising Eagle, he stood with

Never Sleeps raised high, the eerie white light glowing in flashes around his entire body.

In seconds, the light disappeared, and Rising Eagle sank to his knees, then slowly lay down on a blanket, still holding Never Sleeps. He wrapped the boy into the blanket, and the drumming and singing stopped. The clouds suddenly vanished, and the night sky grew black again, except for the thousands of stars. Buffalo Dreamer felt warmer, and the night seemed all at once too quiet.

"We must all sleep now," Rising Eagle told them. "In the morning we will know if Never Sleeps is healed of his weaknesses."

Everyone believed the spirits had revealed this to Rising Eagle when the lightning surrounded him. Why should they doubt or question a man who had twice been visited by the Feathered One? They all quietly retired to their tepees, but Rising Eagle and Buffalo Dreamer remained at the center of the Medicine Wheel. The fire, struck by the white bolt of lightning, dwindled to a tiny pile of embers.

Buffalo Dreamer pulled a blanket around herself and Big Little Boy, and all fell into a deep slumber.

Morning brought sunshine and warmth, even at the mountaintop, unusual for Mother Earth at this time of the season. Drifting fuzz from a wildflower brushed Buffalo Dreamer's face and woke her. Surprised to see that her normally active, noisy son still slept, she sat up and looked over at Rising Eagle. To her surprise, he sat staring at her with tears on his cheeks.

"What is it, my husband?" she asked in alarm.

He closed his eyes. "It is something I cannot explain, except to say that I am too humbled to even *try* to explain." He swallowed before continuing. "I know now that the life circle of the Lakota will never be broken, no matter what lies in our future. We have received a sign like no other in the history of the Lakota, like none that will ever be given us again. The future holds much for us, Buffalo Dreamer, and I pray that we are strong enough to face it together and accept whatever is to come. Surely the promises of the Feathered One are true, and we must be strong now, for the coming of the white man."

Confused, Buffalo Dreamer moved closer to him, astounded that he wept. She had never seen her proud warrior husband in this mood. "You speak of things we already know, Rising Eagle, for the Feathered One told you. So far, life has been good, and we are prepared for the coming of more *wasicus*. Why do you weep?"

Rising Eagle wiped at his tears. "I have seen something . . . something so miraculous that I realize *Wakan-Tanka* truly does control all—the earth, the sky, the winged ones, the four-leggeds, and the two-leggeds. I always believed this, but not in the way that I believe it now. Our future holds much, my wife, and we must cling together through it all, until the day comes when we join our ancestors. Until then, we must do all we can to teach the young ones the Lakota way, to make them understand that they must do the same, from generation to generation. The Lakota are the only true human beings."

Buffalo Dreamer shook her head. "I also know all of this, Rising Eagle. What have you seen that has touched you so?"

He drew a deep breath. "I weep because I am humbled to be chosen by the Feathered One in such a way that my prayers have power, more power than I ever realized." He looked down at Never Sleeps, and he slowly unwrapped the child.

Never Sleeps kicked his legs and flailed his arms, and his skin color looked richer and healthier. No longer sickly, he appeared to have put on weight overnight. But that was not the most miraculous gift of their prayer vigil. Buffalo Dreamer gasped and put a hand to her mouth, as astounded and humbled at what she saw as was Rising Eagle.

Never Sleeps had ten fingers . . . and ten toes.

AFTERWORD

There really is a Medicine Mountain in the Bighorn Mountains of northern Wyoming. I have been there twice, and have studied the stone Medicine Wheel. To go there brings to mind the sounds of drumming and singing. You can almost hear them in the constant wind. I first visited the Medicine Wheel in 1985, and ever since then, I wanted to write a story involving this mystic place.

Mystic Dreamers ends in the year 1834. The Lakota did not number their years, but rather recalled certain years by major events. Years were termed "winters," and had no true beginning or end. They were simply given names, as 1809 was the "Winter Little Beaver's Tepee Burned." Eighteen forty-three was the "Winter of Stealing Arrows From the Pawnee," when the Sioux recaptured Cheyenne sacred arrows stolen by the Pawnee, but that is an event reserved for one of my future "Mystic Indian" books.

History Keepers, men who could be called the "scholars" of the Lakota, kept records painted in circular form on a deerskin. The first event depicted was at the center; future years were recorded by drawing pictures that spiraled outward, with new events added each year.

The year in which my character, Rising Eagle, experienced his vision of being visited by the Feathered One on top of Medicine Mountain is 1833. I chose this year because in 1833, a meteoric shower actually occurred. The Lakota call 1833 the "Winter of the Shifting Stars." Today the Feathered One is called the Phoenix, and the Lakota still believe he will return. When he does, the Lakota will inherit the earth.

Watch for future "Mystic Indian" stories, which will be the continuation of the lives of Rising Eagle, Buffalo Dreamer, and their children. You will learn what becomes of little Never Sleeps as he grows into a man.

Until I meet you again in my next book, may we all be *taku-wakan,* kindred spirits.

—Rosanne Bittner